THE OTHERS

Siba al-Harez

THE OTHERS

Translated from the Arabic

TELEGRAM

First published in Arabic by Dar al Saqi, Beirut, 2006

This edition published in 2009 by Telegram, London

ISBN: 978-1-84659-042-9

copyright © Siba al-Harez, 2009

The name of the translator is not listed here at the translator's request.

A full CIP record for this book is available from the British Library.
A full CIP record for this book is available from the Library of Congress.

Printed and bound by Thomson Press (India) Ltd.

TELEGRAM
26 Westbourne Grove, London W2 5RH
2398 Doswell Avenue, Saint Paul, Minnesota, 55108
Tabet Building, Mneimneh Street, Hamra, Beirut
www.telegrambooks.com

L'Enfer, c'est les autres.

Hell is other people.

Jean-Paul Sartre

1

And so there was a long line of them, and I admitted them all. I let them come in through my front door. It was the front door of *me*, and I, for my part, was about to become something new: an occasion for entertainment, a spectacle. A museum with a few paintings hanging prettily on the wall, a spiral staircase provoking dizziness, pieces of a puzzle scattered about. Anything may leave a pleasant impression, but when it lingers, it is bound to turn aggravating. Humdrum. Dull and heavy. Yet it also slips easily away, and in the end, is apt to be forgotten. What matters is for the queue to wind up at the opposite door, where no sign offers any help. *Exit.* The door that plays its part flawlessly and controls only one direction: out. That's all.

Very few, indeed fewer than few, are those who have broken my private law, breached my private space. Yet over time, the lower floors of me have transformed themselves into a human garbage dump, trash piling up inside. Other people become corpses that loiter within me and turn to rot. These others refuse to go away. These others refuse to leave me in peace. They forget the parts they were to play. It may be that they assumed their parts too thoroughly, or perhaps they never grasped what those roles really were.

The nights are unbearable here—the screaming, the scratching and wrangling, the massing and piling of bodies. They redraw the borders of each one's dominion over the territories of my body. I would have preferred dust and cobwebs to rats chewing relentlessly at my heart, leaving splinters of wood behind. Splinters everywhere inside of me.

Dai was one of my miracles. Or to put it more accurately, she was what I thought of as my miracle. She did not enter through a door, which would have meant my sending her out through another. Perhaps she came from somewhere overhead, sliding down the banister or hanging from the ceiling. Something did compel me to swing my gaze in a particular direction: above. And when I did so, my compass swung out of control, and the fall, which came next, shattered me. Maybe I got careless about keeping my red lines clearly defined. Perhaps it was she who exceeded the boundaries. Maybe, in this game, there were things I did not see; maybe all I was conscious of was its red-hot pleasure and its enormous impact on me. Whenever the balance sat cupped in my hands, the scales were utterly still, but Dai could deftly keep them in perpetual motion. She knew how to turn things on their heads, how to fabricate a long chain of reactions to the single and sickly action that I was.

Throughout that meteoric interval during which we were serious enough for me to tell her it was time for her to leave, she looked very sad, with a sort of surprised grief that was supposed to work up my sympathy for her. But even after I told her to go, it did not seem to really matter, and she stayed on and on. She stayed until she became my illness.

That was it, yes. I sickened, and the sickness was a creature named Dai.

Dai. The talisman that I so feared to hear recited, lest it be thwarted. If it were touched, violated, I feared my talisman would disintegrate into tiny pieces. I was so very fragile, so transparent—an enlarged negative—and she was my original, my nucleus. Time after time, I was moved around. I was rearranged and ultimately forced into the shadows. And when you are in the shadows it is quite a joke to discover how much you fear the dark—that darkness which is your own special maelstrom, and from which there is no getting out.

2

In my childhood, the old-fashioned air conditioner in my room was my hero. In my mind, the control dials were a pair of amber eyes, and the whirring blades a mass of tousled hair. The blades made a delectable light scratchy sound, an echo like the one that seems to rise off your skin when you wake up. Every night, the air conditioner was my own brave warrior, facing off against my nightmares and fears and the dampness of my bed. The ceiling of Dai's room had the same effect, even though I was never able to fashion a moving image out of its stillness. The ceiling was a dumb witness; perhaps it even made a choice, somehow, to close its eyes and sleep through everything. I fastened my eyes on that ceiling and engraved that word onto the surface of my brain—the word I would have to say without any stuttering or hesitation, confidently and calmly.

A few encounters had been enough to apprise me of Dai's temperament and essential character. I knew when she would be ready for a lull in hostilities, when she would grow angry, when she was gambling on my intelligence, when she would have me, and when she was about to let go with that laugh of hers, the sticky gluey laugh that disgusted me. The laugh of the *bu'bu'*, the bogey.

Soon enough, I could read her signals. If she was wearing her sky blue cotton shirt, she was in a happy, serene mood. Her braided hair would tell me that she was feeling cheerful and lively. And the movement of her fingers along the seams of my jeans would let me know that she was feeling her way toward me. Before she arrived, I had to set our destination.

Let's go there, I said, waving my hand in the general direction of the mirror. She turned, a skeptical question on her face: There? Are you sure? Before she could actually ask it, I had her by the hand and was pulling her over to the mirror. I needed something that would save me from myself. I wanted to come out the other side of this new experience with credit in my account. And I was beginning to find it stale, this cat and mouse game, this habit of pushing things as far as they could possibly go and then suddenly announcing one's unavailability. I undid a button and left the rest of the task for Dai's hand, and suddenly, what seemed like it would take endless time had truly happened, startling me and riveting me, too. I hung onto the mirror, my flagrant nakedness sending me into a state of rapture I had never experienced before, a feeling of bliss at seeing myself desired like this, and escaping the laws mandated by my own body.

I was liberating me from myself. Turning my face toward the mirrors that Dai exposed as she opened the doors to her wardrobe, I was thrown off balance, distracted by these sudden and multiple images of myself. It was not just a matter of being released, of feeling free, but rather, it was a sense of no longer being able to exert a guiding hand over myself. My authority over whatever part of myself I owned was worthless. My body, dissolving beneath her and melting into clear liquid, was no longer mine to own. From that moment, Dai was my body's commanding mistress and I became simply an organism whose body lies elsewhere, and lurks in obscure isolation, a remote, secluded place that allowed me to witness—but only as an outside observer, one who does not react. I am not part of it. I feel none of this. All I can do is to stare, my face featureless. And so I fix my gaze on what appears to be no concern of mine—or would not be, if it were not so conspicuously there, in front of my eyes.

We finished. A contorted, artificial smile lingered on my mouth as she spattered my face with her wet kisses, in her usual way. She chewed on her lip for a moment and then handed me a cotton wad, saying a few words that I could not make out. But I knew these signs—the chewed-on lip, the cotton wad—and so I knew that she had left the marks of her passage on my neck.

Far away is Dai. And my body has left me behind to travel toward a point that I cannot see from here, where I remain. My body has gone about establishing its ordinances and putting in place its distinct arrangements, devising plans for what it may reap in the coming days and weeks. Its intentions frighten me, for they are both obscure and absolute. Meanwhile I remain in my dreadful solitude, not because I don't belong to the world, but because here I am without even a sense of belonging to myself.

The calmness I felt in the beginning turned into fear, and then into a blind capacity for anger. It was not as though I had sobered up after a spell of intoxication, for I had not been intoxicated in the first place. It was just that, of the three fingers on which I had been counting up my intentions, I had lost the third one, where I had lodged the answer to the all-important question: what shall I do? I came to Dai intending to say, Take me, and I said it. I also came to share my body with her, and I did. But then ... what to do with this *then* of mine where all the details lay, details that I could not remember! I had not intended to stand there upset and unsteady, unable to resolve anything at all.

I began to regain my senses somewhat, to come out of the jelly-like bubble that had wrapped itself around me deceptively. I found everything around me irritating. Dai grated on me: her smell, her strong breaths, the nakedness of her body, her weight pressing down on my ribcage, a few tiny hairs sprinkled around her eyebrows, her forefinger playing in my mouth, her voice, her mouth, everything that was a part of her, everything that made up her *I*. Her sweet little singularities that had dizzied me time after time now showed themselves as petty details. This, I had not been able to see. Or rather, this—these trivialities, unrecognized—gave me purchase to diminish her. And the *other* one remaining between us, in the form of a lavish register of quarrels, insults and ruptures, grew to fill my eyes beyond the limits of my visible horizons.

I shivered. And shivered and shivered. She covered me with her body and began to rub my hand in hers, but it had no effect. It was not the cold that was making me shiver. It was something else, something unknown, buried somewhere deep. I could not stop shivering. I could not control my limbs. I tried hard to fix my mind on something, anything, a particular thought that could extract me from this suspect impasse, but nothing came to the rescue. I wanted to escape Dai, so I turned away from her. I pulled into myself, jerking my legs upward and close to my chest and covering my face with my arms and hands, palms interlaced. She began to lick the abrasions on my back, her own fingernail scratches and the other light marks caused by my skin rubbing against the carpet's roughness. I could not help seeing myself as a swamp, a marshland of saliva and moist breathing; she was a cat, licking my wounds that would not heal.

Her fingertips played with my ears. Any regrets? she asked me. I shook my head, no, I didn't regret this. The truth was that regret was not on my list when it came to anything in my life. I would do something or not do it—in either case, I would not have a lot to lose. So it was an experience: I went through it, and I learned something. Regret would mean backing off, distancing myself from my own action. Regret would mean erasing some experience, taking a brick out of the structure that was me—and no structure remains standing when it loses a foundation stone. No, I did not feel any regret. Just loathing. I was full of disgust. All at once I had seen my body's power to turn animal-like. I had realized how very faithful it could be to its basest instincts. How completely shameless it was. And who was I to curb its reckless lusts?

I would not be one to ban my body's longings, if only I could understand what they are and fathom what they mean. I wish my body had been kind enough to begin a little conversation with me on the subject. If only my body and I could sum up my longings in a few clear points. I am not an angel and I do not proclaim any pure and perfect virtue. And this would not have been my first baby step toward hell in any case. The whole deal is that I just need to understand. This dark, murky chaos is killing me. It kills me to be driven straight into this nighttime of the blind, where at the end there is no daylight to look kindly down on me.

I must get away now. I am choking to death. My chest floats in a bed of dark mud, and kisses steal my breaths from me in a room where the air is foul. This is not happening. It has not happened. I will go out of this room now, and I will fall. I will tumble into a well of oblivion. With a little bit of effort, I will be able to forget. I will be able to slip out in silence, outside of Dai. If I open the door, new air will come bursting into this room and I can fill my chest with it. I can run. Memory does not have two legs that can carry it against the wind. I can pray. God will be generous with me; God will wipe from the list of my sins another black mark. I can kiss my mother and I will not find that bitter taste returning to my mouth, the taste of my burning intoxication: Dai.

3

My filthiness is not the kind I can wash away with soap and water. I am tired of repeatedly washing my hands and my mouth, tired of bathing so often, tired of the fear I cannot help feeling every time I sleep on my back or part my legs. After all of this has happened, I cannot wipe an enormous eraser across my body and mind to bring back the whiteness of their surfaces, the whiteness of the page. Dai sliced me into two parts: my body, glorying in its confections, and my self, so determined on purification from its offenses. How horrifically enormous my offense was when measured against the authority of the morals I had amassed through years of instruction. That accumulated moral sense of mine gave pride of place in its statutes to my body, for that was the measure by which I would be evaluated and judged, and then moved into one of two categories: pure woman or slut. *Taahira* or *aahira*.

And so I was *aahira*, a slut, and I had conducted myself to hell. Before me lay two solutions by which I could bring back my twin and regain the duality that was me, unalterable and coincidental, body and spirit. I could seek forgiveness for my sin, or I could live under the protective umbrella of denial, not simply denial of what I had done, but also of the painful notion that lay hidden behind it, which told me that I was something other than what people naturally are. I could deny it until, with time, what I had done would be forgotten, so that the sin would lose its stark sin-like image. That way, I would always be a guilty corrupt victim ready for the guillotine known as my conscience. But when the burden of that image would fall from my back, my feelings of shame and ignominy might end.

But I did not choose. The choices were not clear to my eyes, blinded to everything but the horrendous magnitude of my sin. I was alone, left to stumble hopelessly forward. Since our first kiss (with its secretive connivance), everything had progressed so gradually and, it seemed, smoothly, that one would think there existed some prior agreement between us that things would happen just as they did, from the most trivial details, the precise shape of a kiss, all the way to the grandest issues about how it all happened, encompassing along the way all of those shy preliminary skirmishes, and culminating in my complete and utter detachment from my body, my granting her my body in its wholeness through that gradual progression of our acts. I did not even really catch onto how much of a battleground I had become over two months of wars and lean victories. Nor had I given any thought to what the next step might be. What happened was like some cheap poster hung on the wall and held fast by many nails on either end. No sooner would one person finish working on it before another would begin, and so it would start to split slowly, slowly ... so slowly that no one would even notice a thing, not even that the panel had become two sections that were entirely separated, indeed, ripped violently apart.

If only my mother had paid attention, I said to myself. If only Hassan had not been defeated. If only I had not despised Dai and been crazy in love with her at the same time. If only there had been someone there. O Lord, anyone. If only God were not so stern and hard. If only fate had struck a blow the way it normally does, surprising me with some tiny alteration in some little event, anything, in the normal course of my life at that time. If only my final exams had happened to be just then. If only it were not the new millennium. If only I had not been in a state of total exhaustion and overstrain, and if only I had not been totally insane at the time with something called Experience! But at least Freud is not here to explain everything about my present fix by linking it back to my mother not nursing me enough. Nor is there a candle I can light, nor do I have a wailing wall.

I wanted to undergo the experience but I did not balance my accounts: I did not think about the price that would be demanded of me. With the mark of my sin carved into the palm of my right hand, I found myself unable to pay. The cost was huge and my wallet was empty. I tried my hand at concocting a rift, fast and complete; I thought perhaps I could make a total break with the event which I hoped to fix in my mind as a part of the irretrievable past that it was futile to unearth. I immersed myself in an endless series of intense connections, my lines open—and impossibly tangled—to girlfriends who did not particularly mean anything to me. I emptied my datebook of its emptiness, and filled my schedule with meetings, more or less, according to my varying level of absorption in the activities of the Hussainiyya, as the ending rituals of Ramadan drew near. None of it was any use. While I was busy, and my time slipped away in the swarm of appointments, and rarely was I by myself, I could not keep my mind from whirling, gyrating on the same waterwheel time and again, and stopping always at that night of mine with Dai, never getting beyond it, as if all places, and time itself, had frozen there.

We had just finished putting together the program for the Charity Tray, which would take place on the hallowed twenty-seventh of Ramadan, the Night of Power, when verses from the Qur'an were first revealed, as the Qur'an tells us. People would buy food coupons and we would distribute the proceeds to the poor. Now it was time to start organizing the festivities to honor the girls who would successfully complete our three training modules—Prayer and Piety, Morals, and the Articles of Faith—and the women who had served as volunteer instructors. We had to come up with a budget, calculating the minimum funds we would realistically need to put this event on. We had to schedule it, making sure that the date we chose would not conflict with anything that anyone else in any other section was doing, and then adhering to it. It meant we had to assign roles and choose a signature theme for the ceremony. We had to decide on the program and speakers, contacting Hussainiyya women known to be good orators or those who wrote for religious magazines. We would need to select token gifts for the volunteer teachers, and arrange with a stationer to print the necessary number of diplomas. We might ask a group of graduating students to recite verses from the Qur'an. Then there were the opening remarks to write, as well as introductions for each part of the program and the concluding words. The event had to be publicized by means of fliers hung in the front windows of the grocery shops, handed out around the open-air Basta market with its cheap goods spread across the ground, and distributed to Internet listservs. And we were the ones who would spend the two final days before the event decorating the walls and ceiling of the Hussainiyya, reconfirming the time and place with everyone involved, and holding a final rehearsal for the dramatic presentation, if we decided to have one. There would be a few headaches arising from the inevitable last-minute changes and necessary back-up plans, or from disagreements among participants, or because some would count on others to do all of the work.

My particular challenge was that I had to see Dai almost every day. It was not just a question of seeing her as she passed me by in the building, or of the two of us being in the same place. I had to be prepared for long discussions with her since she was an essential component of our small group, and indeed was the one to sign off on every step we took. To all appearances, we gave the impression of a strong and practical collegiality that went no further. Everyone thought we had a great working relationship, judging by our success at jointly coming up with program ideas. Everybody thought that was all we had. To all appearances, we were simply two individuals whose relationship had not undergone any change or had any special or private dimension throughout the nearly three years in which they had been active participants in the same venture.

We had not come to any advance agreement about keeping our relationship secret, because nothing called for such an agreement. This was the best thing to happen of its own accord, in a relationship that in the space of a few months had suffered a great deal from repeated and dramatic starts and stops. I was truly grateful to her that this, at least, was not an issue.

Despite my genuine participation in organizing a successful end-of-Ramadan program, I did not feel for a moment that I had offered an appropriate admission of guilt to God, nor even to myself, not to mention the act of contrition that should accompany it. I remained submerged in my sense of embarrassed disgrace, the tormenting feeling I had that my sin dripped visibly in huge drops off my limbs. I knew in advance that I had been acting out of my need to consume the empty time I had at my disposal, so that I would not actually have to encounter myself and start quarreling again with the reason I was. I had done it to soften the sharp pain of seeing myself so broken and dejected; I had done it so that enough time would pass that I could mold justifications that would convince me, or construct a state of oblivion whose coming would sweep away the images etched on my memory.

My self-disgust underwent a transformation; it went from being a row of huge exclamation points to a series of question marks whose sharp points abraded my chest. That was when I initiated my oddest phase on the Internet, even though all the gateways to sex were firmly shut. This did not mean that there were no peculiar side trips—for example, when I searched Yahoo's listservs. They had not drawn my attention before. I discovered that Yahoo was off limits to lesbian groups. That was the work of the contractor who supplied web access for the whole of Aramco. Male homosexual listservs were legit, and that is why I immersed myself in them, joining one after another, to the point where my daily consumption of subscriber emails was up to twenty different groups and my inbox was polluted by wave after wave of images and tales. None of this gave me what I was looking for. I was in search of beginnings and their causes; I was looking for how transformations happen, how the body's desire is formed and molded. I was searching for the causes provoking a body that had been clean and became dirty.

My most jarring habit was entering particular chat rooms. I had only done this previously on a trial basis. The site would be quiet and very disciplined throughout the day, because censors regularly checked in. Over the last third of the night, though, it would mutate into a sex bazaar. Everyone tossed their most intractable desires into the ring and waited for someone with similar inclinations to show up. I was no better than any of them, and I did attract some attention, from some of the homos of course, of both sexes. With the guys I took up the role of the bashful young man. As fatuous as this role was, it would quickly fool them. I was learning; in fact, I was getting some fast seasoning, for I began passing things I heard from one person on to someone else as my own personal experiences. I would make the details my own, summoning up a personality suitable to the role I was playing. And so I harvested an inconceivable number of weird practices and unruly appetites. Meanwhile, the young women would easily and rapidly discover how very inexperienced I was, or how difficult it was to get to me, or they would unleash doubts about what my sexual identity really was, quickly making their annoyance clear and hastening to distance themselves from me.

It was a while later that I turned to a more serious form of research. I read all the pages the Google search engine would give me when I typed in the English words *homosexual* and *bisexual*. The pages that came up made my head hurt. I felt as though they were forcing upon me awareness, an acknowledgment, of an orientation that was not really mine. And yet the pages that came up on the screen when I searched for the Arabic equivalent, *al-mithliyya al-jinsiyya*, all veered from *tahrim* to *tajrim*, interdiction to criminalization. That would drive me to close the window before I could even finish reading, as these pages screamed into my face that I was rocking God's throne in His heaven. Finally, I resorted to my own thought processes. No doubt, here was where all of the answers were, in my own body. But my body would always shut the doors in my face and recede.

I could not abandon my shame. I would shift my eyes away from the mirror in my room, and I draped a cloth over the bathroom mirror so that I would not see myself naked as I bathed. In fact, I went back to bathing with my underclothes on, a practice I had shed a few years before. I was so mortified that I could not place my hand on any part of my body, even if accidentally; I could not move a bar of soap across my own skin. The shame was like an enormous pair of steel boots stomping across my chest.

I went on like this, in a state of estrangement from myself, while my body began to truly harass me with its demands. I was perfectly conscious of when I could fend it off and when I had to take its desires seriously. But the touchstone here was *what* it was that my body wanted. Not pieces of candy, nor two extra hours of sleep. What it wanted was an *other* sin, one that would lower the water level again, an experience that would break yet another bone and color the skin above it with bruises. The critical thing now was that my body itself had become an offense, a sin, and I must bury it as quickly as I possibly could, for otherwise it would get the better of me and slip from my grasp once again.

4

Wretched and weak, I was laden with conflicting feelings, sleeping two hours a day and then confusing what I saw in my meager dreams with real events. I would accost people I knew on the basis of dream events that they had not shared, pelting them with words that would never have entered their wildest imaginations. I was tottering under an enormous weight of guilt, ignominy and self-doubt. I was sinking under the burden. I was falling apart.

I had just hung up on Umar. Sounding deliberately naïve, I had asked him, Ready to come play a little game? How about some loving? We laughed. We laughed for a long time. At that moment, I was not thinking about what it all meant, the playfulness I was proposing; nor about its well-kept secret content. The minute I closed my phone, though, the thought came to me that likely this was the one single thing that could prevent me from staying completely immersed in the wrong I had committed with Dai. Likely it was the only thing that could protect me from the crimes of my own self.

I was bent on distraction. There was nowhere safe to turn but Hiba. Can you loan me a pillow? I asked her. Ever since that night of mine with Dai, I had not touched anyone in any way, except for those cursory handshakes that my meetings at the Hussainiyya demanded, or the grasping of hands when I met up with one of my friends, someone I hadn't seen for a few weeks or months. I held myself back, not kissing them, and I made do with letting them plant their kisses on my cheeks. Even my own body—I didn't even touch that! I averted my eyes from others, from other women whenever anyone came near. I was completely drained and exhausted by my fear. I closed down my senses; I was terrified of what I might discover in my body—what else I might find in addition to what Dai had already revealed there.

I needed to be near to Hiba. I needed to touch her and I needed her to disclose to me that there was a place in myself that had not yet become soiled. That the cravings which had passed through my body were not a flaw in my physical chemistry that would lead me to commit the offense a second time, and then a third. I needed Hiba's body to be close by, and I needed to find that nothing had changed about what I felt toward it, or my ability to look at it without framing it in sensuous physicality. I needed to find that I could brush against it without the blaze of my lust flaring up. Hiba was in a state of noisy excitement, showing off her new possessions, and so she completely forgot to answer my question. She finally managed a laugh, and said, Bring your own pillow or else pay me for it in advance. Nothing is free, gorgeous! I laughed just as smoothly in response. *Ya hilwa inti*! Speak for yourself, gorgeous! Then you're selling me the pillow, not renting it out!

I do not have a pre-existing framework that allows me to define exactly what Hiba was in relation to me—or in relation to anyone but herself. It is not a problem of ignorance as much as one of knowledge, or more accurately, what my own scheme of knowledge about people is. That is, I tend to be attentive to particular details about people, their finer points which are the traits least likely to draw the attention of other people, and which probably do not mean much of anything at all. For example, the fact that some guy really likes the European football league and the Liverpool team, or that some girl has a room painted the color of cappuccino froth, even though I don't know who is on the Liverpool team or what its history is, or anything about that girl's room except the color of the paint on its walls. I wouldn't set much store by the guy's or the girl's other details, facts which appear to people other than myself more important, more worthy of committing to memory, more appropriate to circulate: how many brothers and sisters they have, what their fathers do for a living, what their mothers are like, what their skin tone is, and what the names of their friends are. This means that I do not often have the correct answers when faced with questions about one of my friends, like How would you describe her facial features? Is she from a wealthy family? Her sister is studying medicine in Bahrain, right? She's reserved for her cousin who is going to marry her after he graduates, is that so? Even I do not understand my particular brand of selectivity when it comes to details; I do not really fathom how it is that knowledge of others, as I gain it, is in the end so abstract—pointillist, if I can put it that way. When asked such questions, the most I can offer are vague and approximate answers, reserving for myself the truth that I do not know, and that anyway, I do not care that I do not know! I do not really see anyone, I guess. That is the truth in its simplest and starkest state.

My relationship with Hiba was a cacophony of memories—long silly conversations, meeting at the Basta market every Thursday, walking along the water, staying up late together when we had the next day off from school, and the walking stick of a grandfather from whose trunk our branches sprouted. We cooked up things that no one but us would possibly take the risk of tasting. We stuck a cardboard plaque on the door proclaiming our names as owners of the room, or to be more accurate, as an owner and her live-in partner, and of course the first of the pair was none other than me. True, I scoffed at some of her craziness. This human being appears natural but she drinks her tea only after it grows cold, reads the newspaper starting at the back page, and bathes in icy water even far into a wintry night for no reason but to spite the cold.

We were two lines that never intersected, and only rarely did we manage a little miracle across which we would truly come together. I am slow, apprehensive about everything, and perpetually suspicious. Hiba is an explosion always in the making, its echo never silent until she has scattered slivers everywhere. She is always on the move, rushing in absurd directions. She considers it an unforgivable waste of time to think twice about taking any single step. She appreciated her life, which as she described it was simultaneously empty and full, whether that life was on its way forward and upward or whether it was heading in reverse to careen downward. Every breath is a sacred blessing from God, she would say, and so why exhaust it in noisy irritation over things we cannot help?

It was natural that we would differ. Everything about our two lives diverged. Only occasionally did my family assess me on the basis of my studies, my volunteer work, and whether I was well-behaved or in a good frame of mind. My uncle and his wife, however, appraised their Hiba according to anything and everything that would enhance her opportunities in life—and according to them, life was summed up entirely for a girl in marriage. As they would always say, My Lord protect her with His shielding Hand. Thus, Hiba's value plummeted every time her weight increased a few kilos or whenever she stopped accepting invitations to weddings and other social occasions for a while. It had all become harder since her decision to stop her studies after successfully finishing her first year of high school. At first, her parents paid little attention; it did not seem to bother them. In recent years, though, university study had newly become a near-universal condition on the list of desiderata for any respectable marriage, and so they wanted her to continue. However, their attempts made no headway in convincing her to return to her place in the high school classroom (and nor did mine, even if our goals differed). She would come up with excuses; she claimed she could not possibly sit at the same tables as children. Anyway, she said, her mind had grown too lethargic to be awoken by the riddles of mathematics and the enigmas of grammar.

The two of us were neither complete opposites nor very much alike. We were a pair of unlike territories, and only proximity linked us, while we had no shared topography to unite us. The yield? When our shared stock was at its highest, the indicator pointed to no more than one in ten fingers. Yet, true to her name, since Hiba means Gift, she gave me something which all the accords and alliances of this world are powerless to give: abundant security, in the shape of a soft, open hand; security crafted frequently like a bar of chocolate, or lit up on a screen where waves of color surged.

Why are you so down?

We're all colored gray around this time, every year.

At the approach of the New Year, the whole world wears a dark grayish overcoat, the whole world grumbles and weeps, and the cold etches lines as long and as wide as it wishes, the scratches crisscrossing along my bones. I had just put on a recording of Fairuz and my hoarse voice followed and soared above her Lebanese warmth.

How often people
at the crossroads see people
and the world goes wintry
and they carried off my sun
and here I am on a pure clear day
and no one sees me

Though I envied Fairuz's voice, hearing it against my own scratchy one, which emerges from a throat that is like an ice grinder, I did not dare enter the paradise of her voice and forget myself there. Or perhaps I already saw myself there. Hiba's face took on a clouded-over byway, her features displaying a query composed of twenty question marks. So what's the matter with you, huh? I opened a secondary road in the conversation to avoid falling into the trap laid by her expression. I posed a question about what I could possibly hope for in any period of time, ranging in length from about now until the end of the year, and then I rushed in to answer my own question.

God would be treating me really well if Hidaya were to be pulled from my shadow.

Does she annoy you?

I'm tired of the whole thing! I'm bored. It's all absurd.

This wasn't boredom, though. It was the overwhelming fatigue brought on by wasted efforts. For every single occasion we concocted the same arrangements: the hollow glamour and pomp at weddings and the gloom at funerals, the words of presentation to which no one listens and whose sense no one understands, the faces that never change, our closed and narrow meetings where nothing new is ever brought to the table. As soon as Hidaya would demarcate the event's theme or focus, and parcel out the roles that each of us would play, we would claim to be hugely busy taking care of extremely serious tasks. Every new idea was a locus of doubt and suspicion. Everything that overstepped some boundary ended up in the wastebasket. I do not understand what we are doing here, then! *People won't accept it* were the doom-laden words that would overpower the simple wooden dais on which we acted out our naïve and repetitive thoughts and ideas. *Fear God by fearing to wrong his people*, we would hear, and the pronouncement would flatten our voices before they even came out of our throats, to resound and tremble through our consciences as if signaling a private hell. *Beware of the zones of evil*. That sentence sent blindness into my eyes and uncertainty into my heart.

I was completely exasperated with Hidaya, to the point of getting a little bit mean and sneaky in my dealings with her. What happened was that in some newspaper I found a report on the suicide rate in the country. I read it to her. The number of cases had reached five hundred and a third of those were from Qatif. Three-fourths were young women, most of whom were legal minors living in very reduced material circumstances. Was this not a problem that deserved somebody's attention? I asked. This is a Hussainiyya, she responded, and not a Social Services Center or a volunteer center where people can call in their emergencies for free! The utter scorn in her response stunned me, especially since this wasn't her usual style at all. I kept silent. But she made a bad situation even worse: she added more moisture to the clay, as we say. Two days later, my mother was telling me about Hidaya's phone call. Hidaya complained about me to my mom, grumbling about the way I did things, about my impetuous ways and my desire to change the world with a snap of my fingers.

Hiba knew that when I started talking like this, chattering fast, my voice resentful, I was bent on escaping some anxiety rather than making my way patiently across its winding turns. Relying on her knowing this, I could be certain that she would spin out the thread of my chatter without breaking it—if, this time, she had not disappointed me and done just the opposite.

And you are not brave enough to leave!

Do you really think that?

I envied Hiba her ability not to care. Her view of things was that whatever does not give you double the enjoyment compared to the effort it drains from you does not deserve any of your brainpower. It follows from this that Hiba thought I did not invest my time well. Time is a life passing, and a life going by is not the hand of a clock that returns to make the same circuit over and over again. Yet, as sharp as she was about anything she saw as a colossal waste, she did not put me on trial. She was never in a big hurry to show how distasteful she found it when I emptied into her ear my weariness with the tone-deaf region where I stood. She did not spout eloquently composed pages of highbrow critique on my behavior or outlook, although in her view I was heading in utterly the wrong direction. I was always aware of her ultimate and decisive solution to anything. *Get used to it or get out.*

I would explain away her canned response to my complaints on the grounds that she had never had the experience of giving to others, giving to the community, something she had produced through her own efforts, something she cared about, in the way that I believed, at the time, that the world would become a more pleasant and better place if we rubbed and polished its outer skin a little, if we plunged a random hand into the world's brain, wherever that was, and reorganized things in there just a bit. The path to God is clear and unobstructed, so why do we always find ways to open new potholes at some points on the road, while we pile up the dirt and create new obstructions at others? That way, we squander the chance that each person has to find his own particular map. Does not God say in His Holy Word, Wheresoever you turn, God's face is there? Hiba's response to all of this was to thump my empty head sharply, as if it were a watermelon, tapping out its long-running delusions and phantoms. Wake up, girl! A time will come in which you will be exactly like one of those dust motes that you try to wave away but you can never get rid of. You will become another Hidaya—whose name, after all, means *Guidance.*

Always before when I had heard this notion of Hiba's, I would not let her get away with it, but now I would find myself asking her, You think so? I was making a serious attempt to alter the face of the world, but it looked like it was only my face that had undergone any change. Now I do not have so many questions that move with the speed of a 260-mile-per-hour wind; I very nearly have nothing left within me. Who gives me the right to be so adrift? So rebellious, such a harlot, an *aahira*, arriving like a prophet who has no miracle to show, who grasps the microphone and with a quasi-artificial humility and a tremulous conviction, speaks to others on the subject of God?

I stared at the wall, on and on, as I traced Fairuz's voice with my own. Gradually her voice faded and my fragile voice could no longer hold onto any substance. On the edge of words: that is where I found myself, thinking something that took me by surprise and filled me with dread. I could not leave enough room there for Hiba to descend into my hell. Rather than letting her in, I would have to give myself an extra layer of protection; I could not drop the veil of my pretense in front of her. Angels cannot possibly fall from the height of seven heavens after a single little error, and was I not Hiba's angel?

I hurried to the bathroom, in a fast attempt to pull myself together, dying for a cigarette. One cigarette that the tightness of my throat would put out, just as the cigarette itself put out an urgent need I felt to drain the filth from my insides in the shape of an incoherent story where the details were missing. If I did it, if I told that story, I would blast a hole in Hiba's heart with the acidity of this old, festering news. Even in the sights of a person who sins abundantly, my sin was not one to be forgiven. And I was blindly taking a huge chance that I would have no roof to shelter me, nor a pillow to give me any rest. I would be an exile from God's sphere and from Hiba's world as well.

Never mind. I am not suffocating now. I will breathe deeply, deeply … deeply. The need in my blood will fade. An evening without cigarettes—the world won't end. Sooner or later, the accursed longing for nicotine will stop knocking against my head. I am fine. I am really well, really well. I feel dizzy, but it is not a problem if my dizziness is still here, the twelfth night after Dai. My body is expelling the filth from within, after all, and my eyes are draining the impurities they hold. Soon, I will be able to see.

The cigarettes are not the worst of Dai's legacy to me. She had offered me a cigarette to lighten the heaviness of the physical blockage that had me in its hold. I took that cigarette. I was sitting on the edge of the bathtub in the bathroom off her room, trying as hard as

I could to keep down the fury I felt toward her, as an alternative to turning the remaining hours we had together into a stupid argument and a series of verbal bombardments that we would launch at each other. I was not yet convinced that I could grant her more than the few centimeters she had revealed by pulling up my shirt, but she wanted more. She always wanted more.

I incarcerated myself in the bathroom. She followed me in, though. She ran her fingers through my hair, but I pushed her away. She knew how much her touches irritate me when I am angry, but she would not stop. She held out her cigarette toward me. This was not quite the first cigarette I had tried, but in a few seconds, despite the coughing and choking and the cloudiness in my eyes, it calmed my feverish blood. With just a tiny dose of nicotine she bribed my nervous gestures into growing regular and quiet. I found in cigarettes and bathtub a safe place where Dai could not reach me, where the pain she could cause was too remote to cast its hand over me.

Since I do not enjoy the taste of Faisal's cigarettes, and in any case it would be too hard to steal from him—this guy who suddenly and for no reason had begun to smoke two cigarettes a week—in the beginning I took all I needed from Dai. Then, I managed to convince Salaam, our driver, to bring me cigarettes along with the beer that he was already smuggling in for me. In my mother's custom, even beer was unlawful: our religion said so. Drinking it in our home was as bad as drinking a whole bottle of hard stuff. No difference there!

My addiction, as I claim, is not to the taste of cigarettes or the way they tame my blood. It is to the feeling that suddenly comes over me whenever I toss a cigarette butt into the toilet and then tug the flush cord. With it goes my entire brain; I find myself suddenly unable to think through anything, as I follow the swirl of the water sweeping away the cigarette and my unease with it, the garbage of my murky thoughts, and those nightly phantom birds of mine that arrive constantly to peck from my brain their fill of worry, fear and suspicion.

I was in the bathroom, overcome by nausea and without a cigarette; all I needed was two fingers jammed into my throat. If we inherit the ways our bodies habitually react to stress, what my genes had given me was a welling nausea whenever things went bad with my mother. I would do better than her, though, by making myself throw up. Aah, the superiority of my inherited traits! This was the only just thing, it appeared, to have gotten mixed into my nucleic acid, from among the interlaced, jumbled obscurity of quirks I inherited, one of which stripped from me the right to eat *ful* beans while another made me liable to break out sobbing at any moment, turning me into a tiny duckling-like creature who had just gotten wet and in the cold could not rid himself of his constant shivering. My parents were kind to me, in any case; I cannot deny it. They did not bestow on me infected blood corpuscles or a faulty pancreas.

I came out of the bathroom depleted, my vision blurred and my head spinning. I grasped Hiba's hand and smiled sourly.

Huuba, dearie, did I tell you that I flunked?

She was so incredulous that she left her mouth hanging open. How could I fail, for the first time, when I was only a year away from finishing my years of study, and capping a span of time that had been full of certificates of excellence and diplomas and my ranking at 94th percentile in my third year of high school! I knew how violently this news of mine would slap Hiba, who was always keeping after me to focus on my studies, who would phone me after midnight during exams to make sure that I was still awake, and who would ask me urgently, What page have you gotten to? All of that stored-up motherliness in Hiba pelted down on me in a concentrated storm. On me, the girl who was one year younger than Hiba, but five years her senior in my studies. I clung to this motherly Hiba as if she were a last fortress that no one had yet been able to breach.

Ever since I began at the college, and ever since I felt sure of a successful first year, I had gotten into the habit of picking up my results late, each term's grades sometime during the following term. The woman who supervised my department in the student affairs office would give me odd looks. What level of unconcern was this, which led me to go all this time neglecting to pick up my grades, not knowing whether I had passed or not? Even worse, I would hold onto that sealed envelope carrying my grades until there came a time in which I needed some happy news that would lift me out of my moody state. Luck had never betrayed me until now. This time around, the result was a complete fizzle.

And, Hiba, you are going to laugh at me when I tell you that I failed in the stupidest, most trivial subject possible. I made a dumb choice, passing up all the subjects in my major, in which failing would at least be honorable, and then I went and failed a general-ed course!

Neither of us could sleep that night. But we both lay there rigidly, neither one wanting to turn over, so as not to let the other one surmise that she was awake. We each passed the hours of darkness counting the lambs of sleep—or the beasts of anxiety.

5

I drew out the black notebook from a shadowy niche inside my chest. I recorded one more stroke, just as before I had recorded my very first sins: the first song I listened to, the first prayer I abandoned, the first ritual ablutions I postponed, the first longing I toyed with, the first fast day during which I ate, the first kiss ... and now, the first full discovery of my body. I documented them all, with their dates and their details.

If dates can be derisive, mocking, and sadistic—and carefully selected, of course—then that precisely was the status of my dates when they concerned Dai. Our first kiss was like the sweets at Qurqii'an, the evening halfway through the month of Ramadan when children gather in their new clothes to celebrate the birth of one of the Prophet's grandsons, whom we revere, Hassan son of Ali. They go round to people's homes to ask for candy. Or it was like yummy peanuts halfway through the month of Sha'ban. The prayer of the body, the night of my fate, my power, my own Lailat al-Qadar, but at the beginning of the final third of Ramadan instead of at its very end. I do not know if she was aware of it at the time, but with perfect mastery and precision, Dai gathered between her thumb and her index finger all those years of mine that were uselessly gone; she rubbed them until they became dust particles so fine that they no longer had any substance. Then she sat back, one leg crossed over the other, a crowned and contented queen. Radia, "the Lady Contented with God's Will," as so many Muslim queens have been named.

In my past few years I have lived a double life. I prepare intensive summer courses in Islamic jurisprudence and the theology of Oneness that is the basis of Islamic belief and morals and the science of logic. I do volunteer work. I write for a magazine focused on the proper cultural education of the young. I march into battles doomed to fail, only so that my voice will have a place to resound, and my steps, a pavement on which to fall. In half of my responses, I am giving myself cover, and I try to leave the other half vague enough so that no one can observe what I have been doing in my life, far from the eyes of others, or can look into my thoughts, which would inevitably appear tarnished by stupidity or their deviation from the correct path of the upright.

From a few stories and intrigues I knew that my life, and the lives of every one of us—by which I mean those whom other people categorize as workers for God—were permanently under the microscope. My errors, any way in which I might fail or stumble and fall, were not private issues concerning me alone. They were owned by everyone, and they were always on exhibit for eyes that had been thoroughly trained to catch any missteps. Whenever any one of us held the microphone or put an identifiable signature at the end of an article for the sake of seeing our names circulate, we were volunteering ourselves as defendants on trial; we would be interrogated, judged and sentenced in tales told at the end of the evening, tales that always got around, leaving sharp reactions in their wake.

We were not saints, nor were we preserved and protected by the name of God alone. We were nothing but a lowly rabble, third-rate workers, which made us nothing more than an onion skin or an orange peel—quickly pierced, thoughtlessly discarded, something everyone was allowed to deal with or dispose of in whatever way they wished. We were held accountable as the vulnerable breach in a long line of institutions and beliefs that protected them, such that people hardly dared to treat badly any person who might try to get ahead of us in that holy queue. The kicks aimed at our backsides continued, and people relished them. They transformed our every little slip into an extremely serious issue that could not, in any circumstances, be hushed up.

Thus, although there was no written statute on the books to tell us so, we had to remain blank slates, perfect in every detail, without a single scratch, honorable and ever lustrous, as extraordinary as prophets and as pure-white as angels. We were what stood in the way of anyone who might try to demolish the structure made up of a thousand stories reaching all the way to the sky, and yet we represented the flimsiest bricks in the building. What is unshakably true is that we garnered nothing from this except some traces of false glory, a few mean compliments, and perhaps a bit of good will. But at the same time—behind the scenes and the tightly shut doors—we were sustaining plenty of blows below the belt, whether we knew of them or not.

I was perfectly aware that my secret life, my other life, was an extremely dangerous gamble and a harmful one, and that was part of what made it so pleasurable. I was gambling straight out, but I thought I knew what I was doing. I was aware of how long the path of retreat was, how enormous my reversal would be if I were forced into it. A measure of intense adrenalin pushed me onward, and I bore real and true dread of God's wrath and felt the weight of a terrible guilt complex. I sensed the heaviness of hell upon me, and the heaviness of the others, and of the possibility that my cover would be blown. I searched for my salvation as feverishly as I could. But the more I tried, the more deeply I found myself divided, hopelessly submerged in my two worlds, as deeply in one as in the other.

I did not leave. As sick and despairing of everything as I was, I did not go away. I went on watching Hassan, and figuring that he was watching me from that other shore of his, though I had not wanted him to see the hasty reaction of mine that followed his final departure. If I had known that he would abandon me and go away forever, from the start I would not have negotiated even two seconds that I could squander in that wasteland I now inhabited. What had started me out was the pull of the adolescent hormones of a sixteen-year-old who needed desperately to see herself growing older in the eyes of others. Hassan infused me with the ability to feel proud of myself, and to spread my wings in the sunshine. Whenever he gave me a pat on the wings, I flew—I was a seagull who never ceased embracing the skies. Hassan remains my eye: Hassan is the eye that sees me, and he is all of my mirrors. He is the eye whose light was put out, setting me into a blind nighttime in which no one could see me or sense that I existed.

From where I had been, I had cut a path that I could not retrace or wipe out. In bright red lines, I drew the letters that composed the name *Dai*. Next to that name, I set down the new date of my body, and I closed the notebook. Something would happen, I decided, that would be no worse than what had already, and really, happened. Her impact had been so overwhelming that now, gradually, my body could only lose its need for her, and eventually I could deflect my longing to love her. I might even learn to hate her if I could see clearly enough how very scandalously she was disfiguring me. I would slide with her to the very lowest place she could bring me down to, and at that point I would dare to leave her, for it would not be in her power to do anything more—anything worse—to me.

Without needing any more justification than this, I went back to Dai. A simple gesture from her was all I needed, a sign, a five-minute phone call. My longing alone, mingling with my physical desire, was enough to make me a pawn to her wishes. She used the excuse of my approaching birthday to propose that we see each other, and for my part, I did not wait for any incitement to rip up the pages of the calendar as fast as I could in anticipation of Wednesday, which was so slow to come, just to spite me.

6

My next task: to convince my mother to let me move into what used to be Muhammad's room. It had been a whole year since his marriage, and the same amount of time since Faisal had settled into his university housing; he only came home on weekends. If our home had shrunk since Hassan's death, it was this double blow that truly abandoned it to an awful, killing silence. It was this that made my mother stare at the belly of Maryam, my brother's wife, willing it to swell, to bring us a child who would bring back the happy clatter the house had once held. Fatima's three children were not enough for my mother. Fatima, the sister eight years older than me who had been married, it seemed to me, since the beginning of time, and whom my mother never ceased to blame or scold for her absence, her failure to visit—the signs, as my mother saw it, of my elder sister's deliberate separation from her. Our home, empty most of the time, left my mother saying over and over again, in obvious distress, There's nothing left of this home but the maid!

Half of my arguments with my mother were about overdoing the solitude thing, as she saw it—my long spells of withdrawal into my room, from which I would not emerge unless to leave the house altogether or to take my food from the kitchen, returning to eat it in my room, or to use the bathroom. My mother blamed and scolded me incessantly for always closing the door to my room and blasting the sound of songs into the air behind my walls.

Muhammad's room was virtually separated from everything else, and it had its own private bath. This was precisely what made it so difficult to get my mother to agree that I could move there. Even though I possessed quite a range of devious ploys that allowed me to unload my mother when I wanted to, I barely used them. She had enough fatigue and unending worries because of me.

Finally, I had no choice but to give in to her demands. Eat your meals with me on days when there is no school. Don't close the door for long periods. I want to be able to check on you, especially if you are taking a bath ... leave the door open! Stop staying up so late, sitting in front of that computer nearly until the sun comes up ... and TV, too—keep the light on when you're watching TV, you're tiring out your eyes for no reason.

Any other orders?

Watch out for yourself, sweetie.

With this last sentence, she touched my cheek playfully. I had come to know this affecting, querulous tone of hers ever since Hassan had been gone, and I dreaded it as much as I longed to answer her with the words, *Mama, I miss him too. Me, too*! I had not wept for Hassan like a proper sister in mourning. I had screamed, on and on, Hassan is not leaving me! Hassan is not dying! Touch him, rub him, he just feels chilled, he isn't really stone cold! He is just making fun of us. Please, believe me, this is a silly little game and he is just teasing us. He will open his eyes in a little bit and say, Boo! And no one laugh. I will kill all of you if you laugh. No one laughs at tricks as stupid as this. He is under the sheet now, trying to get the better of his laughter so that he won't be discovered. Let someone lift off all of this white that covers him. You will see, all of you will see. Believe me. No, wait! No one lift the covers off him! He told me yesterday that he was feeling chilled. This winter is a miserable and mean one—it does not realize how cold Hassan is feeling. Stop crying. You are all letting his hand slip away. You are all letting him go. Stop, all of you! Hassan is not leaving me. He told me that he is a hero and he will triumph. He will recover. He was always saying that hospitals lie—they are the ones who make out like bandits from his illness. He told me that, and he was looking right into my eyes when he said it. He is going to give me an awesome gift for the next big feast, the Eid. On that holiday, my wallet will explode from having so much money stuffed in it! We will go to the seashore together, and to the amusement park, where we will ride the Death Train. I'm afraid of that rollercoaster, I told him, and he said he would hold me really tight and laugh and laugh at me as I screamed in fear. I told him he would never have a chance, no opportunity like that would ever be offered to him. Ohhh, never be offered. Never, never be offered!

I screamed for a long time. But my screaming never went any further than my head. I wiped my tears, the drops swelling out of my eyes in spite of myself. I swiped at them with true disgust. I must not cry. If I cry, it means I am confirming Hassan's death, and then he really will have died, even though Hassan is not someone who dies. Hassan is not someone who goes back on his word. I can give him my blood! But Hassan, my blood is not clean enough. Still, its corpuscles are prettier than yours, Hassan, and they are more fastidious. Mine are round and plump, because I have fed them for eighteen years on sugar and watered them with Cola. With what have you watered your blood to make such bad things pierce its corpuscles, to cause a violent scythe to slash them, reaping all of your dreams, my beloved brother? Come, tell me, with all your usual sarcasm, that no, I am not fastidious, not elegant, that my blood is not exacting. Say that if my blood tastes like sugar, as we Arabs say, it is the taste of noxious sugars. Say that you were just worried about the state of your monthly stipends and you escaped so as not to pay me any cash during the Holy Feast. Do you think that I will go easy on you? Of course not. Just come to me, that's all. *Hisabak asiir ma'aya*! I am going to call you to account. You are not imagining, surely, that you can make what is in your head happen as easily as this, and get away with your very obvious plotting! Just come, just come or ... okay, look, I will not take any of my medications until you back down. I will get sick. You know how stubborn I am. I will get *really really* sick and mother will put all the blame onto you. Mom will cut you off, too. She does not like it when you frighten her like this! She cries, and she says to everyone, Do not put out Hassan's candle. She says that it is not easy for her to see you stretched out full length in this expanse of whiteness, this tall frame of yours, which after today, she thinks, will find refuge only in the soil. Tell her she is wrong. You are totally wrong, Mother.

But Hassan did not speak. The dead do not have anything to say. Their final word is their death. The dead do not talk. They turn their steps toward worlds we have never pierced, and they do not come back. They overdo the silence bit, yielding to us a space that everyone knows is designated for talk and plaint and shrieking and weeping and blaspheming God and all inglorious forms of rejecting what is right and true. They stare into the void, into that absolute space where they fix their grip on all that we do not yet know. They will not connive with us to steal a glimmer of light from that unknown space, a flash that we could hold onto. They will not solve a single riddle for us. With their newfound arrogance, they shut the door, slamming it closed with all the energy of the lives they had, rather than seeing the angels of death suck that energy away. We are not allowed even a keyhole or the sliver of space beneath a door, to make it reveal the momentous secret whose details no one is willing to share with us.

What hurts me so much are the details of him, for they are impervious to my mind's usual ability to forget. With total recall I can hear the timbre of his voice and see the pupils of his eyes flitting whenever he speaks. I can recollect how he waved his hand about and exactly how his fingers moved, the particular ways he walked and stood, and his own special manner of holding the prayer beads or his car keys, how he toyed with his hair if he forgot something and was trying to remember, how he slammed the door when he was irritated, how exactly he balanced his spoon with all five fingers and ate like a child. I remember the mole just where his hair sprang out, as close as could be to his left temple, and how his temples pulsed when he had a headache or if he was seriously angry. And even though he seldom got angry, I recall him snapping *Khudh lak*! when someone stepped in front of him and blocked his way. I remember him praying quietly, free of any care, and I remember him when he got sick and the whites of his eyes turned yellow. I remember him scooping out those miniscule fish, harpoon fishes, from the little dam nearby so that I could raise them in the shiny gold Abu Kursi shortening cans, where they would die. And then I was afraid to cry lest his face melt from the impact of my flowing eyes, afraid that his face and its minute details would leave me, afraid that he would abandon me in my awful solitude.

I continue to try to deal with Hassan's absence by writing, and I deal with writing by making sure of my own personal absence from it, and I deal with this absence of *me* by maintaining a brittle presence that is nothing like me, a presence that could only resemble a creature without well-defined features or a clear demeanor, without even an identity, an *I*, in that world where I could open a computer window and march through it. A world in which I can decant my features simply with the dust particles of words, fishing for laughs and cries with ready-made icons.

Whatever distances I set out to cross, in directions I have already traveled—my studies, my trivial volunteer work, writing, my friends and my mother—all of these are nothing but a long, deliberate, and persistent attempt to keep myself fixed in the image where Hassan left me. I was an image pounded into the wall with a nail with an inscription at the lower edge: as Hassan was this ... thus. I remained terrified of the thought that he might return in the form of a hailstone or a white gull and would find nothing but a girl whose wonderful wholeness had dwindled away in his absence. That he would look down on me from his other world and it would frighten him to see me alone, abandoned and fragile. Inside, I was that girl, exactly that girl, and so I went to great lengths with powder and laughter even when I didn't feel like it—whatever might keep anyone and everyone from noticing the despondent way I had receded from life. In the space of three years, I wilted, and here I was, on the point of breakdown.

If it had been up to me, I would have moved into Hassan's room. In his bed, I would have been able to breathe in his existence, to inhale his dreams as I buried my head in his pillow, and to feel, wrapped in his bed linens, the warmth that had moved and walked among people. Had I done that, I would not have dared to go on and do any of the foolish things that I did. I would not have been able to lead the compass of his mind astray by saying, Yes, I prayed just a little while ago, or to claim that Dai and I had been completely absorbed in the film on the screen and so we didn't even hear the knock on the door. His face was all it took to return God to my heart. I knew that his trusty moral compass, which kept him headed in the right direction, and which had kept me on the right path, too, would have exploded out of its accustomed direction if my lies had been revealed.

No sooner did my mother give me the faintest possible green light than I moved myself wholesale into Muhammad's room. I had already dealt with the chaos of my belongings, certain that my mother would soften in the end and agree to my plans. I did not take any of the furnishings from my room except the television and computer and the tables on which they rested, plus a few picture frames, all of which held Hassan's face. The number of books in my bookcase paralyzed me. I could not possibly move them all at once, and that led me to an idea that I really liked: the notion of having two rooms, completely separate from each other, with two different sets of furnishings, and different capabilities. I would read in one room and watch TV in the other, and perhaps I would sleep one night in this room and another night in that one.

Muhammad's room, with its serious and practical workaday atmosphere, suited me very well. The sparse furniture left a huge expanse of room free and available to the flights that my mood would take. The space allowed me to sleep some evenings on the floor, to stretch out in front of the television with my legs raised and hanging on the table edge, to have my phone conversations as I paced to and fro across the room, to study in its most remote corners, so that I had nothing around me but bare walls and corners, to park my body just behind the door, where I could hide while I got myself through the various stages of my depressions, and to toss out my many pillows and let them scatter, transforming the floor into a space where one could not easily set one's feet down.

What was even more agreeable to me was the bathroom. Late at night I would leave the bathroom light on while I sat in the doorway thinking, planning, writing, finishing my homework. If it had not been for the sound that would echo too widely, I would have brought over my phone and frittered away the whole night chatting with Umar or Hiba. And, once finished, I would sit with my back leaning against the closed door of the bathroom, from inside, and smoke my daily cigarettes, or rather my nightly cigarettes. The scandalous pleasure of the nicotine creeping through my blood mixed with the warm intimacy of my cooped-up berth, and the curtain offered by the nighttime, and the utter silence of our home—all of it sent into me an intense, comforting kind of numbness.

I transport myself to a higher world; concealed, not really there, I follow vestibules and doorways and corridors, secret ones that exist only in my mind. I trace their details and twists and turns, trying to keep hold of them, rubbing my fingers against them and burnishing the truths there until I can see them clearly. I've never had a galloping imagination, not even in the first years of my life. Only the sting of my curiosity got me to approach the earth and its tangible objects. But here in my head—and only in my head—I feel as though I am rebuilding myself, brick by brick. I can decide what I will allow to make its way stealthily into me, and what I will prohibit from entry. I absent myself from the world as a way to bridle my desire to swallow it whole, convincing myself that I would choke on it immediately, for the world is hard and I must learn to let it pass me by rather than enter me with its arrogant self-propulsion. And there are the others, the others always, my first precaution and the cause of my fears. I do not want anyone to touch me, to reach me. No one, and nothing, either.

Being alone is reassuring. It gives me enough space to come as near as I wish and to stay as far away as I want. To choose your own solitude does not mean that you stop being at the heart of the world. In its simplest forms, it means that you are there, or anywhere, only by choice, and that you take in hand your own being-there, holding it within your own personal boundaries so that no one can roam widely enough to steal you from your self suddenly, or mold your face according to his wishes, or harm you, or twist the neck of the compass that guides you.

If my room, before, was my stern isolation from everything outside, the bathroom became my ultimate refuge, where no one could violate or disturb me, nor could they see the marks of violation on me, abbreviated or whole. All I had to do was to close the door to be sure that no one would see me. The door was my trustworthy guard, and the breach through which I could penetrate to my special private world that concerned no one but me. The bathroom was where my brain was—my slate. My thoughts are my chalk, a chalk of pure white. I will color the world in the light of God, and my own world is no exception.

7

Wednesday came, and with it came Dai. When the clock hands met atop the four she was kissing me, and with her lips she closed the final moments of my first year as an adult—or a rightly guided person, as we say—before taking me by the hand as I stepped into my new year. For an entire twelve months now, I had been lifting one foot, and with the other leaping into a new hopscotch square, but I did not know how I was supposed to deal with any of it, nor what was demanded of me in this new stage of things.

For years, I carried a mental image of the age of eighteen as a glowing lantern, and I had been ready and waiting to cross in front of it so that it would light my face. Of course, the enticements were simply that I had gotten through and beyond adolescence and was entering the university. This made it inevitable that I would riffle out my feathers and swell up like a peacock, as I would raise my index finger and shake it in the whole world's face. Stop treating me like a little girl whose anklebone will become twisted if she plays ball, or who will lose her way back if she sets out alone to the neighborhood store!

I made it past eighteen, and teenagerdom, and the first of my years of university, and no big changes came about. I was still getting an allowance and I still needed permission to leave the house, plus practically an old-style military order, a *firman* from above that carried absolute authority on the acceptance or rejection of every new friend in my life. I hung up my second lantern, twenty-one, with a huge red star and the phrase, *Finally I will be taken seriously*. I was not. In the eyes of Hidaya, whose very name meant *guidance* and who represented for me the power of adults, I remained that little girl who had not yet absorbed enough life experience.

But between the two lanterns something changed. I cannot exactly pinpoint that something's starting point, nor the manner of its first steps. It was not a single thing, but rather many things, taking on new colors and changing shapes and qualities until I was incapable of following the changes closely, let alone monitoring them.

I would put on makeup, pluck whatever extraneous hair I could find, and leave the house without doing more than leaving word for my mother just so she would know I was out. If she were out, I did not even leave a note, since I was a sensible girl, and anyway, my steps were restricted by where the driver would agree to take me. If it was late I would call, since I had a cell phone. And I withdrew into a seriously astonishing whirlwind called the Internet. There, I could address anyone as *my dear*, even though I was daughter to a society where to address anyone falling in the category of *sound male creature* would be considered as either utterly inconceivable or a brand of prostitution, unless, maybe, it was a male parrot that I was addressing. Out of my roster of friends, my mother knew only each girl's first name, and only in a quarter of the cases did she refuse my wishes to spend time with them.

My mother had a tendency to pronounce snap judgments that came as a surprise and left no room for lightening them up. Sometimes she would reject my relationship with some friend or other simply because she did not feel comfortable about the girl. When it came to that, I had only my time on the school grounds to help friendships grow instead of remaining subject to her refusal.

I really don't know: Did the world itself slip out of its old skin and, like me, leave behind the years of harshness, moving on into an open space to which it had never before even seemed headed? Or did my mother age suddenly, so that closely tracking the steps of her children became too fatiguing a task? Or was my freedom among the endowments that always accompany the age of eighteen, but do not show up immediately with one's birthday and the gifts you receive on that particular date?

On her own accord, Dai moved first to shut off the light switch. I asked her if this was supposed to be a part of my gift. After all, she had tried to coerce me with a thousand-line petition asking if we could put out the lights. She answered me with a diminished smile. I know this mood of Dai's, when her mental sky is cloudy and there is a cause for it, but she will not tell me what that cause is, no matter how I try to outsmart her. But, contrary to my suspicions, she just came over and turned my face to the wall and lay down with her forehead plastered to my bare back. She began sketching crazy zigzags across my skin with her fingertip and then she burst into sobs. For several minutes I was so bewildered that I could not react. It was the first time she had cried like this in my presence. I made an attempt to turn toward her but she prevented me, keeping her hand firmly on my lower back. When she spoke, she sounded completely overcome by profound fear. Why did you desert me for so long? she asked. All this time?

I was confused. I needed some time.

Some time! Do you know how many days it was?

I'm sorry, I didn't mean to cause you any pain. And look, I'm here with you now.

You'll leave me. There's nothing that keeps you here with me. You will leave me. Even Balqis left.

I conjured up in my mind the roll call of names we shared between us, from our days at secondary school and then university, and at the Hussainiyya, trying to figure out some thin thread of intent in her words. But I didn't have an inkling of what she meant. I knew nothing that had any connection to this name. Later, in one of our most intensely intimate moments, she would tell me about Balqis, the girl who transformed her into this *maskh*, as she put it. This freak, this deformed creature, this monster.

She began to shiver, her crying a clear sign of the pain she was feeling. She allowed me to turn over and take her in my arms. I'm with you, I said. I'm staying with you. I will not leave you.

Hah!

This explosive *hah* of hers stands at an uncertain point between sarcasm and suspicious doubt. Like someone waving at me and saying, Please—you may give me that bullet shot known as *I will not stay* instead of the slow-acting and fatal poison, *I will not leave you*. Please, do not give me a hope that has such razor-sharp edges!

She got up out of bed, blurting out a half-hearted joke about her sobbing, sounding like a little girl who has been knocked down by one of the kids down the alley who runs off with her purchases. She walked across the room to turn on the light. She came back, mounted my body and began to drown me in feverish kisses. I was used to her unexpected reversals of mood, for which I could rarely find any reasonable explanation. Her behavior was exactly the same way, contradictory and open to various interpretations. One moment, she would be weak and resigned, and within seconds, she would suddenly have regained her despotic ways and her sharpness. Sometimes when she appeared she was as sensitive and delicate as a fine summer morning, and other times she would shatter me to the bones like a hurricane coming through. From the beginning I believed utterly that she exceeded my powers of comprehension. She was simply too cryptic for me to fully understand. So I stopped working my mind so hard to solve the riddle. That way, Dai was more beautiful. She was a secret I would never divulge because I would never really know what was at the heart of it.

No sooner was I engulfed in Dai's body than a knock came

suddenly on the door, doubling my heart rate instantly as various thoughts raced through my brain, colliding head-on. Fear ran a marathon race through my veins. I shot upward in less than a second. Doing up the buttons on my shirt required two tries, both unsuccessful, and then a third, with Dai's hand, as she got up calmly to put on her clothes, without any haste, and without a single change of expression on her face.

I opened the door to see our maid standing there. I let go with my rude tongue as I jabbed my finger toward a sign slashed red to signal NO ENTRANCE. It hung on my door and meant that I did not want anyone to bother me, no matter what the issue, no matter how serious it was, because I was asleep or I was taking a bath or I had gone to hell. All that mattered was that no one knock at my door! For her part, Edna faltered and stuttered as she tried explaining something to me that had to do with the telephone and Hiba. I know Hiba. If something has gotten lodged in her head, she will not retreat even momentarily for any reason at all. She must have called and refused to hang up, letting the phone ring and ring, and then nothing would satisfy her but insisting that Edna knock on my door. I thanked the maid apologetically and turned back into my room, making sure that the door was once again closed and locked.

Hugely sarcastic grimaces had swept over Dai's face. She did not comment; she did not ask, even. Her face alone was expressive enough to fill an entire dictionary of sick jokes and giggles. She stared at me as she would at a clown who has not done a good job of putting on his face, maybe forgetting his red nose in the dressing room, and then when everyone laughs at him—because he is so funny, he assumes—they are actually laughing at him for being so stupid.

Dai treated me as if I were a child of five who did not understand anything yet. When I kissed her, she would slouch into a short and derisive laugh before receiving the kiss from me with a slightly intimate familiarity as if she were a dear and highly respected friend. It was not long before she enrolled me in school. She dictated and made me write out the domestic chores associated with five or six girls' school curriculum options, and she prescribed punishments arising from every mistake I made, no matter how tiny. At the year's end, she gave me my diploma signed off with her professorial moniker. My diploma was a sentence she wrote in black ink onto my body: You are a possession of mine and of mine alone. She said it would be hard for me to understand the full import of this signature if I did not have any immediate feelings toward it. And in truth, at the time two contradictory emotions were sweeping over me: one feeling urged me to hurl my body away from all of this and outside of Dai, and the other craved her power over this body of mine.

I called Hiba because the little demons jumping around inside of her would never quiet down if I did not call her as quickly as I possibly could. Indeed, she had dialed our house phone number so insistently that she had practically scratched out the buttons on the phone. She drummed up a trial against me, with an imaginary panel of ten judges. I was accused of bad behavior on the basis of shutting my door and turning off my cell phone as well, and then additionally of alarming the servant.

Now I'll become the champion of the oppressed and it will all be because of you, she said. I asked her what she wanted in a voice that did not hide the hurry I was in. She wanted me to stay over at her house tonight. The time of Hiba's call, and our phone conversation itself, sent a vague sensation of anxiety moving through my insides, despite the clear enthusiasm in her voice. It was not normal for her to call me at a late hour on a Wednesday night asking me to come and stay over that very night. Indeed, it was very unusual for me to be anywhere but at home overnight, unless it was summer vacation or a Ramadan night, since the timing of everything, and everyone's schedules, was turned upside down during Ramadan. I put my middle finger to my forehead and, my eyes wandering, smiled vaguely toward Dai, who for her part stopped surfing the TV channels. Her question took me by surprise.

What do you think of Sundus?

Several years before, when I had begun to attend summer religious courses, Sundus was a popular and familiar face to all, year after year. Gradually, our reticent smiles had turned into greetings offered from a distance, and then into handshakes and a friendly, casual companionship. Finally, she asked me to work with her, writing for a magazine called *Dawn*. With Hassan's encouragement, and after some hesitation, I agreed. Sundus was the female bridge connecting me to Aqil, her brother and one of the managers of the magazine.

Months later, Sundus and I had weathered the year of true terror: the third year of high school with its awful exams. Together, we were accepted to the College of Sciences in Dammam. My turn came to take the initiative just as she had, and I invited her to join up with us at the Hussainiyya. As I was new to the place, everything there was completely foreign to me; in Sundus I saw a shield to protect me, someone whose confident steps my wary, uncertain feet could follow. (Naturally, when I had offered the same possibility to Hiba—for she was my closest friend—the reaction was a loud guffaw.) Hidaya, for whom the Hussainiyya was a family-founded religious endowment, and who was related to my mother, treated me like the group's spoiled daughter, especially as I was the youngest among them. She did not reject Sundus's membership. In fact, she welcomed her warmly, perhaps because her reputation as a writer in a religious magazine had preceded her.

The two of us remained wrapped up in our own little cocoon. We mixed with the other girls, but we were equally able to do without them. Perhaps this was because of the unmistakable age difference between us and them, with the exception of Dai, who was about our age. At that time, though, Dai made no friendly overtures toward us. And even though the relationship between Sundus and me had not taken on any special warmth, in her I perceived one of those people who make you embarrassed because of the extreme humanity you find in them.

We thought alike. I didn't have to explain myself twice for Sundus to get what I was saying, even if the ways we expressed ourselves differed. Sundus's take on things was that you had to look at everything with reflection and patience. You couldn't even hope to get close to your goals if you did not give them a lot of deliberation. These sorts of things that we were working on required a lot of time to build. I, on the other hand, found this attitude too lenient, too easy going, and it produced no real benefit. The way I saw it, we had to be forthright about dealing with our pus rather than letting our blood corrupt and rot.

I was really put off by Dai's sudden, unjustified question, especially since Dai had never showed any gentleness toward Sundus. So my response was cautious.

Sundus is a great girl!

And pretty, isn't she?

Pretty, yes, very pretty!

Only?

I don't understand what you're saying.

Wasn't it true that before—

Dai had not even finished her question before I could tell, from her raised eyebrows, what she was alluding to. I interrupted her, marked disapproval in my voice.

Sundus doesn't do that.

But we—we do. And she started to guffaw.

Once again, she had caught me, in unevenly applied slapdash cheap makeup, neglecting my red nose, leaving it behind in the dressing room. All of her features bespoke one thing: I found you out! I felt myself shrinking, as she swelled magnificently. She had arrested me in my most contradictory state. She did not even have to strip anything off me. I was already completely naked.

You know I'll kill you if you're unfaithful to me?

I laughed sarcastically, trying to leave an impression with her that I was unconcerned about this threatening tone that she was using with me. And you'll drink my blood, too, I appended to her sentence.

I got up out of bed, wanting to make sure that the door was really shut, since it looked to me that the doorway might bring me breezes I didn't want from places where the sun did not shine. She grabbed me by the arm. I tried to wiggle out of her grip, and could have if she had not pushed me onto the bed. In a second, she had come down on top of me, in her eyes a look that only the devil could produce.

Did anyone before me have your body? she asked.

I didn't say anything.

Answer me!

Stop it.

Answer me, first!

Quit acting like a child.

I hate her when she moves me as if I'm a doll or a dummy—a doll that will not be injured or destroyed no matter how sharply you twist her limbs in the air. I turned my face away from her. She grabbed me at my jaws and forced my face back toward her, so I kept my eyes trained in the other direction. Her voice strained, she went on saying *Answer me* but I did not. She clapped her left hand to my neck while her right hand pulled my hair, as all the while she muffled me with sticky kisses that bore down on me painfully. They were closer to bites than to kisses.

I knew that if I kept refusing, her madness would only get worse. My refusals gave her redoubled impetus to conquer me and plant her flag on the virgin territory of which she had stripped me. Despite her evident slenderness and the feminine softness clear in her build,

Dai was light years ahead of me in bodily strength, which meant she always had a huge advantage in subduing me when I resisted her.

I withdrew into myself. I gave her the side of me that was completely the contrary of what she wanted and tried to impose. I became as cold beneath her as the ice that preserves corpses in fine physical form. By behaving this way, I was training my sights exactly on target, for I was giving her all the victory flags she could want, to plant wherever she wished, but they were lowly banners that she implanted in ground she had not fought to gain, and thus whose conquering was hardly a victory to be deserved or trumpeted.

She finally released me when she saw no sign that I was softening, when she was convinced that I was frost that her heat could not melt. She sat on the edge of the bed, angry. A heavy silence bore down on the room. Very quickly it became a dreary quiet so thick that neither of us could see the other.

One question rocked the stillness of the room and toyed with our heads. Who would be first this time to let go? I chose to be the one. Be rational, I told myself. Be big. This silence will take the two of you exactly nowhere. I started trying to open a door or at least a window in our barren muteness. Her face was blank, her expression transient, like someone who has just recently figured out some slightly elusive truth. I put my hand on her shoulder and she pushed it off. In a voice I laced with pleading, I asked, What did I do?

You're always like this! You get me angry for the sake of nothing. You get a kick out of seeing me beg for you!

I hugged her, encircling her waist with my arms, as I replied, There's been no one but you. Hey, is everything okay now?

She chose to offer an answer heard only by the bedposts and the sheets, and as usual, it was much more like a squabble than like the lovemaking that they always talk about so passionately in films.

I was not yet beyond the hard and rocky road of growing into a mature young woman—I was still getting all of those bruises that one picks up on the way, the many slaps on my body, and now I was feeling crushed beneath the wheels of a million-ton freight train named Dai. It was too early then for me to understand how far her savagery would go, and how every bit of it would be my loss. Did I yield out of love? Desire? Worshipful slavery? The number of candles I extinguished was matched by the hot tears I swallowed while she was on top of me, lighting up and burning and going to ash like a meteor passing to its final destruction. I was paying the bread of my body as a sacrifice to keep her happy, and she was sucking out my embers, so deeply that no trace would remain in my depths.

8

Fadil has asked for my hand.

Eyes shining and face worshipful, she added, I haven't told my family yet what my answer will be, but I believe I'm going to say yes.

It is truly a cause for regret that she was not joking. Neither her features—suddenly those of a woman who has come to own the world in one fell swoop—nor the shy tremulousness in her voice gave any hint of jesting. Meanwhile, something patted me gently on the heart and said, Don't let it get you down. Not yet. Hopefully, you won't lose her, too. All the while, though, another voice was abrading my ear, a loud and overbearing voice that would not stop laughing at me as it addressed its words to me. Do you understand now why she got in touch? It's classic. She is saying a graceful and upbeat goodbye to you, this girl who has finally stumbled upon a man!

I don't remember anything I said to her in response. I must have put on some show of joy and congratulated her, perhaps I even gave her a big, enthusiastic, warm hug and a genuine kiss. I must have said a lot, and together we must have sketched out a pretty image, a nest holding a couple of birds: this one is Hiba, and that one is Fadil. But where am I? This nest is very small, my dear friend! And you won't make any room for me after today. You will leave me to run with only one shoe, in the wild wilderness of my loneliness. You will cease to be either the step beneath me that keeps me steadily going forward, or the road I tread.

We women make the same mistake over and over again, and we've been doing it since the beginning of time. We truncate our lives, reducing them completely to the man who stamps his name on us. We leave our family and our friendships, our diplomas and our dreams and all the small matters and trivial things that make up our daily lives, and we go to worship at that prayer niche—I'm talking about the *mihrab* of a man. For his part, the man does not have to do very much in the way of self-alteration. He holds onto the circles he has, with their constant motion, and they keep widening, growing and growing while we remain simply a still point in the crowd. We are so very naïve!

As I touched Hiba's face—which was both remote and enormously expressive—I kept before my gaze the list of things to be stolen from me: late-night phone conversations, sleepovers on summer vacation, fresh projects, promenades on the shore, our running shoes. And her heart! *Ya Allah*, nothing will remain for me. My fingers burned; and there were not enough of them to let me count up all my losses. No doubt, a few inches away, she was making a list that was similar, except that it was headed by the image of a hero. Fadil alone was the master of her ticket window now, and I had no choice but to stand in line like any common person, like the hoi polloi, the dregs of society, the lower class, waiting my turn, which might well never come.

Fadil had inspired the burning taste of envy in my throat since our earliest childhood. Hiba had worshipped him when she was little and now here she was, leaving to marry him. Son of her maternal aunt, a boy with greenish eyes and light hair—their boy. At the time, there was no boy I hated the way I hated him. He just made me so mad with the way he rode a bike so well, how good he was at it, when I never could do it with any skill. And if there was not a boy in the world who had the right to claim superiority over me, the spoiled and childish girl, then how could a boy have his sort of swagger? That was why I would stir up his rancor by saying those damning words, Hey, you American you! For children who woke up and went to sleep to the anthem Death to America on Radio Iran every day, this insult of mine was a completely unacceptable dishonor, but for Fadil it was a disgrace that could not be refuted. Its scandalous signs were so blatantly there, and could not be veiled.

Of course, Hiba would travel with him abroad when he had a work assignment somewhere. She would drive their car, she would give birth to four children, and she would traverse all of God's wide world. She would summer in Paris, stare full on at the Mona Lisa's smile, make snowballs and fashion a snowman with a cap and red nose ... and so, what else, Hiba? She might barely remember an old friend now and then, a cousin, no less, flicking the dust off that face and sending her a postcard from the last capital city she happened to visit.

Her jelly-like face pains me. Her silence pains me—she who has never been silent. If only she would say something! *Anything*. How can Fadil alter her to this extent when he has not been close to her, has not revealed himself to her, and has not occupied her very being yet? He has not even put an engagement ring on her finger! How can she suddenly be so much older, with secrets and private matters and things that I have no right to unlock and know, when only yesterday she left all the drawers in her chest open for me to riffle through? Why didn't she teach me from the start how to spy and steal, so that now I would be able to know what she was thinking, why she was as silent and still as a wall, her life as secret as a solitary holy man's hidden cell? Now I am the stranger in the room, and I curse my presence, even though not long ago, our phone conversation had been all I needed to make me feel like I was alive.

Say something, Hiba! Anything!

If only she had not spoken!

She dropped her head onto my shoulder, and I could no longer pick up anything but the murmur of lips wanting to say something but stumbling over the words. I put my arms around her and what I heard was like a mighty kick that struck a distant spot behind her ribs. She held my hand tightly and said, I want to call him ... we need to agree on some things. And I want ... I want to do that without my family knowing. I don't want to cause him any embarrassment when we don't agree. Are you going to help me? Can you let me use your cell phone? And stay with me, I mean, while we're talking. I don't want to feel like I'm committing some crime.

Half minutes, or quarter minutes, went by between the end of one of her sentences and the beginning of the next. Heavy—that is how the time going by felt against my body, and a mix of bitterness and sorrow stung me. Something drove me to feel relentless pulses of sorrow, feelings of regret that I did not understand at all, a sensation like that left by an old betrayal. I pushed her far enough away from me that I could look her in the eye. I explained to her that I could not be a third party in a moment so intensely intimate as this. I left my phone with her. I promise you, she said, I will not spy on your list of numbers or answer any of your phone calls or play around with your messages. It's not a big deal, I said in English. She told me to send Salaam over tomorrow, when she would give him the phone along with a few other things for camouflage, and I left.

9

I am not a water-based creature. Weeping is not one of my distinguishing features. Between the two of us—moisture and me—there is no particularly intense, intimate relationship that one can depend ⁱ+ is true that I am the water's child, and my feet carry the flavor salty sand. I am like as can be to a seashell as I move along the ground; in my cupped palms I conceal the reverberations of the Gulf. If you were to scratch at my memory, you would see nothing but astounding blue and boats and the splash of the tides. But it is true as well that I have inherited a superabundance of weeping that goes back to an ancient era. Ever since Karbala, ever since the death of that young man so long ago, we Shi'is have been weeping, and our tears never have dried up. And since Karbala we have come to understand our weeping as an ongoing, never-ending daily act, a deed that is always there. It is not seasonal, selling us its goods and leaving town. And so, I do hold inside of me a profuse reservoir, tears that exhaust me every night, but I do not cry.

Ever since I was a semi-boy or a sexless child, I have gotten used to the idea, never challenged, that children do not gain the qualities of their sex until after marriage, when the girls give birth to children and the boys go out to work. Because I was so naughty, and because I always brushed up against a handful of devilish boys, I was used to not crying. Weeping gave a pretext for sarcastic lashes and yielded an especially painful quiver of jokes and heart-jabbing jeers. I certainly had no need for a tattoo of shame that would stick to me like a buzzing insect. When I got a little older, I told myself that it would be best for me to continue my abstinence, allowing only a few pure white tears for the black days—and at that point in my life, I had not seen a black day. It was Hassan, and only Hassan, who changed my crying habits. He left me a map washed clean of any features and a broken compass, and then he said to me, Go on!

I awoke in a very troubled mood. I was not going to give in to all of the weeping that was accumulating inside of me in a terrible hard lump of melancholy and oversensitivity (not to mention the closed doors—my mouth, my phone, and likewise, the door to my room). It was Saturday, and even my face exhibited an enormous question. Where and how would I come up with enough endurance to get all the way through another day, so that I could fall asleep once again?

Overwhelming feelings of loss toward Hiba blanketed me more heavily than did the comforter on my bed, and my heart remained cold. The night before yesterday, a long, sharp blade had pierced my body's midsection. Yet I could not stop scolding myself harshly for its self-centered reaction. Why should I not be the happiest girl in the world, because she was the happiest? Didn't we always feel the same way about things? But I was not marrying that American Fadil. He had not encircled *my* right ring finger with an engagement ring. No one had released their celebratory trills on my behalf.

Oh, I was not angry at him, nor at her, not at all. It was just that I felt so very alone, and for the first time. And to make it worse, Hiba was so completely preoccupied with other things that she did not even notice! She now had someone who filled her completely, so what use did she have for me? My problem lay not in Hiba's engagement, but in how cheaply she could replace me with somebody else, and how completely, to the point where she did not even have enough sympathy for me to grant me a decent separation period in which to become accustomed to her absence. Or, barring that, time in which I could at least learn to claim that I had forgotten her, or subjugate myself into accepting my loss of her! The swiftness with which it had happened, and my obliviousness had given me no opportunity to consider such a possibility before it landed on me, redoubling my feelings of loss.

I repeated to myself that this was just another difficult day and at least I could count on it coming to an end. I had to bathe in cold water. The water heater was empty but I could not shake the numbness and yesterday's lingering odor from my body without bathing. And then I could not find an ironed shirt or a clean pair of socks, but Edna was still asleep. So I delayed the driver of the car that carried me to the college every day for five minutes. Even so, the day's hardships had not really and truly begun.

With the rain typical of February's first days, a gray sky, and streets blocked by flowing water, it was hard to get anywhere. A drive that would normally take half an hour took twice that long, and I arrived at the college late, a few minutes after eight o'clock. The entry gate for students arriving in private cars was all but closed. Another minute and the only way I could have entered campus would have been to pass by the security guard women once I had shown them my university ID, which I never carried in my wallet unless we were in the middle of exams. It was not a question of neglect so much as it was a little cheating that we had inherited from the generation of girls who preceded us. One could generally and sensibly assume that we would not be carrying our ID cards. If one of the supervisors— these women who watched us so closely—were to seize us for any transgression outside the lecture halls (which they did not enter), we would always make the excuse that we had forgotten our IDs, and then we could use any name we might invent and thereby escape the punishment of having fifty riyals deducted from our allowances.

It was a trick I had not been compelled to use, so far anyway, since the rules were more relaxed for those of us who were in the science departments than they were in the arts, where everything was really intensely regulated. That was true except when the month of Muharram started, the month when we Shi'is commemorated Hussain's death, even if we were not allowed to do so publicly. They would lock the building entries and erect search points that were just like the roadblocks out on the ordinary roads. In Muharram, the major infraction incurring punishment and a fine was the wearing of black shirts. To wear a black shirt at that time of year, as well as a few other special days scattered throughout the year, was customary for Shi'is. In response to this policy of punishment at the college, we insisted on wearing them in what appeared a silent resistance to an efficient and tangible attempt to banish our difference—even a simple difference in the color of our clothing.

We did not give the issue more prominence than it deserved. We got through it with a bit of joking and a lot of looking the other way. We managed to avoid letting the idea that we were being constrained and oppressed control us. And if the microscope we were always under magnified everything, still, we could slip out from under it with ease and without causing an artificial or excessive confrontation. We wore regular blouses over our black shirts as camouflage. Or we recorded our names as violators of the rule and went peaceably on to our lectures, supplicating God out loud to help these supervisors. We reckoned that they would be obliged to count what was almost a third of the entire student population of the college or even more as transgressors. To feign ignorance is also an effective policy. Doing so does not make light of your adversary; it just neutralizes your foe's argument. We would have been far more likely to find this policy altogether beneath us had we been given alternative solutions.

With the human tide we create, and this mark of our difference we wear, we are suddenly manifest and can no longer be ignored. The question of our otherness is no longer left to guesswork, in the shape of our features or the particular sorts of names we bear, nor in our mutual withdrawal into our own kind, looking as though we are accumulations of flesh inside a different and larger body that does not fit us very well at all. Our distinction glares now: it is the black shirt that we have worn with stunning persistence, happily giving up our allowances for the month of Muharram, letting the money go to our adversaries. We give up, too, the peace that we could have been harvesting, had we been content, submissive to our circumstances. Together, as one mass, we turn into an enormous rolling question, like a snowball growing bigger and bigger. What are those people? Where does their difference lurk?

What is so frightening, from the start, about our being different? Is it because we form a storm of question marks, moving fiercely through an undistinguished and previously unnoticed space in this nation, that never before experienced the essence or function of questioning, or of being in a state of difference? Is it because we release an intensity of presence that remains unacknowledged on the map of the world, or between the thighs of a recognized tribe? Is it because we breach an unannounced law, one that requires us to cloud over our dissimilarity from the universal and only mold that the other is supposed to know and follow, and from all that is real and correct?

My late arrival was a parsimonious little smile of good luck, because it meant that I did not have to pass alongside a section of the quad-rangle where there gathered those we had named *banat al-balad*, the country girls, a space between Science Buildings One and Two. Thus I did not have to exhaust the waning energy in my veins with any encounters, any long exchanges of greetings and questions that always come up after the weekend break; specifically queries having to do with Hiba's engagement. A little cluster of classmates had reserved a seat for me so that I didn't have to deal with searching for one in the big hall or dragging a chair from another lecture hall in behind me. Moreover, our lecturer had not arrived yet, and anyway she did not care if a whole half an hour of lecture time was frittered away in meaningless chatter or if students came in late through the rear door to the lecture hall, whether they had an excuse or not.

I made the most of this bit of time. I went down to the cafeteria and ordered a coffee. The woman behind the glass counter front raised her eyebrows when I asked for two spoonfuls of instant coffee and three of sugar. I did not understand what the secret was behind her wonder. Was it the concentration of coffee or the sweetness of the sugar? I did not have any small change and neither did she, so I added in a cheese croissant and a chocolate bar and gave her ten riyals.

I sat down at the white marble table, fished my cell phone out of my bag, and left a missed call for Dai. If she wasn't busy right now, she would call back without a doubt. I needed her voice, with its easy tone, somewhere between gelatin and the viscosity of honey. Whenever Dai laughed, I felt the ether surrounding her loosen its joints in some fundamental sense, to the point of dislocation. I would truly feel that she was curing me.

She did return my call. Her words were two warm palms undoing the nodes of pain in my neck and releasing a faint aah of pleasure. I heard a fine-grained laugh when I informed her that I had bought the cheese croissant for her, and she exclaimed, You fox, you! It only took one added minute to shed my hateful feelings toward this Saturday, the first day of school after the Friday break, and I would even have belted out that old song with her, the one that mixed nonsense words with the days of the week to teach them to little kids, *al-sabt sabamabut, wa'l ahad raan raan, wa'l ithneen* ... My mother would always sing that to me when I was depressed on a Friday evening because the weekend was over and I'd soon have to wake up in the morning and face a Saturday that would drag on heavily forever. I had all but fixed a long-lasting smile on my face when her phone suddenly went dead. Maybe it was the bad weather bringing the network down, or maybe the battery was gone, or whatever—never mind, it was not a problem at all. I waited another minute, and when she did not call back, I headed into my lecture.

The sudden sharp sound of my phone, more like two thuds than a continuous ringing, interrupted the professor, who was immersed in explaining something, and all eyes swung to the back where I sat. I did not show any obvious confusion or embarrassment, so as to avoid letting them know that the sound had come from my bag. The *duktoora* rapped the blackboard with her chalk to regain the attention of all the girls in the lecture hall, offering a bare little smile that reduced me to dumb embarrassment. I had never forgotten to switch the ring on my cell phone to silent; I was not one to take any chances, fearful of being thrown out of the lecture in the usual humiliating manner doled out to those who committed a transgression like this.

I raised my bag to my lap and took out my cell phone with barely a movement. A message from Dai: SORRY I hng up on U. th angels of death passed by, Malik & Ridwan, & I was afrd they wld take my cell.

I gave myself the excuse that the lecture bored me, it was completely useless, and besides, the corner of the hall I was sitting in did not allow the professor to really see me clearly. Then I answered her, Hah! How cultured U R. Such politeness! Remember the names we respect—Shanqal and Manqal.

Among everyone at school there existed a strong competition to determine who was superior, the students in the sciences or those in the arts. This culture had prevailed so strongly and for so long, renewing itself with every new class, that one really might wonder what gave it such a long life. I have no idea who started it in the first place, nor from whom I picked it up. Just as my university ID had been handed over to me, so was the notion of this competition for precedence, and for my part, I supported it. The girls in the sciences faculty would say of those in the arts that they were superficial. They had a faulty way of thinking and they were idle, with enough free time, after all, to paint their nails and dye their skin with those tattoos that fade when you wash. This idea was so established that we thought we could tell where a girl belonged from her appearance—the way her blouse looked, the obvious care she took with her makeup—without ever needing to scrutinize her uniform to see that she wore a black skirt, as distinguished from the official navy blue skirt that science girls wore. Likewise, they had the same sort of things to say about us; we were silly, boastful, and lacked the criteria by which they measured femininity. You could pick one of us out, they would claim, by the soiled lab coat that she never took off and her thick-lensed eyeglasses.

And in what passed for amusement and whiling away time as opposed to wasting it, we tossed the ball back and forth. At the sciences goalpost, the scales tipped in favor of seriousness and practical thinking, while on the arts end, the balance favored relishing and living your life to its fullest. Naturally, practical reality was not exactly the same as our preconceived notions; nevertheless, a clear difference was there for all to see. I found it inconceivable to weigh such different brain types, one thinking about Wolfgang Pauli's Exclusion Principle and the other the victories of the great conqueror Salah al-Din al-Ayyubi, or one contemplating Einstein's relativity and the other, al-Farahidi's grammar. It is true that our difference did not go so far that we would use the equation $\alpha + \beta = \gamma$ where they would use ME + YOU = LOVE (as they do). I certainly did notice students majoring in geography who had a tough time in their first year getting through the computations they had to have for their studies, justifying the difficulty by saying that calculations belonged to the field of mathematics, even though they had barely gone two years since studying math.

Hah, Shanqal she says! God take them, making terror for us wherever we go!

Shanqal and Manqal. These were not the heroes of some cartoon show on the Space Toon channel. They were our nicknames for the pair in charge of security at the college. These two women had arrived a year ago in green uniforms that looked like soldiers' duds. Their presence was something new, and it spurred comments and rumors that flew from one mouth to the next. It was murmured that they were here because of some drug distribution ring. Or, maybe, skimpy-sleeve relationships—this said with a meaningful wink, for we knew well enough what kind of unseemly goings-on "skimpy-sleeve" alluded to. It was said to be related somehow to the scuffle that had happened the year before, an argument over religious doctrine between two students, one of whom was then expelled.

There really had been a squabble over a matter of dogma; it had led to a clear change in the college's policy of banning certain practices. The change was that we were subject to searches at any moment. We could no longer pass religious books to anyone, even if they were compilations of devotional passages and supplications with which one could end one's ritual prayers. Nor could we bring out our rosaries of dried clay beads, meager stand-ins for the symbolic flats of hardened soil on which Shi'is pray when they cannot pray directly on bare ground. Personally, I no longer felt capable of handing out the magazine on the sly, so I began taking a chance on distributing limited copies of it on computer discs. I handed them out on the bus going home to avoid anyone getting blamed at school, myself included. The possibility that what I was doing would be revealed was practically nil, since our second-year courses included computer, and I could rely on our constant exchange of discs for cover. Things like this were certainly going on, but their connection to the expulsion of students or to the appearance of a pair of security personnel was not so clear, since even the announcement of the expulsion, which was posted on the announcement board in front of the Student Affairs Office, had alluded only to either cheating infractions in final exams or moral offenses that took place outside the college proper, in the area where students waited for their private means of transportation.

The two security women were actually rather pleasant and more or less cooperative. We passed through an initial period of lying in wait and extreme caution, and still we could not make out any fixed aim or specified task that was theirs. The students tried frequently and energetically to pick a quarrel with Malik and Ridwan, as Dai had named them, but they got nowhere with their attempts to put these two up on trial. The women would respond that they did not know the reason they had been summoned for this duty, and that all they were required to do was to patrol the college and look closely at anything that seemed suspicious or any clear transgression of college regulations. In fact, there was only one rule: no moving about. On the basis of this restraint, there was nothing that might logically escape surveillance or grilling. Why did you bring a block of halvah sweets into the college? one of us might well be asked. Or, where was the justification for two girls sitting in a spot that was not easily visible to everyone? The two of them rarely waited for any response, though. They were satisfied to issue a clear order to go somewhere else, or to do something else, depending on the situation. I deduced this from the little amount of contact I had with them.

Shelving the lecture and sending messages instead was pleasant. I could understand (me, such a self-disciplined person most of the time) why some students would spend whole lecture periods in the companionship of their telephones. So I finished up with, Do u have a lecture?

No, am free d rest of d day, wanna meet?

Grrreeeaat idea. I hv class 11 to 12. I'll blow t off & c u.

U dn't hv loads of absents in t?

No way. I've gt 13 hrs max 2 b absent & I hvn't tkn more thn 2.

I'll pass by. Ur lecture's where.

No, I'll find u at d Arts Lib. U cn walk wth me in d rain & buy me a Baskin.

Jst dn't 4get my croissant.

Finally the lecture was over, though I had not listened to even ten words of it. I began getting really impatient. At this point, my tendency to always go for the seats furthest to the back of the hall was an irritation, for I could sign the attendance roster only after a hundred or so students had their turns. The wait was a pain, and my whole head was with Dai. I waved at Salma, who was sitting in the first row. I made a sign asking her, Did you sign for me? She answered with a gesture I was accustomed to seeing. The others had snatched the book away before she could write my name. Five minutes passed with me parked sullenly against the wall before I was able to sign and get out.

Those who played these parts infuriated me, whether here at college or before, at school. I viewed such roles—perhaps falsely—as academic put-ons, which some girls seemed to slip into at school. These sorts of students wormed themselves into a niche beneath an imaginary banner declaring their servility, and they enjoyed special favor and esteem. Because I am not one to believe in passing everyone's actions through the gates of good intention, I was always vigilant toward such girls. I might never excel at making accurate distinctions, but at least I wouldn't swallow their sour and their sweet without even recognizing the taste.

Ten minutes past eleven, and I finally managed to get to my date with Dai. I'd prepared a good strong excuse for her—let me call it a clamorous excuse, completely unrefined, totally street, just as she always loved me to be! I paced back and forth alongside the steps to the theater, which was immediately adjacent to the Arts Library. I had chosen the spot deliberately and carefully, for it was our first time to meet in such a public and visible place as campus. Since everyone knew Dai as a classmate, it was tricky for me, in front of any of my friends, to come up with a believable reason for my absence from class and my spending time alone with this Dai, who was no more than a classmate. Naturally, I could come up with some sort of false pretext at a moment's notice, even a perfectly crafted lie that would fool anyone. But I didn't like to give Dai any more reason than necessary to focus on the idea that our relationship could be prolonged only by keeping it secret, and that it was better for it to remain like that, and that furthermore I was so wary about this that I would even lie to guarantee it. The spot here, next to the Arts Faculty Library, offered a territory distant from everyone.

If a satellite photo of our college existed, it would show what looks like two little colonies almost as close together as they could possibly be but sharing almost nothing—two communities, with two cafeterias, two libraries and two campus bookstores. Even the kiosks for photocopying, computer printing and binding were strictly regulated: one was for the sciences, and you were not allowed to have anything related to the arts curricula printed there, and vice versa. Over here, a density of blue skirts, and over there, black skirts. We maintained this sharp separation even though the two divisions lay beneath the roofing of a single internal courtyard common to all of the buildings. Of course, it was not impossible to see a co-mingling of the two somewhere or other, but this mixing mostly remained a potential held within the strict limits of expectation, and subject to counting. What were the odds that I would meet one of the twenty girls I knew over there, amongst nearly four thousand? There was not even a statistically significant chance of it.

The notion of two sharply distinguished settlements could apply to other kinds of difference, and everyone knew which was center and which was periphery. Which group do you belong to? Which School of Islamic Law do you follow? Of what sect are you a member? And what region do you come from? If someone scrutinized our lecture halls really closely, that person would see the section to the right as belonging to our group and the other section as belonging to the other groups (or maybe the other way around). Naturally, to say *our group* and *the other group* is more graceful than calling us by the warring cartoon characters, Shanakil and Sanafir. Shi'is and Sunnis!

Rarely did anyone here take up the opportunity of being in one place for four school years as a chance to foster a relationship less governed than usual by these criteria of belonging, less restricted by borders, less marked by divisions. This was the state of things when we arrived, and it was extremely difficult for us to even attempt to change it. Change is a frightening act, and in an official site such as this, it might well set off a harmful reaction with a likely adverse impact on someone's future. Always there was a concealed, furtive sentiment that being here, and going on being here, were dependent on several conditions, though they were never made explicit. We must remain totally mute, for even a single slanderous rumor about one of us—that she was participating in sectarian mayhem, perhaps— was enough to cause her admissions file to be thrown in her face and for her to be expelled without any possibility of readmission. The very fact that we were accepted for admission here was considered by some people as a handout to an undeserving recipient, too much generosity to those who were closest to being misguided and astray, those who were the object of God's wrath.

Because we were the minority—and in truth we were never a minority in the college, only in the nation—the possibility of some- one else, someone from the other side, being admitted to any of our groups, organized or not, small or large, was an alien idea regarded with utter suspicion. By the very nature of the fear we had imbibed, and on the strength of the preconceived and ready-made ideas with which we had all been injected, both we and the others tended to be on our guard, always self-protective and defensive. It was always possible that any attempt to enter the other's territory might well be veritable trespassing with no good faith behind it. Our chances at entering into their groups were greater, given the protection of their numbers and the indisputable fact that any one of us would always be the weaker element in any comparison. But I had not witnessed any effective attempts at this, and this was my fourth year. Such things most often happened when the person trying to enter the group had already been isolated from her difference, and so could be more easily incorporated as one of the many look-alike postage stamps, emptying this new candidate of her content, not to mention peeling off the distinguishing outer shell. And so there was no real coexistence, no assimilation that you could count on, not even a preliminary and primitive acceptance from one toward the other, no recognition of the naturalness of difference or of the varying things we had to offer by virtue of who we were.

Another ten minutes passed and Dai still had not come. I found my own justification for her lateness in my certainty that it was an instant punishment for my own tardiness. I called her phone, punching *five* on my quick dial numbers, and the recorded voice staggered me. *The number you have requested is not available right now.* I headed for the spot where she customarily left her *abaya* bag, to be ready when she would leave the grounds and have to put on her *abaya* over her clothes. But I did not find her, nor did I see any of the familiar faces that I usually saw in her company. I left the croissant in her bag as proof that I had been there. I began to worry. I am a person who does not need huge and convincing reasons in order to start worrying. Anxiety is a fact of existence for me, a true characteristic of my self, a sharp-edged and vicious presence that keeps me from being able to successfully apply any of the instructions found in Dale Carnegie's *How to Stop Worrying and Start Living.* Or perhaps it is not so much a fact as it is a counter-fact, nothing more than my reaction to my limited and circumscribed choices.

My anxiety mutated into a particular kind of tenseness, co-mingled with a sharp feeling of irritation. It was the sort of irritation that leaves you unable to engage with anyone about anything. You want no exchange of words, not even a passing question about what time it is; this tension leaves you annoyed even by things that have nothing at all to do with you and which would not in themselves annoy you at any other time: a girl slipping her hand around the waist of another, someone wearing gray contact lenses, the sound of a naughty and boisterous laugh, the vending machine you're standing next to that sells hot chocolate and is out of order so that every time someone comes by and puts her money in, she asks you, So, it's not working, right? And you answer her with some stupid line like, How would I know, *ya anisa*, whether it is working or not? Have all four thousand students in this place disappeared so that you have to come and direct this question only to me? And by the way, this friendly smile of yours is really irritating, so you might as well keep it just for yourself!

Forty minutes had passed since the time we had agreed on, and nothing had come of our arrangement to meet. This futile waiting was laying a trap for me, in an open area where more and more people were pushing in, not just because the prayer space was here, but also because of the rain which since yesterday had not let up its ferocious and ubiquitous washing. I retraced my steps to my locker. When I saw an edge of paper lodged carefully into the slit, I was suddenly happy. It was as though there had been no logical reasons for our appointment to fall from Dai's agenda by error or oversight, and now the very existence of the paper, even though I had not retrieved or opened it yet, was a summary of all the reasons that might exist for it.

I drew it out carefully from its cage. I sniffed Dai's fragrance on it, a deep and earthy scent: a potent batter of soil and sugar. How can you describe a person's fragrance? How can you release it? Preserve it in a secure vault in the memory? Hide it away, protected from decay and forgetting and desire for the fullness of others? Dai's fragrance is a story in itself. I always took care when kissing her that I breathed in the odor of her throat, the place where I sensed the concentrated essence of her fragrance was located, deeply embedded within her, pure, uncontaminated by any admixture of other essences. The very air is incapable of altering the fragrance of Dai. Like me, the air can only breathe her in and feel deliriously stimulated.

I pried open her letter with shaking fingers. My heart always trembles when it is facing first things and first times, when it is in front of freshness, when first times move in to occupy their proper expanse of memory and mind, yet to be pushed back into second place, never mind sink into oblivion. I love the sensation that something is forming, that what surrounds me is entering each stage of its genesis and growing, proliferating. I am possessed by a maternal love for these things I have, and it does not matter to me whether they come in premature form or at full term. In my relationship with Dai, I am always on the alert, my gaze steady and my mind welcoming the possibility of being dazzled with the very simplicity of what is happening and how small and slight it all is, with scenes as they are just beginning to take shape. I love the way that every encounter takes on the nature of the specific and fundamental difference between two people—like in hetero couples—to make them able in all of their difference for one to wrap itself around the other.

My eyes breezed across the words rapidly without taking in their meaning for a second or two. With its many flourishes, the slanted script captivated me. The full stops between her words were large, ripe circles, the way they always were in Arabic before typefaces, while the word edges were soft and yielding, without any ragged breaks, slants following slants, the forming of words that are exactly what they are and no other, as if they say, Turn to me. With difficulty, I stole my eye away from her first word and went on reading.

My love ...
You are reading this letter from me because I was not able to come. I am writing in a hurry. I am sorry, I left you waiting. I was afraid I would change my mind and relent. It is hard to look directly at you and tell you what I intend to say. Forget me. As if nothing ever happened. I am not worth it. Forgive me. I am very sorry.
Goodbye,
Your Dai.

Sometimes—like right then, for example—I really need someone who will explain to me what I am supposed to do. As a human being, what am I supposed to feel? What reaction should I release signs of across my face for others to see? Shall I cry? Laugh? Tear this piece of paper into tiny pieces? Curse Dai? If only someone would give me a little guidance, I would take charge on my own of crafting all the rest of my reactions.

I retained the letter in my grip, pressing on it unconsciously, nothing alerting me to this except the slight pain left by my fingernails digging into the flesh of my hand. I went outside.

I needed to breathe, and I needed to not throw up. At this time of day the bathrooms were crowded. I had half an hour on the bus ahead of me.

I was very damp, and I had no desire to sing "It's raining men! Hallelujah" or "Rain, rain, come down rain ... our house is made of rock." My house was only bare and naked space now, and my men were devils of brackish water. It was not a merciful rain, or a loving one; not a tall rain man with calm features. It was only rain. Rain only. Not neutral, just lacking the competence to participate. It was not the rain of Qatif. Did we plant the barbed wires of our borders in your sky ourselves? Oh God!

The bus was late, and I did not stumble on an empty seat. A group of the girls who would fill the bus to bursting stood in front of the door waiting for the official in charge of transport, aiming to get him to provide another bus for them. I was not in the mood to make my way through the usual clamor: We've tried such and such a bus, no ... that bus, then ... try such and such a bus ... I kept to my squashed position just inside the bus, on the first step, and I tried to sit on the step. The rain whipped the bus's door violently. It was such a hard rain that it did not even slide down the huge glass window in front, but pinged back instantaneously, as if it were intent on continually assaulting my memory by means of its presence, angry at my ability to ignore it.

As soon as the bus emptied of some students at the first stop, I took the seat that one of them had vacated, the seat closest to the door. I gripped the metal column and let my head drop to rest on my hand. With the tremors of the bus as it rumbled along, my soul shook violently, up and down, while I kept swallowing it with the air, letting no sound escape.

I was completely wet, the water still coming off my hair and clothes, and the cold was biting me. A hand—I don't know from what hell it came or from what heaven—left its warmth on my hand, pulling away only after a full minute—I think it must have been a whole minute—without my sensing anything at all. It was not curiosity about the hand that compelled me to lift my head and look through the window, but rather the fact that I had not counted the number of times the bus had stopped and so I did not know where I was and how many stops remained before my own. It was the stop where Dai always got out. I saw her unrolling her light blue *abaya* bag over her head, making it into an umbrella.

10

Describing "that inscrutable lad" in her famous song from the film *Watch out for Zuzu*, Suad Husni chants,

> Bless his heart, that inscrutable lad
> Masks his face behind glasses when he's sad ...

This is exactly what the dead do: they mask themselves in their absences. They convert to a shadow that, concealed as it is, shows its reflection baldly in all the twists and turns our lives take. In the first days of mourning, the women, as they came to console and mourn with my mother, would say to her, Be patient, desire is long lived. Now I understand what they meant. I figured that time repairs the breaches in us, not because we forget but rather because, as our lives regain their earlier movement, we get beyond the defeat that absence brings. But the passing days proved it otherwise. Hassan was as much here with us as was his absence, which was always here. Could there be a more bewildering equation?

Hassan curtains himself in his absence so that his presence will better encompass and surround my life. Here he is, going halves with me in all my problems and the choices I have to make, my daily apprehensions, my frail accomplishments and my painful falls. Often I used to see him conversing with himself, or talking to the mirror, the balustrade, his car key, the newspaper. When I teased him about it, he would say, There's someone there who hears! Was Hassan conversing with his absent ones, exactly in the way that he is now my absent one and I talk to him? I hold whole discussions with him. I debate him and I wrangle with him. I whet my abortive philosophy on his words and I pass on silly trivialities and repetitive scenes. I tell him the latest news; I try concealing everything heart-wrenching from him, but I fail. I let him in on secrets that are scandalous, and that he absolutely must not reveal to my mother. Sometimes I want to tell him a new joke, but before long, I realize inside of myself that this was his role to play, and his absence does not give me the right to steal his roles away from him.

So long ago, back in the days when, standing on tiptoe, I could not even make myself come up to his shoulders, I took from his bookshelves a book called *Our Philosophy* by the martyr Muhammad Baqir as-Sadr. It had a blue leatherette cover and the fact that it was cool to the touch even at the height of summer was what made my fingers pull it off the shelf and take it from his library. He did not say that I would not understand it, that perhaps I would need two more years or even three, plus ten additional centimeters, that there were other books there more appropriate to my small brain. He smiled slightly and said, Tomorrow, I want you to come and discuss what you read, do you understand? I answered with a broader smile: Ayy. As I read, I stammered over certain words that were not in my vocabulary, and I would stop at particular sentences for days on end to absorb what they said. It took me seven months to finish that book, including two hours each week during which he explained to me whatever was too complicated for me to puzzle out. He was fairly exasperated with me for forcing myself unthinkingly into a silly competition that I did not need. Finally I gave the book back to him with a sure look of victory and a stinging question: Do you see me? Look how much bigger I'm getting! Fondly, he stroked my cheek a little. He and my mother were alike in the way they would stroke my cheek, with their long and slender fingers. You scare a guy! he said. I answered him with the very newest thing I had learned in English—*Sort of*—even though I was not certain that this was the right expression to use.

I never drew my nourishment from Egyptian culture as so many others did. When I was little, I did not follow the evening serials on the Egyptian TV channel, nor the Ramadan Riddles that the Egyptian stars Nelly and Sharihan performed, nor the puppets Buji and Tamtam. Omar Sharif's looks did not leave me a wreck, nor did I fall in love with the dreamy romantic voice of the famous Egyptian singer Abd al-Halim Hafiz. I was not corrupted by famous comedies of stage and screen like *The School for Troublemakers* and *The Kids Grew Up*. I had no idea what Café Fishawi was, or where the Cairo neighborhood of Hilmiyya could be found, even though I saw them in films made from the novels of Naguib Mahfouz. I didn't read loads of romantic novels by Yusuf al-Sibai or stories by Yusuf Idris and Naguib Mahfouz and Tawfiq al-Hakim—that famous Egyptian trio of mid-twentieth century writers. It was only very late in the game that I even heard of something called Arab nationalism and of individuals named Sadat and Nasser and Heikal and Sayyid Qutb, or a group called the Muslim Brotherhood, not to mention The Project of Arab Unity and the Camp David Accords.

This was a culture that I always viewed with a certain amount of skepticism and suspicion. I saw it as the culture of the generation before me, who in any case had gone right into their elder roles, playing paternalistic games with my generation, confronting me from a position of studied superiority. It was a generation of people who, at the age of sixteen, hung pictures of the "Cinderella of the Arab screen," as-Sindarella, Suad Husni, on the walls of their rooms and plastered them to their closet doors. They lived their stories of first love to the voice of Abd al-Halim, and they participated in the events of Muharram 1400. They had witnessed close up Qatif's transformation from its rural youth and its blue attire—the blue, blue sea that its pearl-divers frequented—into a quasi-city whose watery margins they were gobbling up, and thence into a network of pavements edged in yellow and black, asphalt streets, armored houses, and wells in which the water, if not the oil, had dried up.

What inscribed my childhood and animated my early teen-agerhood was the channel coming out of Dhahran, run by the businessmen at Aramco. My personality was sculpted, and the sphere of my attention defined, by a channel actually named Dhahran. It had American basketball, slow and boring golf reportage, and tennis matches—yaaah! Tennis! Wimbledon championships, the good-looking blond Boris Becker, and the inscrutable Pete Sampras. Matches held on grass courts and others on courts composed of finely ground red sand. And bananas. Back then, I did not understand. Why bananas, specifically? Films were another story. There was the solitary *Rain Man* Dustin Hoffman with his unparalleled athletic abilities. *Edward Scissorhands* Johnny Depp, that wicked Johnny Depp, with his sharp-cutting fingers of flashing silver metal, a machine with the power to love. *Scent of a Woman* and Al Pacino, always stirring up chaos, shouting, "I am in the dark!" These were part of an era that no one but my generation could properly experience. And then, on the pretext of cost control expenses—that is what they said—Dhahran was dropped from the list of available channels. It was an atrocious loss, certainly not compensated for by my ability to beam in Channel 55 from Bahrain or Channel 33 from the Emirates.

The Cinderella of the Arab screen is one of those images that always accompanies Hassan in my memory. Hiba loved her, too, and put her at the very top of her list of favorites, memorized her songs and knew her films, recorded haphazardly on videotapes. And then there were the poems of Salah Jahin, the popular Egyptian vernacular poet, which Hiba recited, chanting them in imitation of Suad Husni's style, her Egyptian pronunciation, and the tone of her voice with its tremors and the shroud of tears it seemed to carry. I heard her singing them and I memorized them from her. I remember once, Hassan had just bought new sunglasses, and he began to act up and swagger like a pampered young guy, acting the way he always did whenever he bought something that he really liked. So I began to chant to him.

> Your words to him, they glow,
> But he answers you just so
> Bless his heart, that inscrutable lad
> Masks his face behind glasses if he's sad
> And how does he live?
> He's just that way, that's the way he is
> And how does he shout?
> He's just that way, that's the way he is
> And how does he pass you?
> He's just that way
> And he stops and he says,
> I'm that one, I am,
> I'm that guy, I'm that beau,
> On this block in this town
> I'm the tallest lad!

Hiba disappeared. To be more accurate, I made her disappear. My choice. Sometimes it is useful to be proactive in organizing your pain, to cut it short rather than letting it remain a stagnant vessel for more pain from others. Hiba was going to disappear in any case, and all I was doing was hastening the appointed time for her disappearance. The Cinderella of the Arab screen had an appointed time, too: she committed suicide, or illness killed her, or fame did it, or her girlfriend, or Jahin's passing, or the Egyptian Secret Service, or the British police. She died. But Hassan's memory does not die.

Hassan's leaving is the very peak of what I am capable of enduring. It is the high ceiling of pain beneath which all else is indifferent. His leaving is pain, bereavement, the ache of missing someone, rejection, emotional breakdown, the fissuring of the soul, the body's deterioration and collapse, the reign of absence that you cannot shake, the curse of fear, the savagery of the death endured by the bereaved who is sadly left behind. Death makes everything else an everyday mundane triviality, and makes me look at life with disdain. How can I take life seriously? I funnel half of my questions into a single answer, which is itself a question: So what does it mean in the end, anyway? What does it mean in the end for Hiba to disappear? What does it mean in the end for Dai to say goodbye? What does it mean in the end that I sin? What does it mean in the end that I fail the school year? What does it mean in the end that the winter is cold? What does it mean in the end that Umar's phone is off? What does it mean in the end? It doesn't mean a thing, it doesn't mean anything at all. Life means nothing, my questions mean nothing. Life is itself the nothingness of my convictions, the nullity of my stances, the nonexistence of my existence, the nonexistence of all the others. Everything in its reality is the nonbeing of a being who has faded away. The remains, left to be sensed by him or by the others, are merely the traces of an old fever whose core was afflicted by frostbite.

A third window—but Umar's phone shuts it in my face, just when I am in urgent need of using his presence to charge my spent battery. Moments like these take me back to the same old notions. How very exhausting the act (and the fact) of love really is, in whatever shape it comes and under whichever category it is lodged. What factories human relationships are for producing energy, or for depleting it. Need consumes me, though I despise giving in to my needs. I do have that complex—believing that if I could tame my needs and regulate them appropriately, and control their income and outflow, I would be able to manage life without anyone. On my own, in solitude, sufficient unto myself.

My longing to be independent established itself very early, as early as my first attempts to put on my socks by myself, tie my shoe-laces, and sleep without my mother crooning nearby. I splattered my face with food rather than eating with her help, and I stung my eyes with shampoo as I avoided her bathroom supervision. I was always poised to work harder and to repeat my attempts time and time again without her extending a hand to me or guiding me into a particular way of doing things. My illness, too, buttressed my fear of collapse, of reversion to the uncertain steps of a toddler, of my body sinking under someone else's sway. Old age scares me, too. I am afraid of suddenly having to face paralysis or senility, and being forced to have my needs met and my body cared for by someone whose duty it would become, someone other than me. I pray to God constantly that I may die before I see this dreaded fantasy of mine come true.

The time for retreat had passed. It was too late, also, for Umar to answer me. I had made a tape of Kazim's song, "I Am Afraid it Will Rain and You Won't Be with Me." On it I wrote, Have I really and truly lost you? I stuffed it into Dai's *abaya* bag. One try will not cause any harm, I convinced myself. I did not know which song I should choose. When it came to knowledge of Fairuz, I was still in first grade, as Dai always said to make fun of me; and Dai loved Kazim. Not to mention that we always listened to foreign songs, even in languages of which we didn't understand a single word. Our tastes merged only in that we despised rock 'n' roll songs, even if they were by U2. I preferred pop, while she really liked rap and was always listening to Eminem. She laughed when we discussed his dirty pantomimes.

She sat down next to me on the bus going home. She had gotten on the bus after me. Lifting her face veil, she began staring around at everyone until she came upon me. She edged over to where I sat and asked, Is that seat saved for somebody? I picked up my bag and answered, No, please sit down. We did not say a single word the whole way.

Did I say, The act of love is exhausting? Then what about the act of desire! An eye to the window and an eye on Dai, and I was split between two opposing longings: one, that the bus would swallow us up into a trip that would never end, where we would have no chance of arriving, even late; or, that the bus would fling me out exactly at my front door. I craved the possibility of our bodies touching, of her fingertip engraving something onto the palm of my hand, either by pure coincidence or intentionally. My nerves would come apart completely, my neuro fluids would zoom around erratically in all directions if even a touch as slight as that were to happen.

The bus arrived at her stop. She tugged me by the hand. She was already half standing up.

Get out with me?

But ...

Yallah, come on!—for my sake?

What about my mother?

Give her a phone call later on. Hurry up, the driver is going to scold me and we'll miss the stop, too.

I do not know which of us was more insane. I felt acutely shy and embarrassed as soon as I entered her house and her mother greeted me with a dazzling show of welcome. I claimed (lying, and giving Dai some fierce winks all the while surreptitiously so she wouldn't expose me) that I was fasting. I did not want to crowd them at lunch. It had not been arranged in advance, and Dai's mother had not prepared for a guest who—according to customary hospitality—would be expected to take half of what was on the table while the rest of the family filled up on half a plateful and on watching the guest eat. Her mother responded, If the noon call to prayer had not already sounded, I would have absolutely insisted that you eat! I answered shyly, *Khairha bi-ghairha*. Another time, I hope.

I called my mother to tell her without giving it much thought, even though I knew that she was seriously dubious about Dai. But it was my mother's usual way to not demand any explanations from me as long as I was outside the house and as long as I called and could tell her that I was with someone she knew. My mother has that nice quality that makes her sensitive to the limits her children set. Motivated by her self-respecting desire to preserve her children's images in their friends' eyes, she does not overstep those limits. Or perhaps it is her certainty about having implanted a dignified pride successfully in her children's blood.

Shall I say that the hearts of mothers are testimonies, the places where revelation descends, where inspiration is heard? Are they the voice of God in one of its most brilliant earthly manifestations? I had explained the rapid acceleration in my relationship with Dai to my mother by saying that it was a good fate that Allah had willed for me. Was it not splendid that I had found a friend into whose soul I could melt so easily and fluidly, as if I were a stream of water, and she, a delta? A friend who clapped her hand over my fears and stood with me on firm ground?

Even an attempt to explain our contradictory and difficult relationship is beyond me. How can safety or security come from someone whose ability to harm you is a fact that you know well? Since you do understand it, does this mean you prepare yourself thoroughly for it? You know it is coming and you are ready for it, but still, will it not be a shock when it hits you? Does putting yourself as close as this to the source of your harm while somehow retaining your sense of reassurance mean that you are comforted or immunized by knowing from where the weapon will be pointed, when the blow hits the vast body of your aching squarely in the gut?

If only we arrived at birth accompanied by an illustrated guide that we could open and read. If only it would tell us what we need. How do you operate us? How do you shut us off? How do you recharge us? What are the best ways to employ us, to maximize our functioning, and what are the best ways to maintain us so we won't go bad? If it were possible to have such a thing, I would be grabbing the user's guide to *me* and comparing it to Dai's. Then I would understand something about the enormous hollow that she seemed to have filled in me, even as she opened up an aureole of fear. She stopped the irksome ringing that seemed deeply, permanently etched in my ears, resounding as soon as I tried to exchange hellos or handshakes with anyone. My anxiety would immediately tell me that I was in an unsafe situation, and it would push me to withdraw, to retreat far to the rear, inside the cavity of my heart, after closing my outside doors upon me. What was it that Dai did, what extraordinary miraculous thing did she do, to get me to rely on her enough to smother the frenzy in my blood and the promptings of extreme fright?

I fancied that we had erased Dai's insinuated goodbye and the nine days just past, had leapt over both without either one of us falling. We prayed, and Dai brought in a plate heavy with food. We ate with one spoon and listened to Kazim's song, and she said that I knew how to appreciate good music. We chattered about the college and plucked out all the feathers of our strutting professors. We grumbled over the exams, for the doors to the examination halls were just being opened and they would not close until the year's end. We tried to figure out a way to hasten the upcoming Eid al-Adha holiday. I got into a discussion with her over a few choice ideas from her stock of observations concerning the Hussainiyya. I read the first proofs of the article she was engrossed in writing.

I really believed that no chasm had opened between us after all—until we got in bed. She took off her clothes and mine, and slipped on top of me with a few kisses, then pulled back slightly and gazed at me sadly. I was touching the pair of dimples on her cheeks.

Now I saw the rift, utterly wide, in Dai's eyes. She turned her back to me. That was what gave me the view of dark traces across her skin, some of them so clearly etched that I could almost figure out where each one started, though staring at her back gave me no power to envision the kind of madness that had caused them to be distributed so randomly. Other marks left me powerless to understand how a human being could be responsible for a disfigurement such as this. The sadness of it was mine now. My heart tried to entice me to redraw those traces with my kisses. I should devote myself to her, gently and carefully, but I drew back. When was my role ever to smooth out traces made by someone other than me?

I was not astonished by the sight of these marks that stained her. Many times, Dai would try out something to see if it would stir up my anger at her—or my jealousy—what was the difference? She would mount an exhibit for me, an abridged scene of an intense physical encounter between her and one of her women friends, always cutting it short so as to leave me with legitimate questions and scurrilous fancies. I was usually certain that she was mixing some lies with some truth, but still, there was tangible evidence of her multiple relationships. It was the first time I had seen such traces clearly, and in this form, and without any attempt on her part to hide them. It was as if she were saying, Hah! Look how good I am at fooling around.

I placed a tiny kiss on another blue blemish at the top of her forearm, a very small and gentle kiss, out of fear that I might cause her pain. I took my lips away quickly as I heard her moan, not knowing from the sound of it whether it was my proximity that hurt or the particular spot where the kiss had landed. Be mine, I pleaded. I mean, mine ONLY.

She answered, but only after a long silence, so long that I doubted she had heard what I said or intended to respond to it.

But I can't.

I had the tormenting feeling that I fell at the end of her queue of choice partners. She had a yield to equal the number of fingers on her hand, and so what could possibly make her content with only one! One like me. Me, so naïve and confused about my body. I had a pressing feeling that tormented me just as much, which was that her other choices were better endowed in every sense, were wealthier, had more breadth of experience. After all, weren't they purely top-of-the-mattress relationships?

I turned my back to her and each of us sank into the ocean of her own thoughts. Over us slumped the shadow of an excessive and ugly silence. A chill spread across me, starting inside. I lost my ability to feel any concern, to ask any questions, to experiment by heading down some other avenue. I was like someone who has put all of her eggs in one basket, and now Dai had simply given my basket a kick, sending it against the wall to shatter all of my possibilities, without offering any alternatives or reaching toward compromise solutions. It was really stupid for me to come asking her to let go of others, when it was she a few days earlier who had said goodbye, and still, to this very moment, I had not even asked her why.

Imagining our bareness as we lay there facing in opposite directions provoked a naïve laugh in me. Sometimes, laughing creates a window through which you can let things pass even though they have no relation to mirth or teasing or jokes—things like pain, shock, embarrassment, surprise, being dazzled, black ironic humor, and those truths that always show up too late.

I sat up, feeling strongly that I wanted to get up and put on my clothes. But at that moment I discovered that I did not have the energy for it. Even a trivial task such as this would require more effort than I had at my disposal. So I lingered as though I had forgotten what I was about to do. She sat up in turn and rested her head against my back. I guessed that she had her eyes closed since her lashes were not moving over my skin, and I sensed her fatigue from the way she was breathing. Something like sympathy or compassion moved inside of me. I wished I could immerse her, could pass my hand over the place where her hurt began, and open the energy of the hell lurking in the heat of her breaths. That is what I wished, but I was not strong enough to do it.

I worry about you, about what I can do to you. You are so fresh, so frail and sensitive, that I am afraid if I put my hand on you, I will break you. I do not want to hurt you, but this is what is happening. If I get too close to you, I will disfigure you and make you become like me. I am a freak, a monster, can't you see that? It's hard for me to explain! Hard for you to understand!

Never mind.

There was nothing to be said, and I wanted her to be quiet, so I pronounced that *never mind* like a huge period that stops up any opening for speech. My throat was full of saliva that burned. No crying, it was nothing like crying, only a temporary state of dumbness. I felt no sudden curiosity about what she had said, and no desire to get inside of it or to try to understand it. How long she had been saying such things, obscure and vague, things swimming through emptiness. Completely useless things, as if she were plastering all the reasons for our stumblings along a secret wall, and leaving to me the labor of evaluating them. I had no desire to play this game any more, the game of making assumptions about what this might possibly be, this thing which is so hard to explain and which exceeds my powers of understanding. And I did not care to negotiate with her over these secret truths of hers.

I got out of bed and put on my clothes. I handed over her clothes, a gesture to her that she should do likewise. As soon as she was done I opened the curtains and sat down on the edge of the bed staring at the view from the window. That Dai's home was on the fringes of the city, in the agricultural area that had not yet been hit hard by the asphalt epidemic, made looking out of the window a true and astounding pleasure. I could see blue skies in which the sun blazed, and an overwhelming green as far as the horizon, as if God granted this land an exemption, and it never lost its virginity.

She came closer to me in search of a kiss, and I made a sign to her: No. Even though the windows of her room were one-way glass, the fact that I could see the street, with people going by and children on their bicycles, and that I could see into the homes of the neighbors, left me with the feeling that they could see me, too. It would make me too apprehensive, as if I were committing a kiss in sight of everyone. Dai smiled. Perfect, she did not understand my refraining from the kiss as a rejection or refusal of her.

Why? she asked me.

I don't know.

She smiled at me spontaneously, and I felt the curiosity in her eyes exposing me. Think of it as a parachute jump. If you get beyond the first moment, you can overcome everything else.

But ...

Come here.

She stole me with a long kiss, I murmured *no* to her over and over again, and in a rising voice she answered me over and over, murmuring her refusal to accept mine. At first, I tried to disentangle myself from her, but then I relaxed and finally I responded to the pressure of the kiss.

So? she asked me, as soon as she drew back.

I did not answer. My heart was pounding and my breaths were overstrained. She winked at me, so as to say, Let's keep on doing that when the curtains are open. We both burst out laughing, despite my suspicion that it was not a joke. My response was that she really had gone crazy.

That look of sadness came back, as my forefinger stroked the slope of her nose. It seemed that there was some defect in my fingers which injected sadness or despair into her. Perhaps I needed to daub my fingertips with a good luck charm, or redo their chemical makeup. With fake annoyance, or with real patience running out, I'm not sure which, I asked her, So, now what?

You're angry at me, aren't you?

Of course not.

Are you telling the truth?

I told you, of course not.

You won't hate me, right? Whatever happens?

I began to grow uncomfortable with the repeated turns that our conversation took, always leading us in the same direction. Batul rescued me, kicking at the door, her words commingled with sobs. Maaamaaaa, come here, come tell them! They won't play with me, I hope they rot!

Dai opened the door for her and picked her up. Her little sister's face was flushed, her cheeks rosy and her eyes cascading tears. Dai brought the little girl over to the bed, next to me, and held her slight form on her lap, a little sparrow whose wings had just barely begun to sprout. She dried Batul's tears and wiped her nose.

Yallah, come on, again. Come on, blow your nose, ha-ar-r-r-d. Dai drew out the word and then made the sound of a nose blowing. The little one was responding to her demand with perfect obedience, imitating the sound exactly.

I'll break their heads for you. Okay, sweetie. Okay, enough, no screaming. She looked at me. It's another *mawwal* every day. A tearful song that never ends!

She opened the drawer of the bedside table and pulled out a Snickers bar. Batul took it and held it between her tiny hands, gripping it tightly. As Dai soothed her, her eyelids drooped.

Why does she call you Mama?

You could say that I have basically been delegated to meet all the demands of her upbringing.

What about your mother?

Busy.

We broke out in smiles at the same instant, me because I had asked such a dumb and prying question as this, and her to let me know that we had gotten beyond the stage where we would hesitate before asking such questions or stick to earlier commitments about where the red lines were when it came to invading each other's privacy.

Do you fancy yourself a teacher?

You mean do I imagine myself being like my mother?

She left no room for me to object to the way she had understood my question, and she rounded her own question off with an emphatic *Impossible*!

And your diploma?

You know that majoring in English gives me a lot of different choices—Aramco, or a bank or a hospital.

Without any preliminaries and in contrast to her usual practice of keeping things to herself, she started talking volubly about her mother. What does daily life mean under the burden of doubting our mothers' love for us? She had been a highly strung, stubborn daughter, to the point where the distribution of roles between the two of them did not long remain those clearly defined domains of a mother and her child. Rather, Dai had been a little one butting her head against rocky ground whenever she got angry, and her mother chose to confine and whip her hard for behaving badly. When Dai grew older she became a very calm person, aware and smart and older than one might suppose. Her grandmother began urging her to follow her path, the one taken a generation earlier by her mother and her aunts. They had all become Hussainiyya reciters. Their voices offered the glow of condolences and mourned along with bereaved women, all of them in black. They revived Hussain, thirsty and alone, on every Ashura. But Dai would slip out of her grandmother's hands. Then, with a young teenaged girl's recklessness and self-pride, she had rushed to try out her gift for writing. She had imitated in miniature the novels of Khawla al-Qazwini, the most felicitous of women writers during a time when our society was very conservative when it came to any sort of writing that fell outside the sphere of the religious authorities or the state's Islamic sensibility. Dai's novel circulated from hand to hand among her friends and received much approval and a lot of praise, but her mother offered nothing but a cold gaze and open sarcasm. *Don't waste your time in such trivia. Concentrate on your studies.* That was when Hidaya extended her hands—Hidaya who tries to nationalize the creative production of talented women in the country, according to Dai's way of putting things. For Dai, this was an opportunity to aim a successful blow at her mother; and for her mother, it was a chance to spread the branches of her tree much wider—that family tree which Dai's earlier behavior had seemed to chop off almost at the trunk. Often, then, when I was with Dai, we would reach a point in the conversation where Hidaya's name was bound to come up, and I would stop talking, for I am not nearly strong enough to take up a defensive position in a scuffle that Dai would start and refuse to let go, the cause of which would be Hidaya.

Even if the world were to love me, she said, the whole world, I would still be convinced that no one loves me. As she finished this sentence of hers, she picked up Batul to carry her to her own bed. I yearned to take her hand and say, No. Stay, just like you are right now, like a mythical goddess, a woman at the apex of her motherhood. If I were a photographer or a painter, this scene would not have faded from my mind before I could recreate it fully: a lap molded to welcome the little body, two hands reaching around to embrace its frailty and drawing out of that transparent form a sprite exuding light and warmth. This is not Dai whom I know, not the sociable and elegant personality at the college, nor the astute artist at the Hussainiyya, nor the ferocious mauler in bed. This is another Dai, one

I have not known before, in whom I did not catch whiffs of heaven as I do now, *ya Allah*! Is this what motherhood does to us?

As soon as Dai pulled the cover over Batul, she woke up and refused to go back to sleep. Dai opened the chocolate bar for her and she took a bite, murmuring over and over, *yummy yummy*. Then she went out of the room, still carrying the little girl, and I heard her scolding her brothers about their Play Station and threatening to make TV watching off limits for a while. Noticing the particularly loud echo that reverberates through a new house, I realized that she was yelling down from the top of the staircase. Some moments later, she returned.

You can't imagine the degree of madness and chaos those naughty boys cause!

In fact, I am incapable of imagining it, having always lived in a home nearly empty of children. She added, in a tone of heavy and almost angry sarcasm, Four demons pouncing on one piece of candy, Batul—my God, it's beyond belief!

She laughed, and I laughed along with her. I love this sunny mood of hers, and it bewildered me to see the reversals and mood swings that I so often saw in her—when, at moments like this, I liked her so much and she makes me feel so good!

I pointed to my lips and raised my eyebrows at her to get her to realize that there was a chocolate smudge on her lips. She shook her head and commented, When will you start really remembering your lessons and begin applying them?

She was on the point of kissing me, but I nibbled on her fingertip instead, showing her that something was occupying my mind.

What is it? What are you thinking about?

Come on, let's go for a walk, how about it?

11

It was a completely ordinary day. Nothing about the way it began or the brilliance of the morning light gave any hint that it might be different. Nothing turned my attention toward any possible breach or miscalculation. At an early hour, I finished reviewing for my exam. I got dressed, waited for the car, got in, and arrived at the usual time, ten minutes before eight with a few seconds to spare. The place was like a beehive; the usual routine of exams never changes. I performed reasonably well on the exam and was ready to leave the hall a little before the time was half over. From the start, my calculations did not include setting very high expectations, but nor did I predict the worst. I went out and searched for Sundus unsuccessfully, but I knew which lecture hall she would be in for her last lecture on Wednesdays. Room 7, Building 3, the guillotine of the math wing, as Sundus calls it. I was sure to find her in the end.

It had happened before that Aqil had given me a two-day deadline, insisting that I finish my article and turn it in, or he would be forced to finish writing and editing the magazine without my essay appearing on the next-to-last page. It had never happened before, and it would not be *his* choice for it to happen. I hated this promotion, as Aqil asserted it was when he removed me from the trial list and added my name to the roster of the magazine's essayists. At the time, I got very annoyed at him, and so he told me that he knew my interests better than I did; what an overbearing guy! I was so irritated that I took my time coming up with a title for my corner of the newspaper, and so he named it for me. He called it *I Hear You*. And because I was the last to understand the intent in naming it that, just like any reader, he explained the whole thing in Platonic fashion. My writings as a whole were insistently focused on one idea: we must listen to each other instead of screaming into a void, in a miserable, futile attempt to make all the others listen to us—those others who were older, more mature, more seasoned and farsighted.

I had finished my article the day before. When I turned on the computer to make a copy and then send the file, I discovered that the computer was frozen, suffering no doubt from stress and over-exertion. The only thing I could do, then, was to hand it directly to Sundus.

I took a chance and dove into the cafeteria to do something about my hunger. The hideous crowd kicked me outside in a hurry. I returned to the spot where the country girls would gather. I had dashed off my article in a hurry and had not bothered to write a clean draft. It looked like a mass of hieroglyphics whose code no one but me could decipher, so I set to the task of rewriting it in a readable hand. Otherwise, Aqil with his biting tongue would transform my poor handwriting into his latest joke and would make it a stimulus for general amusement. However, I was interrupted constantly by girls asking about the exam. I had no choice but to engage in the conversation; we exchanged the answers we had given and I talked about how to understand the questions with some of my classmates who had been in the lecture hall. All of this meant that by the time the break was over, I had not even gotten through three lines of my text. Oh well. In any case, the next two lectures would be by video hook-up, since male professors were not allowed in the same room as female students. While in class, I could finish what I had just started.

It was a third of an hour into the lecture, and so far nothing truly deserved attention. A very short time later, I sensed a bitterness in my mouth and my tongue began to go numb. Tiny delicate ant feet seemed to crawl from the tip of my tongue to its roots. I took a deep breath in order to avoid a frightened panic that might lead me to act in a way that would prove embarrassing. These were the familiar early signs of my spells. At this point I would know that I had before me a little respite of somewhere between two seconds and one minute before the spell would attack me and my convulsions would begin. Sure enough, as soon as I stood up and asked permission from the supervisor to go to the bathroom, I felt my tongue getting heavy and the words began to stumble from my lips with a lisp. It is one of God's protective ways that this lecture of mine was in Room 24, exactly facing the bathroom, so that I could run inside and lock the door before the seizure really struck. It was a simple one and ended quickly. I stood facing the mirror over the sink, my eyes reddened by proliferating blood veins and heavy tears that clouded my vision. I washed my face and took some long breaths and returned to the lecture hall.

It was not the spell, which lasted under a minute, that drained me completely of energy, but rather the fear. It had only happened once that the spell had struck when I was in public, and it was so long ago that I had all but forgotten. It happened on the day my cousin—the son of my father's brother—got married. The spell took me by surprise. I was next to my mother, who took me in her arms and concealed my crying beneath her *mishmar*. One of our relatives asked, What's wrong with her? And with a frank sincerity that I did not understand, my mother began to explain my health condition and the nature of my illness. I hated my mother that day. I hated her furiously. I hated the feeling that she was stripping me naked, in all simplicity and cheapness, and that the secret I had been determined to preserve—indeed, I thought, the secret we would all preserve— was now out, and she, my mother, was the first to let it spill!

Every evening, in my final prayer of supplication before closing my eyes, I begged God that my condition not become scandalously public, that I not be forced under the guillotine of sympathy, that my spell not drive me into the maze of loving but enervating kindness. And God was kind to me, so generous indeed that even my unending prayers were not sufficient to thank him. And now, nine years on, my praying stumbles on its way to the heavens. My prayers do not ascend high enough now to reach God, who does not answer them. Why doesn't God answer my prayers? Why does God leave me on my own, now, after I had become so certain, across the space of nine years, that he would not? Why does God set me down and abandon me so close to another spell, when not even five minutes have passed since the last one? And if my mother could explain away Hassan's death by calling it an act of a mercy, then why is death not merciful to me, taking me along, taking me to where Hassan is?

The seizure had puffed my eyes to slits. Because my spells are the kind that leave me extremely alert rather than putting me into a faint, I could see everyone around me and I caught glimmers of their reactions. And the terror I felt was just like the terror of all the other girls, bending over me in a miserable attempt to lighten my condition: the terror of my own hell, to put it bluntly. This was not simply a spell: this was the most terrifying of my nightmares. Under the influence of my desire to reduce my convulsions to nothing quickly, and despite my certainty that it was futile to try, I was working very hard at it; yet, my spell just got stronger and my convulsions increased. All I wanted was to close my eyes, or for God to grant me the hands of that girl who was half earthling and half Martian in that foreign TV show, when she puts her two forefingers together and the earth stops. Or for God to draw over me and everyone else a temporary blindness so that none of us could see.

Umar said that I was accustomed to my seizures occurring in front of the emperor who has no clothes. When he first said this, I answered him with a giant *Aaaah* but then I retreated to ask him, Uh, what do you mean? It was odd that I did not fully absorb or understand the expression despite its obvious meaning and the familiar context in which he was using it. I had been telling him that I was used to the spell coming on in front of my mother. But who can ever get used to falling into a dark chasm day in and day out? Now, I missed her hard grip on my right hand, squeezing the palm, and her voice as she called to me, as if she was trying to bring me back from the far and isolated place where the seizure took me. Perhaps it was her hand's presence that made me able to regain control over the right half of my body and sense its movements during the convulsions to a far greater extent than I could with my left side.

My entire face was like a burst of gunfire floating on a dark and empty expanse. The faces of those women were like reverberations from a game of roulette that began as a joke and ended in a wall of blood. I saw many faces lowering their gazes toward me, most frightened, others haunted by worry. Even when it is not contagious, illness strikes fear in people's hearts, for it offers observers a live show of what could easily happen to them under similar circumstances. Illness exhibits to all watchers just how fragile our humanity is. Even so, I do not doubt even one part in one hundred that the effect of illness on witnesses to it is nothing compared to the reality of how illness disfigures a human body, gashing open the soul and mind of the invalid.

As it happened, I had not had occasion to be embarrassed by one of my seizures. My illness was a serious defect when it came to questions of physical perfection, but it was a recognized human deficiency that could happen to anyone. What embarrassed me was the saliva flowing out the sides of my lips and rushing downward toward the collar of my blouse. I wiped my mouth in disgust while my other hand covered my forehead to shade my lowered face, so that the few tears welling from my eyes would not be visible, nor my shortened breaths obvious. I do not understand how the details of my spells became a personal shame, just as no woman understands why she feels so ashamed when her underclothes or bed sheets are soiled by her menstrual blood. Perhaps I could attempt to explain the matter to Umar by asking him what he feels when he wakes up damp from a dream. He would be likely to respond, *A little bliss*! Or, *Not a whole lot to concern myself about.*

With difficulty, I was able to leave when the supervisor let me know with a nod that I could go. In the bathroom, a vile desire to cry engulfed me; I felt I would release a veritable flood, the kind that sweeps everything along with it and shatters the landscape completely. I was incapable of releasing it, though, of letting myself cry. Here, and at this moment, it would mean increasing my stock of gratuitous scandals. My feelings were so confused and heavy and chaotic that they left my legs too weak and tired to hold me up. My heart was beating erratically and I felt all mixed up inside, and there was a colossal, tyrannical ringing in my head, and the sort of heavy headache that normally hits at the earliest after a third seizure. As happened every time, my mouth smelled disgusting, an odor something like a chemical of unknown composition or a medicine bottle filled with rotting capsules too unbearably noxious to swallow.

I recalled the little character Cole in the film *The Sixth Sense*, when he wakes up with an intense longing to go into the bathroom. He stands in front of the lavatory and is surprised by one of the dead who pursues him. He runs out of the bathroom and heads for the little tent in his room, and mutters in a voice trembling with shadows, This isn't happening, this isn't happening ... this really isn't happening. Then he feels the heavy jolt on his shoulder when the ghost's hand lights on it. When he turns, he sees the dead man directly behind him, and so he flees outside, terrified, screaming. He later recites a talisman in singsong Latin, something like "Grant me salvation O God."

Clinging to the face of my mother and the reassurance it gave me, I repeated what she always said when my spasms arrived, *kaf ha ya ayn saad*, those letters of the alphabet that so mysteriously appear in the Qur'an, at the beginning of the Chapter of Maryam, like the letters that appear at the start of other suras in the Holy Book. Some people believe they have healing power when you say them. *Kaf ha ya ayn saad*. I repeated them until I was completely quiet, still and motionless. I washed my face and left the bathroom. If I stayed any longer, I feared, someone would come looking for me.

The supervisor smiled at me and walked over. Do you want to go to the clinic? she whispered.

No.

Some classmates clustered around me in a sincere attempt to give any help I might ask for: the clinic, tissues, water, even permission to leave the college before noon, when the authorities would open the gates. I responded with a stern *no* and a friendly, even ingratiating, smile to everyone's overtures. The supervisor rapped on the door and ordered the students to attend to the lecture. After two or three reminders, their offers began to flag, until they stopped completely. I felt enormously thankful to the supervisor for thrusting away from me the difficult burden of sympathy.

The first time the warning siren reverberated during the second Gulf War, it was a drill, an attempt to teach people how to vacate the streets and rooftops where they had congregated in the fastest possible time, to hide like rats in tightly shut rooms with all openings blocked and with huge Xs on their windows. Isn't this the sign the two heroes of the *X-Files* series make to each other that going *into* a building is forbidden?

On that occasion—and it was the first—people fled in terror at the reverberations, their children tucked under their arms. The sound of the siren convinced them of the danger. They wept and prayed and prepared for a long period of misery and exhaustion, as if the war had wrenched away doors and windows to enter as a ghostly evil spirit whose breaths we could feel on our bodies and whose footfalls we sensed, even if we could not see him. It was very real, because it was the first; utterly frightening, because it was the first; and savage, because it was the first. That is exactly how this spell of mine appeared to me. It was terror that stayed on for years, not mere months, standing just behind the door, and now, with a single kick, the wall had lost its façade and the shadow came to rest inside, unwanted and unwelcome.

I was uncompromising about giving myself strict training for just such a moment as this. I set up mental classrooms for myself, and in my mind's eye I erected horrendous scenes I could imagine facing. I lined up a succession of possible scenarios, though over the years I did change their order. I persisted in my peculiar drill, which was to make myself summon up model reactions to these mental scenarios. When a seizure actually arrived, though, it would be overpowering, pulverizing, and I would be unable to remember a single element of my scheme. My cautious, conservative nature did well enough to protect me from the well-intentioned but quite possibly dangerous interventions of others, those well-intended people who had the effect of trampling my honor to shreds without being aware of what they were doing or understanding my condition. Without necessarily meaning to, I would meet these interventions head-on, protecting myself behind a shield of outright rejection and self-assurance, attempting to plaster onto my features an enhanced confidence—or a forged one, what's the difference—behind which I was concealing a body cracking into pieces, a devastated soul and a sense of security that was suddenly gone from beneath me.

An hour passed, and another half an hour, and a new professor took the old one's place on the screen, and there was still another half hour to go before the day's classes would end for me. The crying inside of me was picking a quarrel with the rims of my eyelids, and accumulating beneath. I pushed the tears back, but I could not keep them from their steady push toward the edges. What to do? What does a person do who finds herself pierced through and rigged to sail, being carried on a cold wind, alone in the most savage of her solitary moments? What was I to do when I could not hide my face from the curiosity of others, nor my eyes from unintentional humiliation, nor the writhings of my body from scrutiny? How was I to say what I needed to say to the sixty girls who sat with me in the lecture hall? I am fine, take your eyes off me! I am not an object to be stared at or a procession of gypsies, or a circus hopping with clowns! Do you not understand that there is a slick surface to your gazes on which I will slip and fall, breaking the neck of my pride? The interest you are taking in me, your overdone concern, has a stink to it, a smell I won't accept. The way you are gathering so tightly around me like this makes me think of a cocoon, one that suffocates whatever is inside. I am living these spells, they shatter and wreck my soul, they ravage my body, wreaking it with exhaustion and illness. But I cannot cross over your sympathy as if it is a bridge, nor can I go on living beneath the mercy of its very low span.

I had thought that the fast circulation of talk, its spread outward in such rapid waves, was only to be found in rural areas, or perhaps in cafés, but only on the outskirts of town or in small and intimate evening gatherings. I also assumed that our college was a microcosm of an urban society, civilized and above suspicion of being ruled by empty chatter, the leakage of story after story. But now, my attempt to philosophize all of this does not look so logical or realistic. I left the lecture hall and went straight to my locker. I remembered the business of the article and Sundus, so first I passed by the hall where her lecture was, but did not find her. Next, I went over to the girls gathered nearby to ask whether anyone had seen her. I sensed something suspicious, but my extremely sensitive emotional radar could not give me a precise reading. The stares that followed me and the odd questions about whether I was well seemed more numerous than usual, and more intense, as did the whispered offers to save me a seat on the bus.

I was very skilled at closing up my face behind a neutral and perhaps ambiguous mask which allowed no one, however hard she tried, a glimpse of what was really there unless I wanted her to see it. In a scene from *The Man in the Iron Mask*, after the iron mask has been stripped off Leo's face, he fishes out his mask and puts it on once everyone has gone to sleep. He has gotten used to seeing the world through it. The mask is his safest place and refuge. That was the way I was, putting on a jellylike mask and sailing through others, practicing a murky withdrawal that gave others only a noncommittal expression. My face was not a little transmitter broadcasting my news out to them, so I figured that others had taken it upon themselves to spread this news item around. I felt an overwhelming desire to laugh. For it is laughable that, for an entire nine years, I kept my secret so well, even from my closest friends, from girls who were so often in my company, and then one single spell scattered all of my long efforts like particles of dust or soot.

My illness had always been a secret. For long periods of time, even speaking about it was a disgraceful act that could trigger a scolding in our household. It was as if the illness was a sin without possibility of forgiveness, a flaw it was necessary to hide, a little scandal blemishing the family that must not get out beyond the most intimate circles. I understand the logic that equates illness with a bad reputation. No one is going to come forward promptly to pick this up and carry it for you; no one wants to take it to his bosom; no one will be in a hurry to procure such a thing for his sterling family tree. Until now, I had been utterly grateful for the secretiveness that gave me a life no compassion disturbed and no sympathy interrupted. But my questions, now, were slaying me: What will change? What has already actually changed, since this happened? What more will happen? I am afraid my questions are many, and there are no easy answers.

Before she was near enough to my ear to whisper *Give you a hug*? I knew who she was, by the sound of the heel of her shoe on the tiling. There is a distinctive character to the way she marks out her steps, one after another, a series of sharp *taps*. Her perfume penetrated my nose as she leaned over me, confirming who it was. I took the hand that had come to rest on my shoulder and turned her toward me, and as soon as she faced me I saw a quality of anxiety in her face, stimulated by my paleness and the rising flood of tears that my eyes concealed. But I had singled out Dai to read my pain plainly and in all of its horrid details.

She crouched down at my knees and began to rub my cold palms. She put her hand on my forehead.

What's wrong? What have you got?

Nothing.

Are you sure?

Yes, I'm sure.

To change the course of the conversation and dispel her worry, I said, Tell me, how did your exam go?

Fine ... *I guess.*

By the looks of you, I swear, you made a mess of it!

And you?

Very well.

I said it with a broad smile to reassure her. I picked up my bag, took Dai by the hand, and led her out of there. First, though, passing by the vending machine, I put in two riyals. The machine spit out two cans of Pepsi. I plastered one against my cheek to lighten the redness and fever, and I set the other one in Dai's bag. We went out and sat down on one of the white stone benches in front of the glass wall that lets us see half of the inside courtyard. I gave her my article and then I handed her some paper and a pen so that she could rewrite it. I chatted with her about the morning's opportunity that I had lost in searching for Sundus. I don't know, I said, where this girl hides when I'm searching for her!

I hate Sundus! she said, but she said it the way a child would. She looked at my handwriting and began to laugh. She had every right to laugh, since the article looked like a toddler's brash scribbles: after all, I had written it on the bus yesterday, with the pen jolting and sliding across the paper every time the bus shook or bumped. She sighed in near-wonder. *Ya quwwat Allah*!* One, two ... whoa, only seven words crossed out! I began to dictate to her as she wrote, and I shaded her eyes with my hand so that she could see what she was writing down. Now and then, she would stop me to give her opinion. I knew what she was likely to say. If you would write it like this instead of like that ... if you expand a little on this thought ... if you open the door to that idea ... I know Dai, and I know her desire to make everything in this world perfect, superlative in the appearance it makes, even if it is just a one-thousand-word essay.

We feared we would not find two empty seats together, more than we feared the hardship of sitting on the steps going into the bus or being jammed in the aisle. From where we were, I could not make out Sundus's form, so I cut the effort short and began simply calling out her name. All the way at the other end of the bus, she raised her hand. *Here ... here ... come on*! I scolded her a little for making me go to all that trouble searching uselessly for her. Her justification was that she was spending all her time outside of lectures in the library, looking for sources for her final research paper. I handed her the article. She read the beginning of it and then inserted it carefully in her bag. It needs some concentration to read, she said. In other circumstances we would have chattered a little about Aqil and given him a sharp little ear pull in absentia for acting the pharaoh toward

---

* Invoking the strength of God.

us. But in the bus, where even a whisper was audible, we always had to restrain ourselves sharply, putting on a simulated gravity. Who would understand here that there might be a good reason pushing two girls to joke about the brother of one of them, without putting the conversation on trial, criminalizing the speakers, or interpreting it in some other shameful way!

She invited us to sit with her, and of course it was not appropriate for us to refuse. Dai pinched my arm forcibly and I began to laugh as a way to get back at her. The forty minutes before Sundus would get out went by slowly. We talked about our final papers that we had to turn in to graduate, the demands of various professors, the narrow range of topics, the scarcity of sources, and our doubt-laden dread of that day when we would face our oral defense. Dai commented on the matter sarcastically.

Even a rabbit scares me, and yet I'm the one who will get the lion!

It was Dai's good fortune that Sundus was invited to lunch at the home of one of her sisters, for otherwise she would have been the last girl to get out of the bus when Sundus had left. Dai pressed against me, let her head drop and stay on my shoulder, and said dejectedly, I hate you!

12

The cell phone's ringing woke me. Groggy with sleeping too long and too late, I felt my ears echoing with the dreadful tolling of winged creatures that flew through my dreams. I could not figure out where the sound was coming from. I flung off the bedcovers, ran my fingers across the surface of my bedside table and searched through the drawers. I turned on the lamp and finally stumbled on my phone somewhere under the bed.

Two minutes and I'm there. Open the door for me.

Sure.

I dragged my comforter along with me as I left my room. It was the first time Dai would see me in such a state, jolted right out of sleep like this, in a skimpy nightshirt, my hair uncombed and my mouth tight with dryness. The minute I opened the door for her, she deposited a kiss on my cheek big enough that I felt its wetness even against the cool freshness of my skin and sensed its warmth against my cold flesh. It was the kind of kiss that says, *Ya Allah*, how much I love you! And it came from Dai, who had never actually said such a thing to me, not once.

I took her by the hand and we went into the kitchen. Would she like something to drink? I asked. I did not really even need to ask what she wanted, since I knew she drank mango juice if she wanted a *cole drink*, as she calls it, and cappuccino if she wanted something hot. So before she could answer, I pointed to an upper shelf too high for me to reach. Dai had no more than two centimeters on me in height, but as I watched she stretched her frame upward and placed the tin in front of me. Next, she taught me the trick of heating the water and cappuccino powder together in the microwave to boost the amount of thick froth the powder would produce. It was the latest in a series of useful lessons: on an earlier occasion, she had coached me on the ploy of putting batteries in the freezer to lengthen their life. Another time when we were together, she showed me how to whack jar lids to make them easier to open.

Still hand in hand, we went up to the room. I put my finger to my lips with a *shhh* after every naughty chuckle that Dai's little tales sent rocking through the stillness. I detached myself and headed into the bathroom. For a couple of minutes she left me alone, but then she came right up to the door and began to chatter away. Like a bratty child who can't stay away from mama for even a moment, I thought. I was not accustomed to this bathroom chitchat. Whenever Dai caught the sound of me moving around, or the echoing tap-tap from the tiled floor, she asked me at once, urgently and insistently, what I was doing. I did not know how to respond. What does anyone do in the bathroom? I opened the door for her and began to brush my teeth. She leaned comfortably against the doorframe. Her eyes on the bathrobe I had carried in with me, she asked bluntly, Are you going to take a bath *now*?

I sensed what she was getting at. No. A little later on.

She came a few steps closer. I made it obvious that the last thing I wanted right now was a kiss from her, not while my mouth felt thoroughly scoured by the artificial mint scent of toothpaste. Dai's response was to say that she would love kissing me even if I were coated in mold.

She came nearer still, put her arms around my middle, and began staring at my reflection in the mirror, exactly as I do myself. Her gaze, fluctuating with unveiled contrariety between the transparency of fine molasses and the opaqueness of deep black, left me doubly flustered, because I could not enter in and probe what lay behind those changeable pearls. She stared as though my reflection were someone other than me, as though that reflection did not belong to me or resemble me; indeed, as though someone she had never seen before was staring back at her. As though, there in the mirror, a creature was caught and frozen, imprisoned inside the glass, obliged to await the moment when I would turn my eyes to it, so that it could emerge from its murky surroundings.

Is there something different about you today?

You haven't figured it out yet?

Just the day before I had cut my hair without telling her—or, to put it more plainly, without getting her permission. So I was expecting to find a harsh punishment lying in wait for me, or a fight that I couldn't see my way out of. I had chosen the timing deliberately, because today was the day we had agreed on; today she would take me to the *mazraa*,* and introduce me in person to her friends. Naturally, she would not want to risk our showing up in front of everyone looking in any way unacceptable, one of us clearly irritated with the other. She would not want to gamble on losing her chance to display how proud she was of me. Here is *sahbati*, she wanted to be able to say. Here is my friend.

In the mirror I saw those eyes suddenly widen. She was truly staggered. Likely, I thought to myself, she has been betting on my lack of nerve, counting on me not to exceed the restraints imposed, or at least implied, by the rights possession gives her. She has been assuming I would not take any liberties with my body. I would not act on my own. I would not act like *this*, without first seeking her reassurance. Now she sees that she has lost her gamble.

Her hand went around my neck as we both stared at the image

---

*   Farm or plantation.

of us reflected in the mirror. She moved her hand slowly, so slowly that I almost did not believe that it was moving at all. She pressed slightly and my pulse was palpable to us both beneath her hand. I closed my eyes and breathed, very slowly because I did not want her to suspect my discomfort. I sensed her trying to calibrate exactly how far up my neck to go in order to find the best position for choking me. Ferociously, almost maliciously, the higher her hand crept, the more feverish seemed her pleasure. She kept her hand exactly in position for what felt like a long time, her palm and fingers mantling my neck entirely as my jaws made contact with her index finger on one side and her thumb on the other. Then a sudden movement took me unawares—she yanked the short hair covering my neck and put her lips to me. Her quiet, restrained little mouthings struggled to free themselves and grew into fierce whole kisses. A colossal hunger was what seemed to drive her, propelled equally by anger and a longing for revenge. I tried to push her away from me with my own protest. No—that'll leave marks on me!

So you don't want me to do it?

Dai, stop—it hurts.

Who said I don't want to hurt you?

I ducked away but I could not get very far, not far enough, because with both hands clenched, she gripped the rim of the basin that we were shoved against and blocked me, enclosing my body in her strong arms. The only space for maneuver I had now was a little circle, inside of which I had already half spun away.

Do you know what they call that mark?

My mood had not yet gone sour. But being imprisoned like this by her presence, and the fact that we were standing so very close together, motionless and face to face, and her expression as she looked at me, resentful and provoking, sent a spark of irritation shooting into the emotions already churning between us. She answered her own question.

Love bite.

Love bite! Hah—it's a hate bite.

I was on the point of giving myself five stars for this reckless little verbal arrow I had launched, except that I caught a flash of anger, derision and rejection all at once in her eyes. She yanked me away from the sink. Once we were back in the room, she handed me a red velvet box. *Haak*! she said sharply. There! Take it!

I opened the box and saw an engagement ring. She pulled it out of the box, and under the light she showed me the name engraved there, a heart bracketing the letters on either end. She spread my fingers apart and slid it onto my left ring finger. She pulled my hand downward and kissed my palm.

Some scene flitting across a screen, that's what it seemed like, a flimsy, inept scene created by an actress who truly outdoes herself at falling flat. Dai did not even manage to close her eyelids as the kiss descended, but rather aimed her gaze directly at my eyes to search out her effect on me. I could not keep this fantasy going, though. We were not in a scene from the cinema. This was something more than that, something much more substantial. Dai had brought all of her considerable cleverness and intelligence to the task. She built a trap for me and I promptly fell into it, easy enough prey. With an engagement ring engraved with her name on it and a kiss on the palms of my hands, Dai would bring this scene of hers to its dramatic fullness before an audience of her friends—her other friends. She would be able to say, this girl is my possession. She's mine. Don't you see what swirls around her finger, the sign and shadow of my ownership?

It stayed in my mouth, that bitter tang left by a perfectly contrived and executed deception, the taste of stupidity and an unbelievably easy capitulation on my part. It happened so fast and I was not equipped for it. I was not capable of reviewing quickly enough in my mind the assumptions that lay behind it all, especially when she was right there next to me. There was no chance to stop her and ask, Wait, what is this? What does it mean? How am I supposed to handle this? And why now?

What was so strange about it all was that this attempt, a premature one that would miscarry, arrived only in time for the words *so long* to form themselves quietly between us. For Dai's too-hasty bid gave a strong push to our relationship. Everything that occurred now, whether on the positive pole or the negative, utterly horrible or terribly good, stable or shaky, recurring or new—every little event now had a different and uncommon impact, an echo that would not quit. That *so long* forced me into a reevaluation of our relationship, and I came out of it with the realization that whatever occurs in the course of a day may never come your way again. At any moment, our relationship could collapse. It could dwindle to nothing just as it had emerged from nothing. Somehow, now, my ability to sense her hurting was twice what it had been. The return on my pleasure at that hurt doubled as well.

She argued with me. I was feeling so resentful that my desire to maneuver against her came back in force, my desire to tease her, to pick a quarrel with her willfulness. I liked best to bait her by behaving in a way that slowly intensified her possession of me while making her nerves gyrate, swerving from rejection to acceptance, submission to tyranny. She would hang between her entreaties and her ability to surmount my *no*, every time I said it—not to the point where she would take me by force, but to the very brink of doing so. She was the one who had taught me the ground rules of the game. And she was the one who wanted to be the ground on which I paced out my moves. Her maddening way with me would just grow more intense, putting me on the verge of reversing the game.

But then suddenly she opens a door in front of me, a doorway straight into hell. She puts her hand on the flesh of my leg, ready to move my thighs apart. I have always hated this. I hate it when she puts her hand just there like that, to push my legs apart like this.

I jerked and pushed her hand away from beneath my leg. No! Why not?

I made it up—the first lie that came into my head. It tickles!

Just as I had delivered an offhand lie then, I improvised a quick climax that (my body emptied of a sense of there-ness with Dai) I was not to reach. I don't know how the idea came into my mind. I don't know how I managed to carry it from idea to act. It was as difficult to force Dai into retreat as it was to force myself to enter a state of mind with her that was wakeful to her desire. A lie such as this, I figured, would cause no harm if only she would swallow it. Just then, though, I did not even care whether she swallowed my lie or choked on it.

After two hours and more prodigal cravings, here we were at the farm and she was giving me a private introduction, under her breath, to all of the girls who were there. It was the third time Dai had recited these names to me, hoping that they would float on my memory, coming to the surface just at the right moments so that I would not have to face the embarrassment of forgetting one of them.

The girl eating corn flakes is Janan. The one in the white blouse, Ghada. That one, who just got up to go into the kitchen, is Basma. And the girl who is tying her hair back right now, that's Miral. The one over there who has no chest is Duha, and over here is—

I know her. Yes, I know her—it's Dareen.

Not a name easily forgotten! And then there was the touch of her hand as she greeted me warmly. Since I arrived, we'd exchanged a few furtive glances together with smiles quickly suppressed, their minute transgressions swiftly concealed. Only rarely did I ever encounter someone whose form would mold itself into an urgent and alluring question mark before my eyes. Someone who could get to me so easily. That moment of greeting with Dareen had not been a friendly handshake; it had been a brush against the membranes around my heart, a pressure upon the sensitive nerves of my soul. The best way I can put it is that the flesh of her hand had gone deep inside of me and flung everything there into disarray.

I had expected—or feared—that I would not prove able to feel quickly at ease among strange girls with whom I had never shared Basta market day hours, or middle school classrooms, or Um Hussain, who had been our teacher in the *kuttab*, our religious kindergarten where we first learned how to read and recite the Qur'an. Yet, even with all of my apprehensions, I forgot myself completely, balling up my *abaya* and piling it off in a corner, and entering right into the commotion they were creating in the kitchen with the help of lettuce and tomatoes and the salad slicer.

Are you from Qatif? one of them asked me immediately.

That's Amal, Dai whispered in my ear.

Yes, I am.

Your mother is, too?

Yes.

Where do you study?

Here in Dammam.

So, why do you talk the way you do?

I looked at her, puzzled.

Like, you speak the way Egyptians do. *Mish 'awza. Taale ala baali. Aysh. Barduh. Libayh.* Like an Egyptian and sometimes a Lebanese.

Dai rescued me, rushing into the conversation. You know the girls at the college. They come in from the villages and think they can shrug off their old ways of talking. They get swollen heads.

Amal's wary questions were not new to me. So often, my speech had stood out from that of others, even my siblings. It was not deliberate. It was not an adopted dialect. It was just that words slid onto my tongue so easily, and then slipped off just as easily, words from the television, from my girlfriends, from my Internet buddies and my reading. I would stack them unconsciously in my store of daily vocabulary and they would emerge in my conversations. Even in chat rooms, I used a language that you might call neutral, unattached—or perhaps to put it more accurately, a language that was not identifiable as belonging to any one place. A mixture of dialects, where I could not pinpoint the origins or sources of the words I uttered.

The low, round table was brought out and a variety of dishes rapidly covered its surface. I heard invitations from every side, entreating me to try this dish or that one; more came my way than anyone else's, since I was the one outsider in a group of obvious familiars. Dai finished eating before I did and got up to wash her hands, leaving me on my own for five entire minutes. Her slowness to return was suspicious and embarrassing all at once. When I finished my meal, Husna showed me around. Here were the bathroom, kitchen and a room to the side. Here was the passage that led to the swimming pool, and over there was the other corridor, on the farm side, where I had entered; here were the birdcages and animal pen. She showed me all of this through the screen door, which led from the kitchen directly outdoors. She pointed out the rows of trees and gave me their names. She began recounting happy memories of visiting a woman named Um Jawaad, who sold native roses to make a living. *We were always running out of money*, she said, *all we got for pocket money was two riyals.* The rays of the sun were so blinding that I could see nothing; she promised me that we would go out just before the sunset. We would pick sweet basil leaves and make necklaces for our mothers. Then she excused herself and left me in the chaos of the kitchen and my loneliness.

Stacked with dishes, the kitchen sink did not look inviting, so I turned toward the bathroom, opened the door, and saw Dai standing there with her friend who wore gray glasses and whose name I had not been able to remember and then had not thought to ask. The two of them were standing exactly in the same pose that she and I had assumed in front of the basin that morning. She was staring at their reflections in the mirror. Her arms encircled her friend's waist and stretched toward the sink: she was rubbing her palms together beneath the flow of the water. She rested her chin—or more precisely her lips—on her friend's shoulder. There was nothing in this picture that I did not know. I swung the door shut. The whole thing took no more than half a second but it dug itself deeply into my head, etching caustic furrows and filthy oaths at Dai's expense, yielding imagined scenes whose beginnings I knew but whose endings I did not fathom.

Once everyone had finished eating, we headed like one large wave to the water as if we were fly-by-night waifs who hardly ever got the chance to relax and have fun in nice surroundings. The air was electric: laughter and splashing, little tricks and transient touches. And I was fully charged, the tension flooding through me, too strong to dam up. Even the water could not drink it out of me. I had never before attended a gathering like this and so I had no idea what might happen. My expectations were flung as wide open as could be, although so far, I had seen nothing more than a surreptitious kiss, and even that I had witnessed accidentally.

By prior agreement, Dai was to show absolutely no signs of physical attraction to me. I could not be sure of Dai, though. I had no confidence that she would stick to her word, especially since this was her chance to parade her skills—and she loved to be the one on the dais, immobilized by applause from all sides. More important right now, though, was the doubled sense of revenge she bore toward me. It wasn't only that I had cut my hair without her permission. I had forgotten her ring. I had taken it off to do my ablutions before prayer, I insisted. And then I had left it on the basin in my bathroom. She saw through my lie, I was sure of it.

Now I felt sick with disgust at Dai, and if she got near me, it would just work up the demons in my blood. I grabbed my first opportunity to get away. In the pool, on my back, every time I closed my eyes I could sense the pool roofing about to collapse onto me: it would only take a second to squash me flat as the floor. And then, the moment my eyes opened in fright to stare at the ceiling, I would feel overwhelmed by how very far away it was, imposingly high above me, and how I was so very alone far below, deafened and silenced by the clamor around me, just all alone, so completely isolated. It was only my sense of hearing that let me know where I was and where I was heading, and all I could hang onto was intuition in figuring out whether I had reached the edge of the pool and should push off in the opposite direction.

I closed my eyes, struggling hard to get the better of my sense of falling, of collapse, of my body bruised and crushed. I imagined myself as a mote that the current was pulling into the depths. And then I was swelling up like a kernel of popcorn and blocking the opening of the pool's drain, and this way, the water could not swallow me.

Dai took me by surprise, laying her hand on me and whispering, The honey—where'd it go? Her morning kiss and her sweetness now were gestures that made my heart tickle, so rarely did Dai act like this with me. She pushed her fingernail into my palm and scratched, lightly, and then, pointing to the visible red line that her nail had left behind, said, Look, your skin has drunk its fill of water and now it's really soft and fine.

She drew me with her—we sat on the edge of the pool. She didn't leave any space between us, and her hand went around my middle. We were whispering because anything anyone said, next to the pool, produced an echo. She asked me whether this excursion we had planned was to my liking. And did the girls please me, and the lunch, and the swimming pool? I was answering, yes, yes, and then, it was sudden, she moved away from me, far enough so that she could look into my eyes, and so my fingers went caressing the dimples in her cheeks, which is what I always do when I'm longing for her. She backed off and said, And me?

You what?

Do I please you?

Oh yes, always!

Always always?

Sometimes not.

Then she was right there again, very close beside me, exactly like in those moments when she is about to take my ear between her lips, and she delivered me the shock which I did not take in.

I love you.

After five months, the total sum of my acquaintance with her, our relationship had begun to take on its own character, with the kind of struggle only intense closeness creates, the summits of long-ing, the particular stupidities unique to us, the ferocity of it, and the way it could shake my life to the core and completely alter the person I was. Throughout the whole of this time, we had never once said to each other, I love you. I can almost, almost believe that it was never there in any of the plans or expectations that either of us had; it was so *not there* that I would not have dared to put it on the list of possibilities that I was hoping or waiting for. It was, simply put, the thing that could not be said, and likely, it was the dreaded phrase desired by no one. From the start, talking about our feelings was not in the picture. And only now do I realize that we actually said very little to one another. Considering how long I had known Dai, there was a lot that I did not know about her. About the human being in her, about her dreams and hopes and fears, the projects she would have in mind, her desires and her past. Right from the start, it had been the body that had steered our relationship, and the body remained alone under the spotlight, unaccompanied by any supporting actors.

So I smiled.

That grin was utterly the stupidest reaction I could have come up with when faced with an *I love you* that arrived like a belated award of merit. I needed to rework my response very fast, and so I hauled her away from the swimming pool. I did not wait for us to be alone somewhere empty and enclosed, though. I pushed her back against the wall, exactly as she does each time I visit her. At the door to her room, she blocked me so that I couldn't move. Then I caught her lips, breaking up a half sentence she was about to finish, my head going round and round as we fell dizzily into a prolonged kiss. A very long kiss.

I told myself that suddenly jumping for once over my red line— after I had just squandered an entire morning sketching out that line with her and convincing her that it was necessary—would not mean permanently violating it. One kiss would not kill me. Anyway, what I was getting in return from her was greater than any loss I could possibly have. I wasn't intending anything more than a kiss that would barely nibble her lips. But my gratitude and the way she melted like sugar in my mouth hadn't together pushed me far beyond. Swallowed up in her, I was brought back into the world only by the exclamation *My eyes!* uttered in a clammy voice carried along on footsteps that had just gone by on the way to the pool. I heard a low murmuring and then an explosion of laughter.

My face must have gone completely crimson. Opposite me, Dai was totally flustered, I could tell. My reckonings had not been at all misplaced. Dai felt proud of me but she was not interested in showing her pride at my expense. That was an enormous distinction. Of course, I could not overlook the satisfaction she took in herself. She was the one who taught me how to draw on my own store of cunning, after all, not to mention how to pass my clever observations to others without having to snap my fingers to get their attention, and ruining the effect.

I hate performing roles for free, though. That is what I had not given any thought to, when it came to kissing Dai, which was what put me directly under the hot spotlight of curiosity. It wasn't the kiss; it was me as a new arrival, an unanticipated and unknown element. It was my being fresh and untried; it was also that I was off limits. And the kiss which could have easily been taken for insolent behavior or a cheap attempt to get some attention was taken instead as a first step toward getting inside the mystery of me and undoing my own reticence. Then I thought, It may well be that everything Dai has told me about this world of hers is a pure lie, and if so, I have fallen into the trap made up of her lies, I have crashed through unwritten boundaries, and concocted unacceptable roles, but all without any understanding of what I was doing.

Dareen winked at me from behind her friend's shoulder. She stood up from the poolside and asked who wanted to help her out in the kitchen. No one responded, and then I caught on to the little conspiracy in which she was including me and I volunteered. I weighed up the two sides of the balance in a matter of seconds. Yes, there was no doubt that I would stir up Dai's anger and jealousy; but I would get to know Dareen and her way of thinking, at least a little. It was well worth the attempt and it also meant I would buy some time away from any attention I might be getting, especially if it was clouded by greediness or envy or mannered behavior toward me. I would remove myself too, I hoped, from any disgust anyone might be feeling at my bad behavior.

When I got up from where Dai and I sat and turned my back to her, she pinched my bottom. I all but turned and slapped her. With a single stupid and mean move, she had just blasted apart all that had happened the moment before. She had crushed my desire to love her, torpedoed the pure memory of that *I love you* instant, done away with the flash of absolute contentment granted me by that moment between us. What I felt was something that went far beyond anger and disgust and nausea and feelings of inadequacy or lowness. What I felt eclipsed anything bad I had ever felt toward Dai in the past. What I felt exceeded my powers of explanation and my ability to respond. And so I did not turn in the direction of that pinch; I did not slap her, I did not spit at her or kick her or push her into the water and force her head beneath the surface until she drowned. These images went through my head, but that is as far as it went.

I asked Dareen's leave to give me some time to dry off and change my clothes, and she said she would do the same. I went into one of the bathroom cubicles adjoining the pool. I squatted, letting the heaviness of my body slump over my feet. I was a pair of legs pressed together, arms encircling them, my bowed head above. Like a clock pendulum, my body swung back and forth, back and forth.

In the film *Seven*, as Kevin Spacey is arranging murders that echo the seven deadly sins, he strips off the skin on his fingertips to rid himself of fingerprints. Without knowing for certain whether or not it was even painful, now I saw this as a truly appropriate punishment for Dai. More than a punishment: the only hell I could find that was truly worthy of her. I would skin those two hands that had moved across my body, strip her fingerprints from her, strip away the possibility of solidity, of always being there; strip away that soiling presence. Strip away any possibility of her passing across me, which meant the possibility of her very existence. I would banish her from me. If I did this, I would be free of her. If only I could do this.

I followed Dareen into the kitchen. We stood side by side in front of the basin and I began to wash the dishes in soapy water while she rinsed them. I don't know exactly how we began talking. What I do know is that we were in high spirits. She was telling me about yesterday's dreams, a mixture of fantasia and legend and action films. She had an appealing way of pronouncing her words; her *s* seemed always on the point of timid flight and her *r* sort of slithered across her tongue. She left a second's silence after every sentence that deserved reflection, and then resumed with a little *Naam, naam*—Yes, oh yes—before she went on to the next thought. What also truly struck me was how vivid the scenery of her memory was. As she spoke, I seemed to have a movie opening before me, a film that offered me the entire stretch between her eyes and the very limits of human vision. It ushered me into the magical captivity of her remarkable screen, to the point where I was practically reacting to everything exactly as she had done, even though it was she, and not me, who had seen those images.

We awoke. When I say *we awoke* I mean it literally. We woke up from the bewitching trance of words, from the honey sweetness of dreams, to an electric shock that flew from her bare forearm to mine. We both caught our breath and stared, blinded by this touch, our senses, our breathing, stolen away. Staring through the window at some distant point, she whispered, I want to kiss you. I did not say a word. She took my hand, pulled me to a door that opened into a little room off the kitchen and slammed the door behind us, and suddenly we were in an intense kiss, our hands moving freely beyond our control, our breaths short and sharp. I kissed her and kissed her and kissed her, and I moved downward to her neck and then to her chest. I was in such frenzy that I could not be sure which one of us had asked and which one had given. She followed my lead, her body yielding, and the way she responded to my crazed kisses ground my nerves to nothing. She was so delicious that I didn't take my lips away until I had used up every bit of air that I had stored away. *Yikhrab baytik*! *Jnnantiini*! I said in a sloppy voice. Go to hell! You've made me crazy! She laughed, the sound of it like a hot lick across me, pumping into my blood an unstoppably willful desire for more madness.

What spoiled our moment was an uproar outside. Dareen put her hand over my mouth and plastered her cheek to mine as she listened hard to the screaming. From the smell of the place, its stagnant feel and the dust, I figured that we were in a storage room: in the past five minutes, I had not noticed the surroundings. It was very small, so cramped that when Dareen had rushed onto me my back had crunched up against the metal shelves. I did up the buttons I had opened down her blouse, straightened my own blouse and patted at my hair, and then kissed her instead of saying *thank you*. She went out ahead of me. After making sure that no one was in the kitchen, she called me to come out. She laughed once more and it made me want her all over again.

Haifaa and Ashwaq are fighting.

About what?

They're always like that. Give them a few minutes and they'll calm down.

We went back to the sink. I noticed the barely perceptible *love bite* I had left above her breast. I told her to button her blouse over it and she said she didn't care; her friend didn't say no to things like this. Basically, their relationship was falling apart, and anyway, from the beginning it had been an open relationship. *She* had not made that rule, and it wasn't the way she had wanted things to be, so now let her friend swallow the results of her own decisions. She let me know that, starting right now, she intended to see their relationship off to its final resting place. For the first time, I was hearing expressions like this: *open relationship*. And I suddenly understood why Dai had been treating me as if I were a child who had not learned her lessons yet, and she was the one who had taken on the task of teaching me!

Dai will kill me! I said.

Dareen's face took on a different expression, shaded with regret.

It wasn't your fault, I added.

Do you regret it?

No way!

Her face lit up again.

The shouting faded away gradually until all was quiet. She grabbed me mischievously and said, Come on. We tiptoed toward the room bordering the kitchen and pressed our ears against the door. We heard the sounds of crying, excuses and pleas, breaths sliced short by longing. We went back to our tasks in the kitchen. We got the dessert ready to go, served it onto plates and carried them on two trays to the sitting room where we had eaten our meal. She let everyone know that dessert was ready.

We all re-gathered. As Haifaa and Ashwaq showed their faces, Dareen and I both giggled, though we swallowed our laughter as quickly as we could. Dai had sat down beside me. She began to grill me about every moment I had spent in Dareen's company. I answered her casually, with no show of concern, hoping to put her off track. Her finicky questions made me want to scream: the only thing she neglected to ask was the color of the sponge I had used to wash the dishes, and since she didn't ask me about that I told her voluntarily. Dareen broke into our conversation with wicked smoothness, demanding my phone number. I began repeating the numbers but she was scrabbling around in her bag. She looked up at me and said, I don't have any paper, and then got to her feet very quickly, before she could be waylaid by some offer of a piece or two of paper. She sat down squarely in front of us, leaning against Dai's legs and putting her left hand in my lap. She handed me her pen so that I could write my number directly onto her skin. I could feel a coming storm: Dai would explode in anger at the very moment I would erupt in malicious satisfaction and Dareen would blow up in ecstasy.

As evening came, after prayer time, Husna brought out a massive tape recorder. She plugged it in, turned out the light, and tried out several tapes. I couldn't make out what they were; I must not have heard any of them before. Almost everyone stood up and readied themselves to dance, swaying and bending as though they had to warm up their hips and heat up their appetites. This was surely a recurring ritual, I thought, but it was one in which I had no experience. At first it all looked quite abstract, but the dance steps quickly assumed a more shocking definition.

Just then, I had an image in my mind of Umar saying, *Here's all you have to do—just let your spirit go, and free your body.* Or maybe it was the opposite, I'm not sure. Crazy Umar finds a philosophy for everything that makes whatever it is simple. I would never know whether these ideas were the product of original thinking, or mostly a matter of words carefully crafted in advance, or whether he was just making it up as he went along according to the needs of the moment. Or was this philosophy of his a truth bestowed on everyone, like the aphorisms of the famous medieval writer al-Jahiz, which people might encounter anytime? But since I am not someone who is particularly interested in staring at the middle of the road as she walks along, I don't stumble over meaningful and awesome notions such as this.

Dai, who is jealous even of her suspicions about me, and who imagines the air as a creature with many hands, all of which are touching me, and who thinks of the sheets on my bed as a vast body that gives way to desire, had given me an odd image of her world, as if it were a world where everyone had gone completely mad, a world of rabid dogs rather than of humans. It is a mistaken image, perhaps—or maybe one that is accurate, yet hideous. My badly shaken confidence in Dai would not give me any definite answers, nor grant me the truth, nor confer on me the ability to offer such judgments. Caught between her hesitations and her inconclusive stance about my dancing, she would flaunt me proudly all the more, exhibiting what my body hid. This was exactly what made her step into the background, leaving my revealed body susceptible to the other girls and to the looks they sent my way. Caught between Dai and Dareen's secret summons coming to me in ghostly forms through the darkness, I chose to dance. This was what I had never done in public, indeed what I had wished never to do, even covertly, except in submission to Dai's commands.

I danced. I wished that the tambourine interlude would never come to a close, that I would never stop dancing, that the nighttime would never end. I yearned to spend myself entirely, to annihilate myself, to fade to nothing. I became as light as air. I was ethereal, and I did not want to return to my humanness, my solid and visible body, where the luminosity of my spirit was held captive, unable to emerge through its pores. There is no one who can hold onto the air, no one who can grab it by the wrist and refuse to let go, and I did not want anyone to hold onto me. My dancing was akin to pleasure's fulfillment, which is also its loss. After it, you absolutely do not wish to wake up. It was a total, crystalline absence into otherness.

And then a different sort of music began, and Dai cornered me. She ruptured my wings and returned me to the wobbly, uncertain, gelatinous world, and I wanted so badly to cry, to cry and not stop.

Dai and I returned from our excursion quietly and safely. I sat apart, glued to the window, my eyes on the dusty street. Dai pulled me toward her, but I would not move. She placed her hand over mine; I pulled my hand away. She slid closer to my side, and I squeezed harder against the window. She shoved her hand between my thighs and I all but screamed at her. I hugged my bag and hunched my body into a ball, pushing Dai outside of it. Outside of me.

13

Always and forever, any kind of math had been my worst subject when it came to grades, and I was the dumbest of the students when it came to understanding it. Honestly, my mind turned instantly into a machine out of order whenever it came to math. With truly gigantic persistence and patience, my father tried to reformat my brain into compatibility with the requirements of mathematics, or at least to improve my ability to learn, but in vain.

It so happened that our neighbors' daughter, who was in her second or third year at the university, was a mathematics student. My mother made an arrangement with her to take me on as a pupil, for a trifling fee to be paid at the end of each month. With an enormous sense of grateful obligation toward her, every school day afternoon my mother would nudge me out of the house and over to the neighbors', where Balqis always gave me a warm welcome. Very soon, my grades were hiking above their usual level, and my eagerness to be at the neighbors' shot upward, too. The amount of time I was spending in Balqis's company would exceed the single hour agreed upon in advance, inching toward two hours or even three. My parents were delighted with the results, and viewed Balqis's genius admiringly, praising her astonishing ability to tame and cow my stupidity into obedience.

Balqis might have been almost a decade older than I was. In my first year of middle school, I had already seen my friends reaching the stage of being women, their chests mounting and rounding enough that they concealed them beneath bras. I would catch them talking in a language of strange words about their secret blood. I was still a child most of whose companions had grown up, leaving her in the isolating company of her dolls.

I would hasten away from the odor carried by adolescents, because it sparked in me a disgust and aversion as nothing else in my life had ever done. Only the smell of Balqis bewitched me, capturing me in a mantilla of pure white expanse and goodness. She was an angel gliding, swaying, borne along on her pure wonderfulness. And I wanted to think of myself when I would be older smiling exactly as she did, and walking and talking just like her, dressing the same way and entering university as she had. I even wanted breasts exactly like hers. Naturally, back then, I did not think about all of this in such detail, but I saw in her a complete woman, utterly mature, and I wanted God to make me exactly like her. She was the only one who did not treat me like a little girl, and at the same time she did not demand of me that I be bigger or older than I was. She stayed—and allowed me to stay—on the edge of both childhood and adulthood, at a midpoint, and she was the only person who could do that for me, maneuver that edge without teetering and swaying.

I reached that moment. All of a sudden, on a heavy summer day, I felt as though I were melting and flowing. I panicked, a terrified girl huddling in the bathroom. Everything I knew about blood I had gleaned from the odd words I heard my girlfriends say about it, and basically what I had learned was the imperative of remaining utterly discreet. Had it been something proper to talk about, then my father would have talked about it, I figured. I did not know how else to think about it, or what to do. My relationship with my mother could not endure such a scandalous event as this. It was a relationship that had never been exactly bad, but neither had it ever been good or comfortable.

And so there I was at lesson time, in Balqis's company, upset and confused about the miniature flood on my underclothes and apprehensive about whether my clothes themselves bore visible stains. I crouched instead of sitting all the way down, balancing on my feet, afraid that I would spatter something on the carpet in her room, and very uncomfortable as I shifted my weight back and forth from one foot to the other. She gazed at me attentively and then lowered her head toward the book. Then she looked up at me again, and then a third time, just as my face was tensing up under the impact of a sharp pain in my gut. She asked me, What's wrong? I was at a loss, confused about what to respond.

I do not know how she knew so definitely the enormity of my problem: there I was, a girl child of twelve whom blood had taken by surprise, and who did not know what to do! Balqis reached into her wardrobe and took out a sanitary napkin and handed it to me. I took it with a stupid expression on my face, for I had no idea what to do with this object. Hah! When I catch sight now of the how to use *lettering on a packet of sanitary napkins, I laugh. The instructions must have always been there but I was too blind to see them. Just imagine it, my dear! Something as silly and small as this would have, could have, kept Balqis from her passage across me!*

She sat down on the edge of her bed and enveloped me in a mother's arms and a houri's perfume. She taught me how to use this thing, and with a little smile she said, Don't be embarrassed. There's nothing to be ashamed of. This is where children come from. You'll have children as sweet and pretty as you are.

That day, she talked to me a lot about blood and other things: scratchy hair; pain; and my body, where the clouds of childhood would lift and disappear to reveal the body of a woman with transparent wings, who bore the home of her children wherever she went. She worked on me until I was no longer afraid, and until I felt grateful to the blood, indebted to it, happy in its intimacy.

Days passed, and more days, and the beads of the prayer rosary were counted and recounted. (I love Balqis, I am crazy over Balqis, Balqis is so so lovely with me.) My grades in math were higher than ever. Then there came the day in which I got an "excellent" on the examination. Close your eyes, she said. I have a gift for you. I was very excited. My soul trembled. She kissed me. That was her present, a kiss, lips on lips. She said, People who love each other give each other kisses on the mouth, and I love you. And then she added that this had to stay a secret between us, and if I were to tell anyone, or love anyone else or kiss anyone else, she would stop loving me. I didn't understand why this was so. She said, Do you want to never see me again? Do you want me to not love you at all? Do you want me to be angry at you? These questions of hers and the spark of suspicious light in her eyes as she asked them opened a fissure in my heart. I shook my head in fear. No, no, no!

Naïve, that's what I was. I was a child. The slightly threatening timbre of what she said did not arrest my attention. I was not put off by a vague sense that there was something amiss about the whole picture. I felt that she was granting me something special, something superior, that no one else could possibly share. I believed, too, that she was acknowledging my merit and deservingness, and elevating me above my child's sense of inferiority. I didn't just love her, I worshipped her, and from that time on I began to do whatever she told me to, exactly as she asked and without any discussion.

That kiss did not reoccur in the days to follow. She treated me as if nothing had happened. I made tremendous efforts. I outdid myself, hoping to win another gift from her. She did not grant me even an ordinary friendly kiss. I would take full advantage of the quickly passing seconds when she was absorbed in explaining things, writing out a problem or reviewing a basic rule, to stare at her lips. Her gaze would fall on me like the eyes of an eagle, sharp and wounding, and I would take my eyes away immediately, for she had caught me, eyewitness to the crime. I was thirsty. To the point where I would start weeping, I was thirsty. I thirsted so much that I was groveling. Because of a kiss, I no longer slept. I would lie down, my head on the pillow, tasting my own lips with the tip of my tongue, biting them, closing my eyes and going over it all again and again without ever growing weary, that half second, that kiss.

Then she did it. Without any preliminaries, without a perfect score on the examination, without any appended command. She kissed me. The kiss grew and swelled and filled out and matured, and slowly and gradually and deliberately it became an entire body, a tremor, a sticky moisture, a release, a liberation. And this was what happened time and again: a moment and then hunger, a single time and then hunger, an instant and then hunger. Balqis trained me and tamed me—or should I say the opposite? I had been a little girl, and I had become a wild mare. I had been a girl and I became a savage cat. I had been a girl and I became a monster, misshapen and deformed. Isn't that what I should say?

A   m o n s t e r!

At a moment when my desire was at its most vulnerable, she asked me to slap her. I would not do it. She raised an angry palm and slapped me. She asked again and I refused, and she slapped me harder. A third time and I cried. She shook me and said, Don't cry! Don't be such a child! Don't close your eyes! Give it back to me! Hit me, get your revenge on me. Didn't I hurt you? Her slaps were harder or softer, I would not know in advance, and when she got to the fifth slap and my ears were ringing and I could hardly hear at all, I raised my palm and slapped her with all the strength that this pain had thrust into me. A fierce pleasure suddenly overtook me. It made my bones shudder and it set my temples on fire. I had no power of recall over this act of pleasure, a boon granted by might, greatness and tyranny, no matter how many times I slapped or however much my store of wickedness was used up.

That was the miserable beginning of it. The more accustomed I got to it, the more she raised the threshold of pain, until my body lost whatever share it had of contentment, going insane if it was not in pain, collapsing into distraught uncertainty when it was not being hurt. Pain became its profession, its craft, its route in search of pleasure. In a certain way, my body did continue to resemble its original human formation, a human body's limited capacities for endurance and the particular qualities of flesh and bone. But it went beyond those human characteristics to attain an advanced stage of I don't know what! It was a body whose capacity for feeling and reaction had grown very weak, had all but left, to the point where a terrible blast of pain could not even shake its nerve endings. I would try harder, try to return the merciless exhilaration of pain to my body. Every time I reached a new and exorbitant threshold, my body grew accustomed to it after repetition, and I would demand more, more and more and more, and every time, a question pelted me until it was breaking apart the very cells inside of me. Is there more? Something more than all of this, is there more?

At the time, I held myself in the category of an observer, for only a few moments, watching what she was doing to me, and simultaneously I was the recipient of its impact. As time passed, she transformed me into an active participant, discovering and experiencing and inventing. People become addicted to drugs and alcohol, they become addicted to the television or Internet or video games. I became addicted to Balqis's body. More accurately, I became addicted to what she did with me, the ruthless force, the slavery. Beneath her, I was a jariya, *a slave girl, whose life was given over to the pleasure of another. She was a goddess who could kill and bring to life. I learned how to exchange roles with her. I was not serene until I had acquired my share of her, nor would my agitation abate until I had made her a plaything in my hands, just as I was in hers. These were dalliances whose danger I recognized, but the more clearly I perceived the danger, the stronger was the impact on me. I no longer cried. I had grown up, and grownups don't cry.*

And at the height of talk, all words ceased.

The words grew silent. Balqis's craziness over me went still. Her desire for me disappeared gradually until it went completely cold. She made excuses to my mother, using my high grades in math to claim that I no longer needed her. Three years of private lessons—it was a long time, Balqis told her, and it would be better for me to begin to depend on myself. Thus, my lessons at Balqis's ended. One day passed, or two days, between meetings, and then three, four days, and then a week. My heart was churning and my body was seething and Balqis was not distinguishing what was correct or reasonable from what was spurious. She used the pretext of "things she had to do," events that were keeping her busy, and I understood perfectly well that her excuses were lies. I did not understand what was behind them, and because of them, I went round and round in the vicious circle of doubt and jealousy. I would make up silly reasons to stop by her home, weak excuses, completely illogical ones. All I wanted was to sniff the fragrance of my houri and regain some reassurance from her. I noticed that she had a new visitor. I took note of the times of the new girl's lessons. I noticed her breasts, which had not yet swollen to their fullest. I noticed how she was still growing and developing. It was as though noticing everything, at that particular time, was a kind of drug that I had to have, or a state of stupor that preserved me. Belatedly, I noticed Balqis's disgusted reaction to me, mounting to the point of nausea, disgust at my body, at the growth and maturity of my femininity, at the child's body now vaulting toward its adulthood, at the growing accentuation of my waist and hips, the rising mounds of my breasts.

They say that memory grows tired and falls asleep, and then, if it is not constantly whetted, fades and dies amongst dreams and drowsy images. Every day, I had some memory of Balqis. Not a day would pass in which I did not think of her. In my mind, I would embrace her so hard that her ribs would hurt. I kissed her so feverishly that I stole her lips from her. I slapped her on account of her absence, and I slapped her for the sake of the new little doll that she crushed beneath her body. I would slap her and then I would regret it. I would love Balqis and hate her, worship her and denounce her. I reconstructed her over and over, tens of times, and then I demolished and scattered her. I no longer had access to her body and so I played with her image. My heart was a vast pump sending delusions across my body, and my blood was polluted.

Often the thought came to me that I was going to live forever in extreme hunger, that a greater hunger would come and accumulate along with the hunger I already felt. Balqis would not return. Her doll would not resist becoming her new plaything, just as before, I had not refused. I went into a state of hysteria, shutting all the doors to myself. I was in an entirely closed-up hell. If my condition had lasted even one more day, I would have started a war of blood and dust against Balqis to force her to come back to me or have no one. All that kept me from it was a hand that reached out to me. Given the circumstances, it was merciful, though it was made of the same kind of pain and the punishment it visited on me. It soothed me and returned freshness to my body with the abundance of its waters. That is how I grew addicted to a first-rate alternative, which I exchanged for another, and then a third, a fourth ... my relationships lasted exactly as long as I was in raptures over their sharp and spicy taste, but as soon as I became accustomed to their flavor, I moved on to another.

And then I met you and loved you. I loved you from the very first time we exchanged greetings in the Hussainiyya, when you apologized for not wearing stockings because the maid was too busy with other things. It was the worst excuse I had ever heard. If you had not pointed it out then likely no one would have noticed. Three years, when I closed and opened my eyes on you every night.

You were an untouched little bud yet to open. I was the bud that had opened prematurely, its petals falling one after another. In you, I caught new scents, the fragrance of firsts, of pure things, of a time that had remained unpolluted. I loved you and you made me forget Balqis, and my pain, and the brutal stamping over of my childhood. But not the wildness of my body. I loved you the way men in heaven love their virgin women. I loved you even more. I loved you and I was afraid. I must not touch you. I must not come near. I must not soil you with me, or with my madness, or the commanding force of my body. I loved you and I protected you from myself, but I had not yet learned to resist the lush ether of you. I thought you had the power to make me pure. I thought that impact on me would be stronger than my demons, able to hold off the bats that inhabited my black world, the darkness of my soul. And so I drew nearer to you.

You had a black shirt, a V-neck that buttoned. Whenever you wore it, I would give you surreptitious looks, catching glimpses of that little birthmark just below your neck, with a sigh every time I saw it, slightly above the visible parting of your breasts, the size of a little red ant, and also the very color of a little red ant, spilling onto your milky chest, and I thought I would die. I want you! That is what was in my mind. I know that I troubled you, even harmed you! I wanted not to hurt you, I really did, I meant that and felt that and willed it strongly. I stayed in those relationships of mine so that I could pour into them all of my violence and my desire for pain, so that I could empty myself of them and not hurt you. For my body demanded its share of pain. But I could not do it. In some secret way, you deflected me from truly betraying you. You prohibited my body from being totally there with anyone else. From every direction, forces turned me back toward you, and even so, I felt unfaithful. You were so soft and kind, softer than your ability to hurt me, and I contained more violence than you would be able to stand. I failed several times because of you—yes, because of you. You would be there, your image, crumpled into a little heap between the two of us, me and whoever I was with, somewhere or other. My eyes closed, I would see you. I would all but swear that you had been there. I found the idea of doing this to you indecent, and I would shake the stem of my longing with someone else, when you were all I longed for—not just your body, but you. You, what I desired out of life, what I wanted from love. You were the salvation and release that I implored Allah to grant me. And now, when you are mine, my possession, I have learned that this mark of yours is a little closer to your left breast. Now I can stroke that red ant of yours, kiss that red ant of yours, lick it and sleep on top of it. And I am afraid, after all of this has happened, I am afraid that you will grow tired of me and leave me.

My chest, and the exact spot where she lay her head, had become a pool of salt water. She had rinsed her body of the intense, heavy, accumulated odor of the secret grief imprisoned within her, the sadness that had settled there so heavily, so dreadfully, so long ago, leaving her to suffer. To tell the story was to bring back to life an interlacing of deaths and disappearances. Her limbs were cold as her breath burned my body. She got to her feet, drained of energy. She turned on the table lamp, diffusing a pale light. She took my fingers and moved them across particular places on her body: her arms, the top of her right forearm, her palm and her thumb, her back, along the side of her leg. I probed small swellings that I had never before seen under a light, and had not noticed, as she told me what had caused each one. This one is because of a skewer hot from the flame, when we were eating chestnuts! That one—she broke a glass on it, she has a swelling too, just like it! Here, this is because the clasp on my bra stuck and she tried to pull it out by force and the edge of it poked me and broke my skin. That one—oh, we were imitating a foreign film in which we saw a scene about blood brothers and the ritual of brotherhood!

This one ... that one ... this one ... my head was spinning. Her words were pounding relentlessly against my brain. She spread my hand out along the right side of her body. Here, I was really hurt, right here. She would dig into me with her knee. Huh! Look, when I jab my knee in your belly suddenly, what happens—the pleasure of your tall body suddenly folding, your back bowing. Look, this is for real, I'm not just pulling some trick out of my pocket.

I bent over her. I kissed the place where my hand had rested. The kisses would not do anything at this moment; they would not make up for what had happened, they would not erase the traces or replace them with traces of something better. I kissed all of the swollen places on her, one by one, and she moaned in a way I was not used to, the moans of a memory overflowing, bringing back scenes, pushing them to the surface.

Don't feel sorry for me! And don't hate me.

I'm not.

I love you. I love you, you've given me forgetting.

After the seventh *I love you*, I lost track of what was going on, although I had been trying to keep everything sequenced in my head. I wasn't just taking note of her explicit expressions of love; I was observing all of her reactions as closely as I could. Her eyes, which bore such a flood of gratitude and hope that poured over me; the way she clung to me; her kisses; the unaccustomed form that her desire seemed to take; her crying, so quiet and still, which she said was caused only by how much love and pleasure she felt; her stillness on my chest.

If troughs and crests exist as part of relationships, as they do for waves, then that time was the highest point on the highest crest we ever reached, the absolute pinnacle, the very best time, without any hurt and without any painful aftermath. It was not just a matter of our bodies. I saw Dai, for once and only once without anything obscuring my field of vision. Without any closed doors, without any secrets, without any hiding places. I loved this Dai, and I fixed her in that image. And suddenly I felt certain about it: Anything that might happen, anything that did happen—nothing would disfigure her for me. I would always bring this image back, revealed, alight, perched between my trembling hands.

14

At the start of it, disgust and nausea were my overwhelming reactions. I had no idea that a mouth-to-mouth kiss was something that actually happened—and just like that, so simply. I warded it off, rejecting her, refusing to witness her fall from her angelic height. She took my hand, held it tightly, and in a voice of entreaty asked that we forget the whole thing and go on with our friendship on the old basis. I could not get the better of my feelings of disgust toward her whenever we met, however, nor of the fear that entrapped me whenever we were together behind a closed door. Gradually, our friendship flagged, until it ended of its own coldness.

The second time was different: it stirred up in me a lot of questions and doubts about myself. What was it that had made me experience the very same circumstances, the very same reactions, twice in succession? Did that happen to everyone? Why had no one taught me anything? Should I conceal what had happened? Was there some defect in me? Was it my childish shirts? My running shoes? My short hair? Was it the slightly formal way that I say I? Was it the way I drop the feminine *t* ending whenever I message girlfriends? Or was there some deep-rooted imbalance or disorder in me that I could not see, but that was visible to women who wanted relationships like this? Of course, by now I had grown a bit older, and I did understand that a kiss could be just a kiss, or that it could mean a relationship with all of its intimate details. I tried to unearth all of this through questions, but my excavations turned up nothing useful. That friend of mine seesawed between acting naïve and an inability to explain the reasons for it to me, giving only improvised and illogical possibilities whose details she would not elaborate. I did not understand anything. I examined carefully my every step, and searched my body, my behaviors and reactions, and the way I acted when I was with my friends, but I found nothing to cause any suspicion or doubt.

When it came to Dai, years had gone by and my questions were all but submerged in the fog of lost memory, as was whatever acquaintance I had had with her. But at the college one day, she stopped to pass the time of day with me—by which I mean, with the country girls. She said hello and chatted a little, and then turned directly to me and said, Why don't we meet, what do you think? Her question seemed a little odd or contrived, since in fact we did meet now and then, here and at the Hussainiyya. She added, You are invited to lunch at my home on Wednesday. We'll go from the college to my place straight away, and don't give me apologies and tell me you can't do it! I did not.

Ever since the moment in which we sat down together on her bed, immediately after we arrived, and ever since she asked me which dress she should wear, and ever since I did up the zipper on her dress with confused fingers, and ever since, sitting next to me, she urged me to taste the dessert and then lifted the spoon to my mouth and fed me—ever since then, in some obscure fashion that I cannot explain, I had known somehow that with time our relationship would end up where it did. I did not know all the details of how this would happen, naturally, but I sensed the essence of the relationship and the roles of both parties to it. Every new thing I discovered about Dai replicated my initial forecast. And instead of bolting, putting myself at a distance, I was there, working hand in hand with Dai to set a decoy at every step that would draw me on to the next step. This course would not make me later into a liar, when I was bewildered at how far we had gone and what we had done, but it equally did not absolve me of responsibility toward any of our actions.

And now an entire month had gone by since the rhythm of our relationship had been at its fastest and most ascendant, a holiday jaunt so pleasant that it exceeded anything I was capable of imagining or supposing, not to mention actually living. It all seemed a pure fantasy of the imagination, or a temporary paradise where soon enough I would bite into the cursed apple and crash to an earth as slippery and as lined with thorns as ever. It was a narcotic pleasure so powerful that under its effects I no longer had any desire to take any precautions or to open my eyes on a tomorrow that would look in any way unlike today. Yet, whatever the extent of Dai's virtuosity with her fingers, and however distant were the limits of her skills, inevitably there would be a wrong note, a finger slipping toward another string, something out of tune. And today she had sounded her ultimate discordant note, her fatal slip of the fingers.

As she gazed at me, I could see in her eyes the usual flash of her craving. I was not really ill, and so my pretext appeared weak. I was getting sick, but I was still in that pre-illness stage of dizziness, blurred vision, jellylike fingers that collapse to the touch, inveterate aching that you cannot pinpoint anywhere particular in your body, and the wild swings of feeling icy and feverish—I had all of those half-visible symptoms, but not yet a tangible illness. So I simply pushed her away quietly. It was the first time that I had pushed her off of me without it being a mere game of tom-and-jerry, a gazelle and her hunter, a desiring person out of patience and a desired one barring it.

She responded by reversing things on me. In Dai's language there is no word for rejection. There is always a *naam* after every *no*. I negotiated with her. *Fine, but just a little bit.* I sensed that she was happy but that was just about all I could glean from her reaction. My body was swinging between two opposing states: a half-conscious stupor in which it could barely sense Dai's pressure, and a doubly conscious one that turned everything she did into a nausea-inducing invasion that practically made me gag. I began to shove her away in distaste, thinking perhaps that the heaviness of my hand against her shoulder would be enough to remove her weight from me. *Enough*! Likely she heard in my voice a sharpness that upset her; my sudden reaction made her ask in surprise, Why? Disturbed and emotional, I answered, Didn't we agree on just a little? Her face angry—I could see it only imperfectly, through my unfocused eyes—she asked, So, what has been making up for me?

I did not understand what she was implying. Please, Dai, I'm so tired, I said. She was shaking me, emotionally, with that look in her eyes that only a demon would offer.

Answer me! Who touched you? Who?

I was on the verge of screaming in her face, Don't overdo it with me, Dai. Don't even think that way. But I also had a contrary emotion, a pressing desire to know just what her limits were, and how excessive she might be with me.

All the details of what happened after that seem unreal when I think about them. Beneath her, my hands bound to the bedpost, unable to move my left wrist, a hell erupted across more than one part of my body. Uppermost in my consciousness at this moment was my shoulder, which must have collided with the floor as she dragged me from her bed, and my lowest rib, where she had used her knee to immobilize me. My breathing was strange, several quick breaths and then a long suspension. I almost choked on a single, interrupted inhalation while my stomach cramped, one spasm coming right after another. There was a pair of scissors—I know it must have been scissors from the sound of them, and from the sharp cold edge boring into my skin, and from the air slapping me. I was afraid to open my eyes until I became aware that she had picked up something from her night table and had bound my eyes with it, snuffing out my sight, leaving me in an unending darkness. She had gotten up to walk toward her desk. I could hear her move; all of my senses were funneled into my ears. I heard the scratching sound of pens in their metal casings, and then she returned and wrapped her thighs around me. She was tearing at my clothes randomly, or to put it more truthfully, in a manner governed only by a wild vengeful anger. I was naked, yet she went on uncovering my denuded surface. She was searching my body for the scent of another, the sticky pollution of *her* fingers, another woman's betraying mark, the signs of her kisses and her tongue, the sounds of her moaning colliding within the hollowness of my body, the signs that yet another relationship was breaking down. Any tiny thread at all, even if it were a single hair noticeable because it was the color of henna! This is the nature of a situation when it has gone as far as this. It grows vicious. I knew I was her prey, and her anger had doubled its strong push. Now she had my neck encircled tightly in her hands. Tell me—who?!

Hassan's face took me away, and I saw the warm eyes whose lively sparkle never stopped shimmering under the light nor in darkness. He had taught me how to be a *heroine*, as he put it. Some self-defense strokes based on his karate, with a few street moves thrown in, of the sort that young men are skilled at launching at the least provocation. That hand planted on my neck in anger was no longer hers; now it was Hassan's hand, stretched all the way around my neck, as he asked me in a gentle voice to sink my nails into the veins at his wrist, my thumbnail to be specific, while letting my fingers curl around his wrist, pressing it firmly into my thumb. He wanted me to press and dig with all the might I could bring to it, even if it took every last bit of vitality that I could squeeze from my being. I am in a real fix right now—that is what he said—and my chances of getting out of it are really slim. If I relax, that means death. Slowness means death. Hesitation means that I die. What situations like this demand is not so much courage, like we generally assume, as the use of that wholly instinctual part of you, the thing that makes cats eat their young and chameleons change color. It is the primitive part of you that human civilization has not yet been able to destroy. If you move fast and without any hesitation, if you plunge your fingernails into the major veins at the wrist, no blood will reach the hand. The veins will be completely throttled and the hand will weaken. The grip will loosen. If you delay, though—and it only requires a hesitation of fifteen seconds, which is the time the body is granted before things start to collapse—you will be the one who is throttled, whose grip loosens, so that you are no longer able to do anything but sense the thread of air that unravels from beneath your collarbone with difficulty. Empty of air, your temples will swell, and the pupils of your eyes will widen at the shock. Finally, your life will be extinguished, you will feel it going out, second by second.

I am sure that I heard Dai say—several times—something like *you whore*. And I'm certain that I heard her crying, and I am sure that the whole thing went on for some twenty minutes. I am completely sure that I am not really sure of anything at all. There is a region in my head, in my memory, which at that moment gave up recording anything, so that at a later time it would not have to attempt to erase it all. My head slipped into the gray recesses at the edges of oblivion, where I can easily manage to not remember something, and where the thing in question appears to me simply as an extremely bad, disgusting joke.

And then, like a person who suddenly wakes up and discovers that he is still sleepwalking, she went abruptly still for a couple of minutes before pulling herself back, still above me. She took a deep breath, almost a moan, and then got completely off me in one sudden motion as if something had stung her. She sat down beside me. I felt the air around her collapse, in the same way that she was collapsing. She was so disoriented and bewildered that she forgot to breathe. Slowly, she undid the ties around my hands and pulled off the band of cloth over my eyes.

I flicked my eyes from one side to the other in search of something to cover me. I tugged at the top bed sheet and wrapped myself in it. I got up to go into the bathroom. I shut myself in as long as it took to regain some balance and steadiness. Meanwhile, my mind was a horrid black hole, my face washed clean of features. I returned to the room. She had shredded my clothes, even the bits that required no more than her two hands to yank them cleanly off me. I opened her wardrobe and pulled out the first thing I saw. It was the last thing I wanted right now, to wear something that had touched her body, when her touch was why, in the first place, I had to take her clothes.

It was impossible for me to believe that what was trickling from my lips and from various places on my body—this red substance, welling out in drops—was actually blood, that something which had exactly the lightness of water could be such a source of pain for a body whose skin struggled with bruises. The parts of my body seemed unconnected to each other, disfigured as they were with rainbows horrible to see in their harshly clashing colors, splotches ending only to cede the space beyond to another patch of awful color. My body was painful, useless. Even if it might have seemed to me, had I given it any thought, that my left hand was not crucial to my day-to-day life, I might well discover that I did need it, to put on my clothes, for example, to attend to trivial little details to which I had not paid any attention before. I might need it for little things like doing up my trouser zipper, closing the back of my bra, or putting my arms into my shirt sleeves.

I went back into the room. I gathered up her clothes and piled them next to her. Mechanically, I began to straighten up the room, returning things to their proper places, straightening the bed sheets and coverlet. She was following me, first with her eyes, then with her breathing, and finally with her whole body. She edged to the side of the bed and grabbed me by the hand. I escaped lightly, and a second time, too. I fetched her clothes and set them down next to her. I was on the verge of feeling that I could overcome the pain in my wrist enough to help her into her clothes. But just then, she stretched her hands around me and shoved her head into my stomach and began to cry, her tears springing from her eyes without even touching her cheeks, as if they could exceed and escape the power of gravity, falling forward to melt into the weave of my shirt and moistening my body below. I remained a silent tablet, a memory with no space left, a mute wall, anything at all, as long as it had nothing to give it a touch of emotional connection or consolation or understanding or sadness or even a formal kind of sympathy. Nothing.

As soon as she finished putting on her clothes, I left on my own, taking the back stairs, which I had normally used only after visits that ended in quarrels. There had been a lot of them. I went out. And I did not come back.

I stayed away from the college for three days. The semester was in its last month before attendance lists would be submitted, and given what the averaging of my absence record would be, since I had had that seizure, another absence no longer had any importance. In the college, always, and no matter where I was or where I went, I felt her shadow darkening every spot, falling over my shadow and erasing it. I would feel the sizzle of her gaze on my back, the dreadful penetration beneath my skin; and twisting around, I would confirm to myself that I had not simply been fancying things. I could see her half hidden in odd and slightly remote corners, staring in my direction, never blinking, her eyes giving off a terrible sadness that was unbearable to see.

It was April Fools Day, and the strands of my lies were intertwining and forming complicated knots, getting shorter and shorter, revealing themselves as lies. Just as she had come out of I don't know what kind of void, I opened a door in the wall and ushered her back into nothingness. I rid myself of her. I returned to my own room instead of to Muhammad's room, because I no longer felt any fear of my room being soiled. I dropped her number from my cell phone and her name from my on-line lists. Her email, too—I erased her from my address list, and I tore up the letters which she had slipped from time to time into my locker at the college. Her gifts settled into the depths of the trashcan, except for her last gift, a small pillow cushion in the shape of a heart, red; at the center was written I LOVE YOU in English. I was in need of something shouting into my face like this, in big letters—no, in huge letters. I was in need of a single thread of memory that would not become frail, that would not break. I was in need of something that would remind me every day never to ignore what the beginnings of things say, nor to disregard the prophecy of my heart.

The strange thing is that I do not miss our bodily acts. I recall what she said about hunger, yet I do not sense my body yearning for what had been. What I have missed are those little things, the details that do not draw your attention at the time, amidst the complexity and chaos of the way things turn out. My fingers on the dimples in her cheeks, and her smile as the dimples grow deeper; her sadness, and the troubled expression on her face when she gets sad. I miss us when we are going to sleep, me on my back and her on her stomach, each of us looking at the other and the world entirely empty but for us. I miss her voice. I miss more the hoarseness of her voice the moment she wakes up. I miss hearing the phrase *Ya quwwat Allah* in the astonished way she says it, I miss her toying with my sleeve when she is talking away, I miss her finger in my mouth, I miss her pushing her nose into the inside of my elbow and sniffing me—but I don't miss the heat of our bodies together. Worse than this, I miss all that we did not do together, all that we could have done but we forgot or put off. We let things slip away from us, negotiating a time, and now, time was emptying its hands of us.

A week, ten days, two weeks. Time had no meaning now. The minute that my wrist recovered from the bruise and the dark patches vanished from my skin, I buried her in a perfect forgetting. The forgotten, like the dead, never come back.

No door should be opened before
the previous one has been closed.

The Others

15

My prediction this time was different. I knew that I would be opening a door onto hell and that I would not close it until after extinguishing every bit of the coldness that crouched inside of me. My little stupidities, I knew, would have intoxicating effects. My slip-ups would mean I was nodding off when I should be paying attention. Even fear would not stave off my tendency to overlook danger signs. I was unbearably fearful, and what that means is that I reverted frequently to my dependence on the same person who had pulled me to the very farthest limits of pliancy and avoidance. That is, in utter contradiction to my need to keep myself within a reassuring space, I treated myself with the very illness I needed to cure. I submerged myself in whichever behavior appeared more frightening to me. Instead of running off to shield myself behind the rigid armor of refusal when others approached, and sweeping away everything that would give them reason to be in my life, I did the opposite. I would leave my door slightly open, waiting for whoever and whatever would enter, heedless of whether it was the fire of poison or the fresh pure water of paradise.

Dareen called me. It was our fourth or fifth telephone conversation since I had met her at the *mazraa*, and altogether we had spent about ten hours on the phone. Into our conversation I had snuck the observation that, notwithstanding my great esteem for her and even though I really valued her, I would not throw myself into this vortex of relationships where partners were shared, or relationships were open or involved multiple parties, or whatever the particular label or category was, into this world whose practices I had not yet even learned to pronounce with ease. With a big heart, she had accepted my hints with one of her own—she would not argue about this, but would leave everything to time and its dictates.

She was calling to ask if we could meet, her voice tinctured with a slightly dark shade of worry, as if to let me know that she was aware of what had happened recently. I had no objection, I told her, as long as she didn't expect much. I was completely out of energy, tired and troubled, my body and head burdened by a loud clamor inside that would not quit and bad dreams in which, every night, I fell and fell into a bottomless chasm. No doubt my voice betrayed my state of mind. She said she was not expecting anything at all, and I had no trouble believing her.

So I visited her. It was not my body's tensions and nightly longings that propelled me, nor a need for sympathy or a desire to forget. I had been shouldering all of these on my own. I went to her for reasons I am the last to know, if indeed there really were any reasons. Dareen did not hold anything back deliberately—that was her nature, as I knew—but she seemed to be restraining herself. Every time she began leaning warmly toward me, she would recall herself and straighten up again in her seat. She lowered her voice the moment anything other than social generalities entered the conversation. Apparently, the walls of the sitting room where guests were always received held concealed ears and smuggled-in eyes that observed and examined, accused and judged. This at least was the first impression I surmised from her behavior.

For two entire hours, we talked. We chatted about everything and anything. What we were talking about was not particularly important compared to how much enjoyment we got from the act of conversing, and the time slipped away without either of us sensing it. She had seated me in the first row of the cinema, and her words opened a wide-screen vision. Compelling and dazzling—that was what her stories were. Her ability to describe things astonished me, the way she talked about neglected details, how she dissected everything under a strong light. She could remember and describe exactly how the stairway appeared in a certain film. She could repeat two sentences from another film; she would offer up a refrain that some movie star always used or a scene that consisted of nothing more than a few steps on a wet pavement and a black overcoat.

I remember that she started talking about the film *Chocolat*, going into its use of symbols, the significance of chocolate and ash, the kind of role the gypsy played in the plot, the ascendancy of politics over religion, the ascendancy of politics and religion together over society, and the forms that society's acquiescence and its complex adjustments took. I am a person who swallows movie scenes whole, in a single gulp; it never occurs to me that there are meanings taking form behind the translucent curtains of the film, which need nothing more (says Dareen) than a simple hand pushing aside those curtains in order to be seen.

Dareen's only problem—if I could possibly consider it a problem—was that what she projected on her screen was so astonishing that the attempt to convey it was an impossible task, as was reducing it to our linguistic systems of words and meanings. It was so impossible as to be absurd, or stupid; so impossible that the attempt could not but disfigure the image. With that way she had in conversation, she would display images that were sparklingly comprehensive, balanced, and mature—but any attempt to talk about reality as comprehensive, balanced, and mature seemed an utter waste of time to all of us.

When I gave her my hand as I was saying goodbye, she left a letter in my palm and a kiss on my cheek. I'll see you soon, she said. Promise me that? She tugged at my hand as she spoke, and so I answered, Definitely! I had no idea whether my firm response was just a momentary reaction without any lasting value, or whether it expressed something that had touched my heart with need.

On my way home, I opened her letter and read it.

My heart began to simmer and it bubbled over
I don't know what happened
And I am not anxious for the details
Except of course if you have a desire to tell,
and then all of me is listening
What I want to say is, I love you
And I am not asking you to meet me with the same
Likely, you are asking how this could be, so quickly?
I do not have an explanation
Be with me, and I will not desert you
I will not fatigue or trouble you, and you will always be content
And I will not shackle you to me—you can go whenever you want
A chance only, that's all I ask
I want to hear from you soon
I want us to be together
And I give you my love
That is all
I cannot decide for you
And whatever your decision, I respect it in advance
and I will honor it
But if things were in my hands
I would have written on the divine slate that inscribes your fate,
tonight, to get in touch
And to say Yes,
Or to say nothing at all

I will understand you without any words

I love you

Two days later, she was in my room. It had been my turn to call her. I did not know what words to use in response to her letter so I settled on asking her simply if we could meet. I left it to her to pick the time, and she answered me, Yes, the first possible opportunity, right now, for instance!

We had finished; she kissed me randomly and then rested her head on my chest, breathed in my skin, and said, Thank you.

For what?

Because you touched me with love.

Don't thank me, I am simply a reflection of you.

She closed my eyes with her fingertips and leaned over my body to turn on the lamp. She picked up her bag from the side of my bed and began searching for something. She lay down again, next to me, pulled up the cover over her chest, tugged it around and under her arms, and said, You can open your eyes. Her wallet was open to the picture of a girl at whom Dareen gazed with what seemed an old sadness.

This is my little lamb. Nadia.

Nadia?

Yes, Nadia.

Will you tell me about her?

We got to know each other when I was a teenager. I used to suffer from very difficult spells. I hated myself and my family and the world. She was the only one who kept our friendship going. Before this, I used to stay away from school a day or two every week. I got to the point where I had no patience with any day that she was not part of, and so I became more orderly and regular about my studies, and it seemed I had suddenly shaped up and gotten some sense. Yet, there was no end to my problems, no end to my anxieties, to my spells of unexplained crying. But she gave me something bright and glowing, something to make me worth something. She was my only friend—me, who had quarreled with everyone, and I pushed them into staying away from her.

Go on.

At that time, Nadia was the one friend I had a right to visit whenever I wanted, and sometimes without even getting permission. Since we were related, distantly related, and since we were classmates, I would visit her almost daily and spend long hours with her. We would get through our homework, and watch TV and play on the roof. Her brother spent his week in the University of Minerals and Petroleum housing in Dammam. In his room we found a place to amuse ourselves, and secrets to pounce on, and little things to trifle with. One time, we managed to stumble on the hidden key to a drawer that had always been shut in the face of our curiosity, but we were so disappointed to find nothing in it but a few tapes. We put one on and discovered what the secrecy was about. They were sex films. We were totally embarrassed. Each of us crouched in a corner hiding half her face, her eyes spying on the screen, but despite our shamefaced reactions, the way these stirred us up, and our longing to see whatever was there, pushed us to watch all of the tapes, one by one. Time after time, we found that the tapes we had watched had been replaced with new ones. So we got accustomed to our daily appointment with the films. We began to time their viewing to the hour that Nadia's mother would leave the house, after her father had gone to sleep. Since we did not want to be discovered, we were careful to rewind the film to the frame where it had been when we started it.

Then what happened?

We did this a few times, but we were so afraid of the possibility that we would be discovered, or that her family would start getting suspicious about the way we holed up for hours in her brother's room. So we started taking precautionary measures. Like, after secreting away one of the films, she would receive me in her home's formal room, where the men usually sat. We would close and lock the door on the pretext that her brothers were used to coming in without announcing themselves and it would not be proper that they see my face uncovered. The last time—I mean, the last film we watched together, which was a Bruce Willis film—there was a short scene of two women exchanging kisses, then one of them tried to take off the other one's clothes. That was all. It was a simple and quick scene, and there wasn't even any real nudity in it.

She turned her eyes to me and said, Can you turn out the light? I did, and she put her head on my shoulder.

The darkness is another common feature in all of my stories, she said. She sighed, and then added, So we kissed each other. I did not know who had started it, or how that scene could stir us up so.

Were you disgusted?

No, never.

You didn't feel any revulsion about what you were doing?

No, to the contrary, I felt fantastic, elated. My heart was beating massively, and I felt ... I don't know! Maybe I was just dizzy, maybe it was love, maybe I felt like suddenly I knew I had become a woman. An odd thing happened at that moment, some orientation on the map of my life changed, everything changed, the cells in my body changed! I felt as though I had already somehow prepared myself for that kiss, as if I was ready for it, as if it had simply been hidden in some secret place, as if ... as if I had lived this before, like, in a previous life, and ...

And what?

We did not know—what was this thing that we were making happen? What did it mean, to have such a large, such a flagrant explosion in your body? Why the doubting glances that one of us was always letting fly over the other's body? What about our fingers, more firmly intertwined the faster our breathing got? We didn't know, but we did continue, cautiously at first, and then completely abandoning ourselves. Every step led us on to the next, once her last sister had married and she had a room to herself. It was the most awesome thing that had ever happened, or that might ever happen, in my life. When I close my eyes, I can still breathe in her smell, and lift the locks of brown hair from her eyes, and whisper, Death, I love you to death!

So, what happened—how did you separate?

My engagement. I refused at first. I told her I did not need anyone else but her, as long as she was with me. She would answer, But I cannot offer you a soccer team of children! She convinced me. Life is just made up of a series of opportunities, and an opportunity that goes by will not come again. And then, she would argue, there is the fact that he is from a good family, and his principles and behavior are even better than they are, and he works for a bank. It is all very respectable, and his monthly salary is in five figures and he summers in green lands that I have never set foot in, and what being with him offers me is pretty amazing, and it is a lot ... and all that stuff. Sometimes I would start believing that I had agreed to it only because she had been so insistent, only in order to please her and nothing more. The whole engagement, the whole thing, was facing me—the marriage contract signing and the dowry and the party and the dress and the drums beating and the huge hall. And Ali's hands fastening on the *shabka*,* and his hands putting the ring on my finger, and his hands fastening a watch and a gold link bracelet around my wrist, and his hands feeding me cake, and his hands holding juice for me to drink. All of those details looked like a game to me, or a day of fun at an amusement park, something cute and then it would be

_____

* An engagement gift, traditionally of gold. Usually a heavy gold necklace.

over. I did not imagine what I would have to go through, or what kinds of traps I would fall into.

Did you love him?

No. He was a good man. He had a big heart, but my heart was entirely with Nadia. Or, to be truthful about it, yes, I did love him as a person, it wasn't easy not to love him at all, but—as a man? No. From the very first days we had together, she began to get jealous. She would go crazy if he stayed overnight at our house, and she would pelt me with a million phone calls. I was stupid, too, because I enjoyed how things looked on the surface: Nadia loves me and is jealous, how fabulous is this! But her jealousy turned into cords pulling on my wrist, and eyes always searching me out, and fights—she was always convinced that he was sleeping with me and that I was hiding the truth from her. My bad relationship with Nadia affected my relationship with Ali, too. Perhaps I was getting revenge through him. I did really make him suffer. At one moment I would be soft on him and sweet, desiring to make up for my mistakes toward him, but then at many other moments I would slam down the phone in his face for the tiniest slip and refuse his visit. He would be perfectly right not to ever forgive me.

So you separated from him?

Don't be so delicate about it! Why don't you say it straight out: we divorced. It was only a few months before Nadia dropped me completely. Everything had appeared to be ideal, had seemed to be going exactly as we had planned. We had been living in the same apartment, in the same room, and on two beds we had shoved together; we only used one coverlet. We were in Riyadh; she was studying sociology and I, art education, and we had just begun level four of our studies. At home, we curled up together day and night, and in the university we were together whenever possible. Everything was as ideal as could be! But after my engagement she changed. If I happened to run into her at the university, she would claim she was just running between lectures and would make a fast exit. If I called her between lectures she ignored the call, and at home she avoided me. One night she complained that I was stealing the coverlet and she used that excuse to bring another one, and thus little by little we were no longer splitting one bed between us. Then she stunned me by deciding to transfer, just like that, to the Women's College of Nutritional and Agricultural Sciences in al-Milliz! I never could have imagined it. Finally, and in line with her recent sudden decisions, she decided to move to another residence. She complained about our apartment, grumbling that we lived in a prison, a cattle pen, a rabbit hole, a chicken coop—not a human habitation. She could not abide the sealed windows, and if it were not for the thin spaces between the wooden slats that separated us from the world, then we would not even have known that there was a world out there, a sun, streets and people. It was punishment enough to hear the insolent speech of the building supervisor and to put up with the bad behavior of the drivers! These were all she could come up with as excuses. She got what she wanted. My mother was not going to accept my moving to a new residence with an open system, its only rule being a curfew of 11 p.m. or thereabouts. I was not yet beyond my mother's domain of authority, even if I was formally engaged.

By sometime in the next university term, Nadia had disappeared, and with her Hanan, who also lived in our residence. I did not need to hear very many whispered conversational asides to know where she had moved and who her mate there was. As determined as I had been to disbelieve and deny it, even if only to myself, I had become conscious that Nadia was prepping for something to happen between her and Hanan. Surely, she had not transferred to Hanan's college or changed residence for any reason but to be closer to her. I wasn't in denial just because Nadia was in the process of detaching herself from me and living in a state of crazy passion with another woman. No, it was also because she was letting go of her fervor about not wanting to be the first experience for any girl. With one glance, I could tell that Hanan was nothing more than a gullible, raw new recruit, who had not yet lived her life, and yet Nadia was insistent on chasing her and leading her to her bed. I don't know whether she succeeded or not. After she spent one year at the agricultural college, I heard that she had withdrawn and had applied to the Institute of Administration. She would not have done that if her relationship had remained good with Hanan. Maybe she was infatuated with another girl and was seeking to please her! I felt that she had betrayed me. She abandoned me after bringing me into this world by sheer force of will. All I could feel toward her was heavy resentment and a longing for revenge. Her absence was a real blow, and it was frightening for me, too. I was depressed and I cried all the time, and for the most trivial reasons. Ali supported me without hesitation, without flagging, whenever I needed him. I cried in his arms a lot. He would say, If you don't love me, if I don't please you, if someone forced you to marry me, I release you from all responsibility, I can rid you of me if that is what you want. At that, my crying would just get worse and I would cling to him, saying, I love you, I love you, don't leave me! By then, I had come to terms completely with the idea of marrying him. In fact, I thought it was a tremendous idea. I began to treat him lovingly and truly bring him into my heart, and I was tender and gentle with him. It was during this time that we made our first attempts to touch each other, little kisses ... I would close my eyes so he wouldn't sense my disgust.

What were you disgusted at?

Ali.

Ali!

Yes. Maybe you are thinking that he was bad, or dismal at the physical thing, or for instance, that he was ugly. But he was absolutely the opposite. Any other girl would dream of being loved by this man. Any other girl would vow her body and her life, and she would lay all her days at his feet. Any girl, any, but not me. I was not created for a man. I had a dread of his body. He assumed that when I closed my eyes it was supposed to signal that I enjoyed what he was doing. The more I tried to respond, the harder I tried to feel any pleasure from his body, the more nauseous I felt. Once I pushed him away from me and ran for the bathroom. I almost threw up. I felt so much shame and embarrassment, both with myself and with him, for degrading him so much. He did not deserve all the bad things I deluged him with, and so I asked him for a divorce. I know for certain that I did marry a truly lovely guy who had no anger toward anyone before he became attached to me, and I destroyed the vast hopes that he hung on our marriage. I did apologize to him. If I could have done anything more, I would have. I even considered telling him about my relationship with Nadia, and about the desires of my body, but I was afraid. I did not want to disfigure my image in his eyes any more than I already had.

So the two of you ended things without any problems?

My family objected and so did his. They tried to reconcile us but we were determined to keep absolutely silent. We had agreed to keep everything utterly to ourselves. In the end, everyone gave in, and the divorce happened.

You didn't try to get Nadia back?

I tried, but with no success. At that point, she wasn't even coming into town more than once a month. She did not answer my phone calls. I often heard about her; from our mutual friends, I got the details about how she had changed. She was acting completely blind to the world, leaving one relationship and throwing herself into another that was even worse. That was not the Nadia I had known, the one who was maybe kind of dumb and careless and chaotic but who was not deliberately self-destructive. I tried to restore our relationship from the point where she had broken it off. I tried at least to make her aware of what she was doing. I tried to show her how totally pointless this was, and how utterly she was destroying her life, but she kept me at a distance and went on throwing herself into those relationships of hers in a truly repugnant way. Her harshness toward me, the antipathy she showed, froze me in my steps as I tried to approach her in every way I could. For long moments I would feel the utmost hatred toward her. After all, she was the cause of what had happened, so why was she cutting me off, as if I were the criminal here! Finally, I had to tell myself very firmly that there was no use at all, this was what our relationship had come to.

So you weren't in touch after that?

There were only the family occasions, which didn't give more than a superficial glimpse of her. I was as far into despair as it is possible to be, and I was also stupid enough that I practiced total self-denial for her sake. At the time, I believed that the mere thought of allowing someone to touch me was a betrayal of Nadia, let alone the act of it. I wanted revenge on her, though! I wanted it so much that I began to conjure up new and false friendships in front of our friends in order that my fabrications would reach her and stir up her jealousy. I often thought, in my times of weakness and fatigue, that I would get my revenge on her through my body, I would respond to her single punch with two, and I would let havoc rage through my body with one relationship after another, just as she was doing. But I sensed that I was simply falling into the depths, that none of this was any use. Things went on this way for a year or more. Then I admitted to myself that I had to get back to living my life. There was no point in waiting for something that would never arrive.

So what did you do?

Nothing important. I had no interests and I didn't care about anything. I started two relationships—no, three. I got involved with that sort of people ... I don't know how to explain this to you.

You can try me.

People who are pretty much available. They can give; they have some space in their lives and in their hearts. I resolved not to get really involved in any relationship, not to take anything beyond the surface. No consequences, not even temporary possessiveness. I felt so light. I didn't have to carry anything. I did not owe anything to anyone. But I was afraid. I found it oppressive to even think about going back in to the dead-end maze of love, and I was terror-stricken by the possibility of again facing isolation and abandonment, as I had with Nadia. My first relationship after Nadia ended in a matter of days because I felt so guilty, and the rest weren't any better, since I always hurried to put out any live coals before a blast of wind from the other direction could blow it out, leaving me all alone.

And I am one of those who are *pretty much available*?

I don't know. When I met you, somehow I knew that you and Dai were ...

That me and Dai were what?

I saw you looking at her, but you weren't staring into her eyes. The two of you—well, your eyes didn't meet, except maybe once or twice. You were avoiding her, very politely, so it was hardly noticeable. But I am very good at noticing these little signs and recognizing what they mean ... I knew you would not stay bound to her for very long. There was something inside of you that was free. Liberated.

How would you have known that I was bound to her?

I know Dai. Everyone knows Dai.

So how could you have initiated it, kissing me, that day, if you knew Dai and knew what she was like?

You could call it an underhanded move.

I don't understand you.

From the way she was acting so pleased and proud, I knew that you were not out of the same mold. I decided that I wanted to help you get free of her, even if it meant pushing you to be unfaithful. She would not accept anyone putting her hand on *her possessions*, I knew that, and if it happened she would either no longer be interested, and she would drop you, or she would go mad.

And then what?

And then she would force her hell down your throat and you would not stay. Are you finding this painful, what I'm saying? Am I hurting you?

Don't worry about it.

Reassure me. I am pretty dumb about these things. I should not have made you think about this.

Believe me, it is really nothing to worry about. Do you still love Nadia?

Ohh! To say I love Nadia is a very feeble way to express what Nadia deserves. To be honest, my heart is so full of Nadia that it is incapable of really and truly taking in others.

So, what if she comes back?

Don't make me even consider the possibility. It's painful.

Would you take her back?

To the very last prayer I pray in my life, I will pray that she return! And you can still ask if I would accept her or not?

And if she were to return ...

But she won't, you know!

How often I have thought that when someone is gifted, the talent they have is a guaranteed treasure with a lifelong warranty. At the height of my energetic teen years, I saw the world as something that exists forever and never knows old age. And now, when I looked at Dareen, what came to me was that she was just another person who showed all of her confusion as she spoke, as she searched in the depths of memory for some logical procession of thoughts, some way to connect the places of her own little history. She looked for the sentence that she ought to have been able to fling out in silence's face but was not strong enough to say. An ordinary person stripped of the advantage of her talents, with a story lacking wholeness. I considered this. Just because you are gifted, I thought, does not mean that you are extraordinary, or exempt from life's usual rules.

Sometimes, we love for the wrong reason. Other times, as in my situation with Dareen, I did not love, also for the wrong reason. In truth, Dareen is the sort of person who makes you feel that she deserves every breath of life, every moment of existence, every divine gift, every love that anyone is capable of giving. But I was not yet capable of loving. I was not capable of setting myself free for that towering height.

I can come up with interpretations for it, sure. Love is a fantasy, love is a state of attrition, love is persistent, incessant. Love is a maze with no exit, love is … so, yes, I have many pathways I can take to avoid really saying anything about love. Speaking truthfully, I'll say that there is no truth in any of these interpretations, no truth but fear—this ancient and acidic infusion, fear, which etches painful things on my heart. Love is painful, and all of the words paired with it are parallel states that do not intersect with it. Love and loss, love and flight, love and absence, love and sorrow. I surrounded myself with more walls and steel and trenches, and it was hard for love to come creeping in, alone, without an invitation, and to break through all of my barbed wire. I had never filled up on someone before. I had never allowed anyone to be a daily part of my life. I had not loved enough. That is because birds do not visit fields where scarecrows reign.

With Dareen, I felt I had enough reassurance to set my heart down next to us on the table, without having to fear that she would steal it if I stopped paying attention to it, or to her. Not because she could not steal it, not because she did not want to steal it, but because she had understood instinctively from the very beginning how badly I was a losing mare in this race, and so she spared me a lot of hardship by placing no bets on me.

With Dareen, I began to rediscover my body as if it were

something new. She would lure me slowly, lighting two candles and whispering scandalous things that made my skin tremble to hear them. She stayed neutral when there were wars between me and my body, even though I sought to embroil her in those conflicts between us. The parts of my body had their names, one by one, even the most secret; our moments had their private and special expressions; and what I would have believed was a cheap expression unbefitting to Dareen and her immense daintiness turned out, I discovered, to provide a kind of grimy tonic. Who said that mire does not touch or arouse you? Our physical relationship was *sex*, and not what I was used to calling it, allusively and euphemistically: *that*.

We talked a lot about Allah and our sins and the form our desires took. Often I hurried behind Dareen to shut whatever doors she walked through, which she left uncomfortably wide open for me, beckoning me to venture into regions that left me feeling unsafe and always on the brink of falling. Yet she would reopen those doors soundlessly after me. If God created me like this, she would say, what fault is it of mine? In turn, I would ask her, How did God create me? In what form did God make me? Does God create things that are defective, corrupt, depraved? She would scold me then. There are truths, and there are realities, and there are prejudices, and you absolutely must not mix them up. I did not understand her properly. As time passed, though, I did come to understand; layers of opacity were peeled from my eyes. Fine, I would say to her then. I've had homo sex. But I'm not a homo. The constitution of my desire is not ... I would look her way and find her smiling indulgently, but I would go on. I don't mean that it is wrong, I would say. If I were really like that, then it would be my business and I would be responsible for handling it, period. As I said this, I could see that she was laughing.

Don't apologize for what you're about and what you believe in, she would say. And don't try to justify yourself to anyone! So

I would ask her, Is it bad for me to say to you what I am about to say? That what I really yearn for in you is a man—a man who will never show up.

She would respond only by saying, Don't turn your desires into a criminal offense. Don't criminalize your needs, either.

In most of Dareen's conversations, Nadia was the topic of choice. What happened that last time? she would ask. Why did our relationship end? How did it end? I love her, I don't love her. Dareen's vast ability to hatch questions like these irritated me, for the questions were inexhaustible, and every question produced a hundred new ones branching from it. From the evocative expressions that lined her face, and from her questions, I believed that Dareen did carry an image of what had happened and what it meant, and she was trying to make it fit some image of mine even as the form that my responses took did not change. I continued to probe with a few words and a lot of obstacles that stopped me, until there came the day when I said to her, Didn't you tell me before that you are not so concerned about every detail of what happened?

Yes, I told you that.

But that isn't the way you sound!

You left the door open for me to walk through.

I did?

Yes, you. Haven't our conversations about Dai and your relationship with her bothered you, even upset you, starting with the very first question I put to you?

Yes, a lot!

Even so, you didn't tell me that.

I don't understand what you mean!

Yes, you do understand. Don't expect others to be firm about respecting your limits if you yourself are not firm about them.

She never returned to the subject. I was sure that she had a secret crystal ball that gave her the appropriate answer to every question

I would put to her, and the perfectly crafted, controlling sentence with which she could keep the wheel of conversation moving in the direction she wanted. I did not know whether this certainty about things was something she had possessed since earliest childhood or whether, like me, she lost herself with every next step and then found her way again only after a certain amount of time had passed. Time, time, time. Cursed, this time! I was the one who always chanted that song: The snow came and the snow went ... twenty times snow came and went. The more grown up I say that I am, the more mature I become, the more I fall back on the sensation that I am only a little girl whose dress the breeze plays with, making it fly.

Life is nothing but a reflection of you, my mother says. And I reflect on whether her words are correct. Everything my mother says is right, of course, but why is my reflection as contradictory as this? A wounding reflection that sends my face back deformed when I look in my mirrors. Another reflection in Dareen's eyes, that of a lost child searching for a hand that will pull her out of danger. I experiment with the idea that my mirrors are not muddy or cloudy or distorted, that my reflection on the watery surface of life does not wobble, torn up by twenty rocks that poke up through the water.

16

Believe me, the only truth that exists in the whole world is the one that you are living and that I lived: the absence of my father. Not the glory of his heroism, nor the wide expanse of his guardianship, but his absence. As far as I was concerned—me, that little girl whose heart was a series of patched-up holes, a heart rent with overwhelming feelings of orphanhood—these were nothing but useless words and fantastic myths by which I was rocked to sleep. These were the things my grandfather would tell me, his beard moist with the tears of a white dawn, or my mother, whenever I tired her out with my questions and my digging for answers.

When he went away, my mother told me, I did not sleep, not for an entire two days. She would wrap me in something that held one of his scents to quiet me because I would not stop crying, as if I knew that his traveling concealed a black fate for me. He did not return. For eight years on end he did not set foot over our threshold. He was on a trip to Iran to arrange his affairs there, and from there he would come back to collect us. When he did come, they exchanged his home for prison bars, and his bed for a tattered old blanket.

The world was a place in revolt. Qatif was afire, smoky with the bombs of ... ya Allah! The empty Pepsi-Cola bottles, the squares of white cloth, a tank of kerosene, and there you had it, flaming missiles and everything in splinters. It was a very simple and small intifada, when what everyone wanted was something on a grand scale to overturn the balance-scales of the world. The Iranian revolution was sending blinding rays into everyone's eyes, and offering them a shining display, a structure to emulate. I will never understand what happened after that, what came to a boil and bubbled over. What was it? What caustic blend of elements changed the face of Qatif? I do understand perfectly that I lived one of its very worst nightmares.

And I no longer had a father. Fathers do not inhabit images, the pictures we possess, or the tales that others tell. I remembered nothing of him; he had gone away when I was still a crawling baby. Because God is very merciful and erases from our lived days our earliest memories, my father was, in my memory, only a blank, dark space. I grew older, my grandfather treating me compassionately in my fatherless state and my mother pitying me, and pitying herself, sorrowful over our aloneness, over the confinement of her shadow with no one to shoulder her burdens. Meanwhile, my father's brother acted as an unending treasury to be spent on hosting guests.

Zakariyya was the only one who appeared natural to me in my restricted world that was clouded by a peculiar secrecy and confinement. I stuck to him like his shadow and that was the first of my problems. We often quarreled and made our peace within an hour or less after forgetting the pain left by the blows we had exchanged, offering each other a toy or a puzzle, while our mothers remained at odds for days on end. They would not speak to each other, and each would turn her face away when the other walked by. We were just a couple of children, while they were stupid enough to track our silly little differences, keeping them going and transforming them into major issues that could never be shrugged off. Later on, we entered that ring, too; we could no longer escape the recriminations and the punishment that followed every quarrel. We each took our share of blows, not to mention the kicks we aimed at each other. My grandfather would step in to make peace between my mother and my uncle's wife, trying to placate them, for each of them wanted all of his sympathy, wanted right to be entirely on her side, leaving the other woman wholly in the wrong. My uncle just let them fight on and did not interfere.

I grew up with Zakariyya. We were partners and rivals, buddies and antagonists. He was my brother, my father, my friend—for me, he was everyone. Despite his swagger when he was around me, despite his typical boy coarseness, now and again he would come through, showing me some kindness, offering me something unexpected. He often quarreled with his friends on my behalf, taking my side when they were humiliating or making fun of me because I was a girl, and girls don't stand up to much in the savage world of boys. Sometimes this made me happy, but there were also occasions when I would blow up at him for assuming I needed his support. He taught me how to be a boy, how to pick a quarrel and fight like a boy, how to curse like a boy, spit like a boy, steal and cheat and gull people and raise pigeons and play ball and bargain on the price of everything I bought for my mother every time she sent me to the grocer's.

At school, I unleashed my most inventive lies. My father is traveling. My father has gone to heaven. My father is a pilot. My father ... I did not pay much attention to consistency: what was important to me was that no one find out that my father was in prison—that my father was a thief and a criminal! How, after all, at the age of seven, could I understand the meaning of his imprisonment? As far as I was concerned, if he was in prison, he was a criminal, a thief, a murderer! He was anything at all, but he wasn't honorable. I could not understand that there might be honorable reasons to go to prison, or at the least causes that were not evil, that did not bring shame. Anyway, if I had understood—if my grandfather's words had not been so vague and puzzling, and my mother's so ambiguous, and I had understood—how would I have explained it to myself, let alone to the others? There was a revolution going on, and that particular spot in the world where it was happening was no longer acknowledged to exist, and my father had gone there despite the travel ban. All he wanted was to study God and take on the turban of a religious shaykh, and then to take people by the hand and lead them to God so that they would not get lost on the path, and then, when he returned, they put him in prison. It was not really this simple, nor this straightforward, of course. At the age of seven, we do not understand anything about politics; all we know is that we have an inherited hatred of America and we curse Israel and Iblis in the same breath. Whenever my mother happened to get word of my lies from one of the neighbor women or the mothers of my classmates, she slapped me across the mouth as if to say, You have no right to be ashamed of your father. In response, I would simply persist in my lying, as if to say, This man abandoned me and I have the right to do with him whatever I want and need to do. It became a routine, and routines do not cause pain.

Then he returned. My grandfather and my mother had been trying to prepare me for his return, while I simply laughed at them and assumed their heads were in the clouds because they were so insistently expecting him. They would talk to me about it, but then he would not come, and I would slip from their grasp and leave them talking to themselves about his impending return. But then he really did come back. At first it did not mean anything to me except a lot of fumbling resistance and uncertainty and fear and fragmentation. What was he going to change in my life now, in my life and my mother's? What was supposed to happen? How would things be now, having suddenly acquired a father? Who was this man? What was he like?

Our home was transformed into a wedding party for seven whole days and nights, with all of the good wishes and sweets and incense and trills of joy. I saw all of the relatives, our female relatives, and neighbors and other women who had never entered our home. My mother was happy, although she did not sit still for even ten minutes at a time, while my uncle's wife muttered and grumbled over the chaos in her home. The mass celebrations ended without bringing this manifest joy to a standstill. Up to that point, I still had not stopped lying, not for a moment, as my friends asked me about my father's return. How had he come back, and from where? But my mother was too utterly absorbed to even notice this elaborate structure of details that I had concocted, let alone to scold me for it. My questions remained without answers as my mother scurried from place to place and my grandfather closeted himself with the men who were always meeting in the grand reception room and our home filled incessantly with guests passing through. And there was my father, this stranger with a grave and apprehensive face, telling me nothing—those angular features, always so silent and still with misgivings. I was afraid even of sitting down with him at the dining table. I would avert my eyes from him, in constant dread that he would notice if I started giving him sidelong glances, searching his face to find a reason for all that had happened.

Many days passed in this way. The only thing that concerned me was that I still slept in my mother's embrace and in her bed. In our bed. Every night, she would tell me a tall tale. What mattered was that my mother was still telling me stories to get me to go to sleep! Then, one day, I discovered that she was tricking me. I had woken up, afraid. It was the same nightmare that I always had, the specter of a man chasing me with blood coming out of his mouth. I awoke afraid and did not find her beside me. That is how I discovered that she was leaving me alone as soon as I fell asleep. She was going to him in the majlis, *where the men would sit. I was furious at her. I stopped speaking to her. She told me that she was leaving the room only to make him his supper. So, if I had been lying, she was lying too. But unlike her, I did not slap anyone across the mouth. I did not slap her.*

All but collapsing on the floor because he was laughing so hard, Zakariyya said to me, I saw your father doing it with your mother! I saw them in the majlis. *Damn him! All the demons of hell leapt and*

*danced in front of my face, and I went for him. We fell to the ground.
I used all the moves I knew, plus some that I had just now invented,
and started testing them on his body. I used moves both legitimate
and unfair. What he had said was the worst insult and curse that two
boys could exchange, and it enraged me. My mother was betraying me,
and she was doing so with* him. *That strange man had stolen her from
me. Zakariyya was witness to the end of my days of glory. Here were
three blows that I could not endure. My uncle's wife, who was liable to
transform every little thing into a multitude, was shrieking hysterically.
The insane girl was going to kill her boy! I would not stop attacking
and he would not stop laughing.*

My father came to separate us and I flung at him that sentence
which had led to my fight with Zakariyya. I cannot even imagine
now how angry I must have been, for me to say those words in his
presence. There was a moment's silence, and then, his voice raised
as it had never been before toward me, he ordered me to go to my
room. Inside myself, I was screaming. What gives you the right,
you bastard? In reality, I was terrified by the way he looked at me. It
occurred to me that he could easily make my face fly into smithereens
with a single blow, and so I obeyed him at once.

I was commanded to stay in my room and Zakariyya was ordered
not to come near me. Things were at their tensest ever between my
father and my uncle and also between my mother and my uncle's wife.
A certain thought hovered over all, but no one dared to bring it up
for discussion. I saw it clearly in their eyes and in their silences, and
it was at its clearest when my mother inspected my body carefully
as I bathed, searching it for something. As far as she was concerned,
I was still her little girl of three whom she worried about slipping in
the bathtub or getting soap in her eyes. They were thinking: if the
two of us were close enough that he could say such a thing as that
to me, if he could use such a sentence, might that mean that the
relationship between us had gone further than they could see with

their own eyes? Suddenly, they had all sorts of suspicions about what might be between us, and they must have mulled over all of those times, those long spells that we spent far from their eyes almost every day. Where had we gone? And how far? It was a silly thought, the stupidest one ever that came to them.

After an interval, to flee all the added problems, we moved to a separate residence. Zakariyya was not welcome there, while my uncle's wife couldn't stand to see me. It all ended as two cousins exchanging annual greetings for the Eid once a year—at most. Perhaps I forgave my mother her betrayal and my father his absence. But I never forgave the two of them for barring me from Zakariyya.

The business about her staying in the majlis *became my own particular joke. Whenever she slept in his room for a week or two, it seemed, her weight went up and her behavior grew erratic. Soon she would be throwing up morning and evening, spending the entire day in her room with the lights out. I do not know how she managed the apparent inevitability of it—how she arranged for it to happen, and how it became a seemingly permanent state. I was twelve when my first sibling was born. I had the sensation of being exchanged for a baby chick tinier than me, and then another one, and then still another. All I wanted was to hear her give me a single reason for having all of those children. I wanted a reason for her to demean herself, to sacrifice her dignity, when he was the one who abstained from her. But that is the way women are. They need a lot of children to feel assured that they still deserve to be alive.*

What I really do hate is how she put me in an observation chamber twenty-four hours a day for the sake of one single suspicion among those she had about me. And then, when I committed the first of my sins, she stripped me of all of my privileges with the cold-bloodedness of a hired killer. Like one of those single-use cameras, that slip was a single-use mistake. One time only. Apparently, though, we are just like CDs: we are a space that is not rewritable. And the membranes of our virginity—we do not have a spare copy, just in case.

I was always aware that she was constantly watching me. It was so obvious that even my uncle and aunt could see it. She would call my classmates whenever I was five minutes late coming back from their homes, and she would stand at the door of the school waiting for me to come out. Whenever I needed to buy a notebook from the bookstore nearby, she would lead me there by the hand. There were times when I felt she still loved me the way she had in my father's absence and that was why she was throttling me with her attention. But doubt and suspicion have a smell that the senses never mistake.

It was a cold night, one of those nights when it seems like all the threads that bind you to the world have snapped. And it was just a game, as are most of the things in my life. I punched the numbers and lifted the receiver, my hand trembling, and said hallo *in a manner I tried to infuse with the tone of voice of an experienced girl. I tried to give my voice those provocative little flounces and sillinesses in the lilt of girls' voices to hide the fact that I was someone who was merely naïve and trying out what I had never before tested.* Hallo, *then I was quiet. When my silence grew long, whoever held the other telephone hung up on me. I dialed more numbers at random and asked for Fatima. I figured that all the homes here must have a Fatima, since the name of the Prophet's daughter, who married our hero Ali, is the Shi'is' favorite female name. Then it occurred to me, though, that I would be putting this Fatima who was the victim of my random choice in a fix if I called at that time. The world was not as it is now. We would go to sleep at ten o'clock and all of Qatif grew dark except for the streetlights. And there was no Fatima. It seemed I had woken up whoever it was that had answered the phone. The sound of his irritation intoxicated me, and I redialed. He answered me sharply.* I told you, wrong number. *He hung up on me. I thought this was a pleasant enough game and I*

went on making spontaneous random phone calls. More than once, I
happened to call my uncle's home, and Hussain answered so I put down
the receiver. Every evening I would think about Zakariyya. My family
had been able to tear Zakariyya from me, but they did not have the
power to uproot him from my mind.

Before I turned around I was already sure it was my mother. She
operated on the principle that every punishment must be appropriate
to the sin that led to it. When I was little, since I was a professional
at biting other children, she would bite my arm exactly as I did
with any of them. She slapped my hand when I stole, and slapped
me across the mouth when I lied, and cuffed my ear when I raised
the phone receiver and played around. I doubt it ever took her as
much as five minutes' thought to come up with any of those trivial
punishments that made me denounce and regret my errors. It was
enough for her to treat me like a dog and deny me the privilege of
my humanity.

At that time Qatif was a different place. They say it was a simpler
place. But I believe that it did not sleep securely. At that time, the
cliché the walls have ears really meant something immediate and real.
The spies were many and the secrets were even more. The secrets were
exorbitant and oppressive, and it was not possible to live peaceably
or securely in their shadow. Everything was sharp and conclusive. A
religious book had as much worth as a rifle. A cassette tape equaled a
pistol shot. A mourning ceremony for Hussain was tantamount to a
whole opposition corps. Maybe it was then that Qatif learned how to be
on permanent alert, always ready, always closed and incomprehensible
to strangers. Sometimes, I long to see through the eyes of strangers and
look at the place; or your eyes, because whenever I've tried to cover
over the year 1400 with a finger, I see it spilling out from between my
other fingers. I have searched, but I have not found anyone writing any
histories of Qatif for that period. Perhaps it was all an affair about which
we were better off keeping quiet. But it stamped Qatif with another

face that we all live with. We will all go on living it. Our problem,
perhaps, is that we are ignorant of what really happened, of the details
and concealed truths. Or, our problem is that we are too ignorant to be
capable of really absorbing it. Often, I figure that I don't understand
what happened because I am a woman. Women don't understand
history because they did not record it; after all, history is only a corrupt
policeman to be bought with money and power.

Molotov missiles, Molotov cocktails—as if it were all a question
of cocktails. In a distant memory Hassan had talked to me about all of
this, but as usual I was losing my way on history's roads and forgetting
where we were. As soon as I returned home that day, I got onto the
Internet and typed onto the search engine *Qatif 1400.* Most of the
sites were unavailable. From the half-paragraphs that the summaries
offer on the search page, I could not make out any useful elaboration
or find a word that would lead me to other search threads. When the
search took me to History of Qatif I read about Ashtarte, goddess of
fertility and love; Tarut, the oldest human settlement site ever; the
Kingdom of the Sea, from which emerged the Chaldeans, Assyrians,
Babylonians, Hittites, and Phoenicians, and which was overrun
by, in succession, the Accadians, the Babylonians again, Kassites,
Assyrians, then Nebuchadnezzar, the Persians, the tribes of 'Abd al-
Qays and thence the Islamic state, and on to Umayyads, Kharijites,
Abbasids, Carmathians, the Uyuni dynasty, the Portuguese, and
the Ottoman Turks, until finally it became the district of Qatif in
the Kingdom, an oasis in the eastern Arabian peninsula. Even the
celebrated ancient Arab poet Imru'l-Qays plucked and harvested
from Qatif (whose name suggests plucking the choicest morsels)
this vast oasis! Dareen did not believe it, but that poet declared,
Here: we are two strangers, here ...

I did not come to know Qatif until the city began to fill in the
waters of the sea. Since then I have turned my back to Qatif as I face
the water, while behind me emerge streets and quarters and whole

districts. I guide Umar on the map I found by chance on a website maintained by one of the consulates. I attempt to introduce him to the city that he has never visited, and he asks me doubtfully, Will I really be thrown out of Qatif if I try to go there?

They know you, I answer. They would recognize you by the particular kind of band that holds your headcloth in place, or by your tiny goatee, that *saksuka* you wear, and they will kick you out in the worst way. And then I laugh, I go on laughing, and he responds, agitated and embarrassed, calling me *stupid*! I mean, after all, he says, I am a Sunni. Then I feel guilty about mocking his question, so I answer him with a soothing proverb. Come, for if the world has not made room for you, loving eyes will. I point to the map: Look, here is where this is, and here is that, and here ... He interrupts me, But where is your house? But I cannot find that spot anywhere on the map.

It gives me a momentary fear. Dareen preoccupies and disquiets me with the chaos of her questions. She has been smitten with the world, or poisoned by it, for so very long, and attached to its creatures, while I am afraid of those who have granted me a meaning and a history. I am afraid because they grant me something that stays with me after they have departed—just as I am afraid of greeting cards on special occasions, afraid of gifts and letters. All the little sieges that affect us in some way or other, but this never occurs to us until much later. If I did manage to extract myself from the gifts, how would I be able to rid my head of their loud voices?

She would talk about Qatif as if she were living it in all its varied details with every breath, while all I knew of Qatif was a very narrow stretch of history and geography, vacated of people as far as I was concerned. The word *Qatif* held no real meaning for me, no life, no true value. It was just a word. Dareen, on the other hand, adopted it as a name she carried with her and held it as a memory to keep her alert. This is Dareen: she bears with her, wherever she is, places, objects, voices, scents, and specters of light. In her soul. Everything, no matter how minute or weightless, she crafts into a vessel that conveys her extreme sensitivity. She scares me, because I cannot endure being in constant contact with the world. I cannot sink my fingers into the diaphanous veil of its sands.

I despise the year 1415, she said. I feel like it made the circle of treason complete by aiming at me. Why did they have to go through fifteen years of siege and absence from the world and keeping people in the dark, only to reap such a paltry harvest? What real gains did we glean from it? It is still a homeland that we inhabit by rent, and a land where everyone competes to win over our fealty to it and them. It is still the case that we are governed with incredible stupidity, and we are led to our own guillotines as if we are a flock of sheep. Yet, even now we seem astonished by the stench of the changes that the twenty-first of September has created in us, as if we all had opened our arms to the sky, all of us without exception, and prayed. The angels were so kind that they encircled the world in a snare of flame and death so that the winds of change swirled even around us, buffeting us. We are so clueless that we applaud, because from now on the maps will show redrawn borders. Just imagine what it will look like—the day to come when we will be completely outside the borders—and off the map!

A heavy silence, and then she added, I am no longer willing to be anyone's victim, especially my mother's. I do not hate her. I do not love her. But I do not owe her anything. Nothing at all.

Did you think about that in the past?

All the time! I was a faucet for complaints, and the liquid never stopped pouring out. That got tiresome, though. I have a life I want to live and I am capable of taking things into my own hands.

But your parents were responsible for what happened, weren't they?

Definitely. I am not taking what happened onto my own shoulders and absolving them of the responsibility and the guilt for it. And I do not have enough forgiveness inside of me to put everything that happened entirely behind me. I am twenty-four years old, though, and I believe I am old enough to make a life where they are not the *alif* and the *ba'* of everything.

What was the first step you took?

A tiny one, and a very peculiar one for me. Suddenly I realized that I was not closing and locking the door to my room. Ever. Some time after it happened, my mother became convinced of my good behavior, and she figured that I had paid the price of my error. So she gave me back the rights she had taken away, among them the right to have a key to my room and to use it. I was no longer capable of exercising that right, though. She had become my subconscious, and without choosing to do so—or feeling like I had any choice!—I was continuing to carry out the punishment she had decided on, as if there would never be a change. It was as if God had ruled that I could leave hell but my feet would not budge. I realized that she was the one living inside my mind. I was always glancing around and behind me, weighing every detail, and counting even my words because I found her there wherever I went. So that was my first step, to turn the key in the lock on the door to my room.

She seemed to be thinking. I knew that my only role right now was to let her sense that I wanted to listen, and to prompt her now and then with a question. Other than that, I simply needed to stay quiet and await her wherever she was, whenever she was ready to start speaking again.

You know something?

What?

One time when we were still living at my uncle's and there had been a quarrel, my mother spanked me and I hid in Hussain's room. I started the tape that was in his cassette player and it was Fairuz. I fell asleep to her voice that day. And so, I always try to remember that every time there has been something awful in my life, there has been something wonderful corresponding with it. If she had not spanked me, then I would not have stumbled on Fairuz. If I had not flunked the year, then Nadia would not have been my classmate the next year, sitting right next to me in class. If it hadn't been for whatever ... then maybe we would not be together here right now, talking about all of this.

Can I ask you something?

Anything.

Do you still remember all of the details?

I remember the smallest detail you could think of.

Her telephone number, for instance?

Of course.

What is it?

I picked up the receiver, pressed the numbers as she said them and handed it to her. She was shifting her eyes from mine to my fingers on the buttons and she looked to be in almost a state of terror. I don't know why at that moment I thought of doing such a thing, nor how I could have rushed headlong into actually carrying it out—me, someone who believes that I have no right to interfere in anyone else's life, a belief I have adhered to sternly. But Nadia was always there, a figure posed in Dareen's eyes like an opaque black shadow chasing her even through her remote dreams. There was no point in trying to escape her presence. Dareen was in need of someone who would repair her heart, who would help her to regain her life, who would love her without making demands, without disappointing or abandoning her, and without advance payments of any kind. I was not the one to do it, especially not when I hoped and believed that Nadia had all of the right answers to Dareen's questions.

Bewildered, she asked me, What are you doing? She gave me back the receiver. A voice was saying, Hello ... yes? So I answered. Hello, is Nadia there?

Just a minute, he answered. And I said to Dareen, Now we could hang up as if nothing ever happened. Or you can take it and do something. Didn't you tell me you have a life you want to live?

But I don't know what to say to her.

Say whatever comes to you, the simplest thing: You've been longing for her, you want her, you will give her some time to think about things, and then you will call her in two days to hear what she has to say.

I watched the reactions on her face and forgot to follow the words she was saying into the phone. I sensed that her voice was confused but happy. Through the entire conversation, her hand was clutching mine, and I could feel how she was reacting by the varying pressure of her hand on mine. At the end, she let the receiver drop onto her chest. She took one of the small pillows heaped on my bed and put it over her face and then she collapsed onto the bed and said, You ... you bitch!

She was not being insolent or ugly with me. It was understood that I would not get angry if she swore at me, that I would not even anticipate it as signaling her displeasure, as much as I would feel it as her praise. I was her *sugar* when she intended to fling one of her judgmental sentences at me, and I was her *sweet cherries* whenever she kissed me. I was *a bitch* when I irritated her. We were too fragile to accept any unexpected mirth without showing our anxiety or letting out our tension. I was *damn you!* whenever I convinced her of my superiority at something. With her, I had a thousand aspects and a thousand pet names, loveable even if they were swear words and insults.

Tell me the good news—what did she say?

I don't know.

What do you mean, you don't know?

She dragged my hand along her chest and said, Listen.

Her pulse was racing. After a few moments, she took the pillow from her face and asked me with concern, Wouldn't it have been better for me to leave her the freedom to call me when she wanted to?

No, that would be stupid.

Why?

You have to guarantee her that you're the best.

Haaah!

Fine. Look at it honestly. This way, you know you have just a specified amount of time to wait, and so you will not become hostage to another labyrinth, a maze of waiting, a vicious circle that leads you nowhere. What if she were to forget, what if she did not have the nerve, what if she did not know what to say to you? It is better for you to be in charge of the situation if you can, if there is a way to do that.

Do you think she'll accept? Come back?

I hope so.

She thought for a few moments, biting her lip.

I have a question, on condition that you don't get mad.

I won't.

Are you doing this to get rid of me?

Give me a break, Dareen!

Seriously. Answer me.

I am doing it because I ... because I believe it is the best thing I could do for your sake.

Get rid of her! I thought. She did not get that right at all, though at the same time, she was not so very far from the truth. Ever since Dareen had gotten acquainted with me, and then had become practically bonded to my very skin and breath, I had felt that I could not go on with her, on to where the waters are no longer shallow and the tide begins to rise. Our relationship certainly had not exhausted itself, through all of our phone calls and conversations and visits, and our strong emotional bond that had developed. Instead, it had begun to enter a deep, deep part of me.

Saying goodbye to her at the door, I hugged her tightly. I had already primed myself that this might be our last time together, so I gazed at her face intently and left her chatting away, letting myself pick up her fleeing *r* and savor it. I wanted to say to her, Take care of yourself for my sake. But I kept those words from coming out, afraid of making her anxious. She was the happiest I had seen her since the first time we had met, and now I could stop feeling that she was a creature whose soul had been half extinguished while the other half blazed so hotly you felt it might go up in flames. A creature who was singing, for it had no alternative.

I did not want her to restrict herself to the question of what she would do about our relationship, which hung in the air between us like a bell that goes on reverberating, impossible to ignore, the space around it only making it echo more loudly. I was not being noble in taking myself away obliquely and without making a fuss, creating room for Dareen to get Nadia to come back. I was not being noble, because in return I was harvesting quite a large share of contentment, having decided that I was doing a good thing. I was getting a full refund on the cost of this choice I had made: so immeasurable was the gratitude she showed me that her overflowing good will became irritating. It got in the way of our phone conversations, the sort of grateful sense of indebtedness that weighs down the debt rather than lightening it.

Since I was implicated from the start in the presumed return of Nadia, I was determined to stay involved until I could be sure of the results, at which point I would withdraw permanently. At the time, Dareen was a mess, always tripping over her words, since she carried inside her the troubling heavy thought that anything she did at this stage of their relationship seemed equally likely to keep Nadia with her or push her to leave. So she surrendered the reins to me voluntarily. It was not particularly hard on me, since I maintained the position of observer no matter how deeply my hands were in whatever happened.

Let time take its course. Have confidence in Nadia and trust your own heart. Don't overwhelm her, don't let her take fright. Get some distance on what happened before, forget about your absence from each other, don't leave her feeling it was her fault, even if it was. It's natural that she is different, in three years everyone gets older and changes. Don't be aggressive but don't be more submissive than you have to be. For you to love her is one thing and for you to buy her return with your love is altogether something else.

We had switched roles. She was no longer the girl who was my elder by not just one year, but rather by 573 days, according to her calculator, and who put on the eyeglasses of a teacher and scolded me. Now I was the older girl, the one who taught her every daily lesson. The gist of all of my lessons was: How do you build a good and secure relationship in ten days? It was no longer odd or unusual for me to find twice the number of text messages on my mobile screen when I woke up at two o'clock in the afternoon. I would already know the reason: she was to meet Nadia later in the afternoon.

The only thing I could not claim to have professorial insight into was a huge question, one of those questions that seem as huge as a mountain when you begin to consider the endless possibilities it raises. Why was I not feeling jealous? Here I was, opening a door and pushing her through it to reach a riverbank that I hoped would be salutary for her. Here I was, too, giving all of her heart and her body to that other one, a stranger to me, an other one of whom I knew nothing except through Dareen's words and desires.

I was doing this without a single one of my nerves starting to shake, without a single heartbeat screaming out. I was doing it completely confidently, totally calmly, and with utterly loyal determination. All of this to protect the most desolate, wasted areas of my soul, and the doors whose dark recesses were to be concealed from Dareen's light. I was doing it without standing motionless for even one minute of silent mourning for what had been; without the truth stinging me that I was exaggerating how black my blackness was, without a belated slap to the back of my neck at a sudden vision of what I was letting escape me.

Like her, I was happy some days because the thing seemed a success, and tense other days because it was on the point of failing. I would pick up her breathing on the phone and the anxiety of her weeping and ask her to calm down. On the whole, I would tell her, life is a circular path where you always come back to the beginning. Its high points are an exact reflection of its low points, and the highs precisely reverse the lows. Life is just a matter of equivalences, and they are all written for us in advance.

17

Contrary to the way Dareen saw it, I do owe some kind of justification, if not to all who pass through my life, then at least to myself. A justification by virtue of which I could distance the guilt, place it beyond me, make it smaller; by which my hell would feel less oppressive. Passing through my life: this was exactly what the world and all who lived on it were doing, as far as I was concerned. I was determined—and I could not do otherwise—to preserve all of my ties, but keep them weak, intent on weaving the relationships I had into cobweb-like structures. Actually, spider web strands have a stickiness to them, and their ends carry poisonous stings, and these are qualities that I do not have or wish to have. Stickiness means attachment and poisonous stings mean binding another being to me. I am certainly not in need of any of that.

Lightness. That is what Dareen called it. That is what I want. At the age of twenty-two, I have not yet come to think with the lightness of *Mal'uun* Milan—the accursed Kundera. The lightness that is unbearable, the lightness that is a countervailing presence to heaviness and is equal to heaviness in what it does. That is what the physics of nature teaches us. The effect caused by a hundred degrees centigrade is the same caused by its negative equivalent. The lightness of zero is what I mean to have. Zero, the only reality that is absolute; and to each side, objects are merely the reflected images of the same reality.

I can barely fathom now what I am really heading for in my life, this being who is me. I was the absence of the others, and the black hole in their memory. I was another step beyond, outside of who they were, a dirty stain in their datebooks. I caused fear precisely because, before I left them (and that I did often), no one ever assumed that I could cause fear or worry. Having their trust and affection, I would shock them with my sudden departures. Indeed, no one left me! Even Hassan himself did not leave me. Yet at the same time, I had left more people almost than I had fingers on my hands. Likely they are all now somewhere wallowing in forgetfulness, and probably, they are like me. They probably have fallen into the darkness of the fear that never ends.

Dareen has an explanation for my fear. It is the same explanation she has for everything: that my fear is one of the aftereffects of the year 1400. Not just my fear—my urgent need for fear. I think she is making too much of a generalization when she attributes my fear to reasons as inclusive as this. I told her, This is Qatif, it isn't Beirut in the civil war. She answered, Fear is fear, even if the locale has changed! She said nothing for a moment and then she added, And anyway, it is an infectious condition. Isn't infection transmitted through the umbilical cord?

Do you remember the chemical masks? she asked me.

Who could forget them?

After two years of the war, no more than two years, not a single house retained any of the masks they had bought. Isn't that a little strange? There was no motive to hang onto them. The war pretty much did not reach us. Anyway, it ended.

You are so naïve! We felt secure. And then, in a single night, our covers were yanked off and we were naked. Everyone was in an utter state of denial and searching for forgetfulness by any route. They were too eager to get rid of the war, to amputate it from their lives. We'd had one long period of insomnia that seemed to never end, and suddenly it was a thing of the past, something useless to ever look at again. Don't you think we all feel some discomfort when Kuwaiti TV shows the pleas of the prisoners' families, and doesn't let us stop thinking of them day after day after day? Why do we react this way, if we really have nothing to do with what happened? Isn't it because they are reminding us of what we work very hard to bury in the well of forgetting? Now, you are not going to also tell me that what happened was not another cause for fear!

On this at least I agree with you.

Do you know what our new fear is?

What?

A sense of belonging. *Intimaa.*

Intimaa. What do you mean by that?

Before, when we faced anything unexpected, anything different or new, we knew we were sure to have one. One person, one response, one voice—we were united, in unison, like military uniforms. Now it is different. There are currents, perhaps even movements; resonant names; turns of phrase that you or me can barely pronounce correctly. Everything is mixed up now, and we are no longer capable of defining what we want or mean. What are we searching for? What are our choices? What direction ought we to turn? There are a lot of questions and not enough answers, or not enough good answers, to suit everyone.

You like theorizing, Dareen!

No, I just want to understand and there's no one to explain all of this to me free of charge.

Something else about Dareen frightens me. What she says is so like me that I could almost swear she makes a copy of my mind every day and then she brings it out again later, when the edginess of my questions and the sharpness of my apprehensions begin to fade, and she can stoke their fire again. It is not just what she says. We used to fall in love with the same things: foreign films without subtitles, *makaruna* with red sauce, blueberry beer, Fairuz, plain bed covers. We despised the same things, too: okra stew, Jim Carey, yellow lighting, the screech of the printer, and finding someone waking us up. Even the way this could spoil our mood for the rest of the day was similar. All alike. Dareen was like me in a way that made me appear a less mature image of her. She was similar to the point of being exactly alike in some aspects, to the point of being my mirror image. It scares me to be as tremendous as that, it astonishes me to be astonishing, just as it frightens me that my mirror rouses me to live, that it coaxes me toward life in this way.

Unlike our most recent phone conversations, this time she did not mention Nadia's name, and she did not surround her words with apologies and modify them with double thanks for everything. She said, I want to see you.

Me, too. I have something small for you.

What is it? she asked.

A secret.

When can we meet?

Whenever you like, I said. I'm at your command.

You'll be my guest, though, she said.

Ah, contrary to the usual. Are you intending some evil toward me?

I have already stolen you once before. I don't know if I am capable of more than that.

When I got there, she blockaded me at her door. I want what is mine now. Now! I tried playing with her ready ebullience a little, putting her off. This is a truly dirty word, don't say it, period! I was hoping she would let out a string of swear words at me as usual, but she only gave me a big kiss on the cheek, took me by the hand, and led me to her room, where we had never before been together.

Holding the disk I had just given her gently between her thumb and forefinger and staring at it, she asked me, What is it?

"Waiting." *Intizar*. I always think of you when I hear it.

There was a time when I believed that with writing and music I could survive, could open up a free space in this world capable of holding me fully and warmly. Later on, I completely abandoned my faith in writing. Every new piece of writing became a noose that would wind its way around my neck and do its part to throttle me. I had had enough of my horrendous ability to misrepresent facts and make sorrows beautiful. I had had enough of being able to write out my fragmentation between two memory spaces—what happens, and what is written. And I had had enough of naïve attempts to steal my vision and toy with my heart. Writing was no longer giving me life, and now it was taxing me enough that it might be giving me death. Music was what was left for me.

There is a saying: Music is the food of the soul. I do not approve of expressions like this. Music itself is a soul, and how can we draw food from a soul? Anyway, how can we grasp that soul in the first place when we do not know its nature and have no description of its essence? The world is stern with us, though, demanding definitions according to the criteria it gives us, so as to verify the beings and objects that dwell upon it. Names are for one's memory, and definitions are for the dictionaries; and music, even though it may fly, is not a creature whose wings can be fixed with pins on a piece of cork, its body left to dehydrate.

On the Internet I have often typed random words into the search engine and studied page after page of results. Several tries might yield a disappointing nothing, and then one try bears fruit and causes me such sheer astonishment that it can swallow up the whole of my long night. Once I put in the word *intizar*, having already chosen to search images, and then I switched to audio files; surely such a word would yield decent results. I found the song and it staggered me so much that I did not wait for Umar to get onto the web at his usual time. I called him and we listened to it together, and I asked him, What do you think of it? He answered, Aah, I don't know! That's it exactly. Beautiful things always steal the language from us and force us into silence.

It's a piece of music from Iraq.

She put it into the CD drive.

No, not right now, I said.

So, when?

Let's listen to it together tonight.

3 a.m.—does that suit you?

It's kind of late for love.

Love is the only thing that is never late.

She waved at the door. See—it's closed.

I noticed. You're a heroine!

I'm …

You're what?

She came over to me, a trance-like look in her eyes that was like magic. I was already half lying on her bed. She went down toward my feet and kissed them. This time I did not tense up with worry. I did not feel assaulted by an anxious sense of being tickled. I did not start thinking, My feet are too lowly for her to kiss. It did not occur to me to worry that my foot might slip after a spasm, mistakenly strike her and give her a nosebleed. I understood her need to do it, to show her gratitude in the most lucid way possible, so I left her to it. Then I gave her a hug. I laughed a little as she said, Finally—it's only today that my room is having its first experience. I laughed with her, she put her arms tightly around me, and I asked her, Does she treat you well?

Nadia? Oh, sure, of course.

She began to laugh slyly when I pushed her away, and then said, Don't be annoyed, I am just teasing you a little. We were quiet for a moment as I trailed my thumb across her cheek. Her smile, with its inviting, ironic cleverness, gave me the impression that she was serious in what she said. Likely, she wanted to pass on this bit of information to me, and she chose to do it by arranging for a little light banter.

It's true, what you are saying?

Yes.

Why?

I don't want to build our relationship only through our bodies.

We went through a confused moment and then my inner self tried to entice me to say, Fine, you are right. Or, No I won't leave you! But she spared me the sin of either wounding her or leading her astray when she put out her hand to me and said, I want to show you my secret hiding place.

The heavy scent of paint walloped me when she opened the door. She said, Go ahead, please.

It was a large room, with very bright lighting; the north and east walls were enormous windows of one-way reflecting glass. On the west wall hung three huge paintings and others were propped against the wall, showing only their backs, except for a row of seven canvases facing outward. Where I entered there sat a large table with several storage areas, its surface strewn with drawing tools and holding an easel.

I think this place holds everything my father gave me. It *is* everything he gave me.

I was taken unawares by the strength of my reaction, which nearly made me swear at her except that my tongue stumbled over the words.

Uh, you are—

It's just exactly what you see.

Why didn't you ever tell me about this?

Here—I'm sharing my secret with you now! I waited so that you could see it with your own eyes.

A secret—why a secret?

You know what the others expect. Windows, stories, trees, little songbirds. I am as far away as can be from anything like that! I am a crazy woman whose head spins at the color white. That means I do not treat white according to some presumed idealism or goodness. One time I read that art rests on destruction—of ideas, structures, and ready-made notions of beauty. By instinct, I am a really good destroyer.

Knowledge has corrupted you, Dareen.

Dazzled, I studied her secret dwelling place. With an admiration I could not hide, I said, God must definitely love colors, to so fill the world with them.

She raised her finger to me, shaking it as if to say, Give me a minute, and I will remember it exactly.

Don't reproduce a translation that is wrong. The original sentence is *God must be a painter*. From the film *A Beautiful Mind*. She was standing in front of a painting and—

I interrupted her. I can second you on the film, I said, but if you are going to start talking about details on the canvas, you know better.

I pointed to the three works hanging on the wall. Why these especially, and not others?

When I lose my belief in what I am doing, when I don't have enough reasons or motives to go on, whenever I doubt my ability, I look at them and I see what I was and then what I have become and I regain my confidence. My stages—the first was anger, as I call it, all red hues, large mouths screaming, fast steps, and swarming streets.

I don't see any of that.

There is no reason to assume that you will see what would amount to a literal translation.

I don't mean that, I mean ... so, that was your embryonic stage, if it is okay to use such an expression. Writing exactly on the lines.

My embryonic stage, as you put it, consisted of some sketches in notebooks. I didn't yet know the difference between watercolors and oil, nor between abstract art and surrealism.

Yes, I get that. So what was the next stage?

Nothingness. Nihilism. I would fill the spaces of the canvas with more emptiness. At that time, in most of my paintings I used colors tending toward black. I was consumed by the idea of contradiction between black and white. I was thinking that if I had been born in the middle of the twentieth century, like in the sixties, and had grown up watching films that weren't in color, I would not have been very happy.

Do you like naming your pieces?

Her smile almost disappeared. This really is a tragedy, she said. At that time, I was sketching my dreams. Every swipe of the brush was a dream. With a certain amount of conceit, maybe, I really believed that at any given time I had enough images and thoughts crowding inside of me that I could draw and draw without stopping. I didn't really notice that I was just going on and on suspended in the same place. I was not taking a single step forward.

And now?

Have you seen *Shine*? If I am not mistaken, it got an Oscar for Best Actor. It is all about a piano player named David. When I saw it, I heard a sentence I can't ever forget. *Play as if there is no tomorrow.* When I heard him playing Rachmaninoff's Third Piano Concerto, I could never forget it, even after I learned that this David could not actually play the passage. His fingers betrayed him. I am going to risk saying that every painting is a stage, or part of one. But now, I do paint every one as if it might be the last one, if my fingers should betray me.

Why are all the others turned to the wall?

How do you feel about your poems a while after you've composed them?

I hate them.

Yes, it's like that.

Show me the one you hate most.

Shame on you!

She searched among them and lifted out one. You have to really prepare yourself for this one, though I should not prepare you in advance.

I put my hands out to her, saying, Come. She did, and stood facing me. I ordered her to close her eyes, and she did. I took her hand, and passed her forefinger from my middle finger to my palm. Every time she seemed impatient to go faster, I slowed her down. We were so close that I could smell the fragrance of the shampoo in her hair and I felt the heat of her breaths against my skin, and when I again moved her finger across the bump on my palm, I said, This is me!

She had a curious look on her face. You are this wound?

No! I am what you feel when I am inside of you. When my being there doesn't violate any other thing.

She smiled, seeing me fall into the *thing* trap, out of which I had so recently tried to pull her.

The sound of the late afternoon call to prayer rose and it was almost time for me to leave. Wait, she said. I also have something small for you.

It was her turn to order me to close my eyes. We were always carrying out these weird sequences of repeated behaviors. I interrupt her, she interrupts me; I kiss her hand, she does the same; if she starts swearing, I come back at her with something worse. I heard the sound of her making a little commotion as she hurried over, and then she permitted me to look. Facing me was a white canvas, as white as if it were a slab of ice, the very image of what I believe heaven to look like. Not colors but what is beyond colors.

It's for you.

What?

You heard me.

But it is your painting.

I made it for your sake.

I can't take it.

Why not?

Because it is your work.

You can certainly give me, dedicate to me, the finest poem that you will ever write, and then we'll be even.

You don't understand. The poem will remain with me even if I give it to you. But the painting, no.

Take it! Hang it over your bed.

Why specifically over my bed?

Because you are the only crazy woman who sleeps the wrong way around in her bed.

Meaning, it will be the first thing I see when I wake up.

And you will remember me.

You mean, I will think about you.

And you will remember me, she repeated firmly.

I really wanted to say to her, but didn't, Hide me, Dareen, here, in this secret place of yours, hide me between your fingers. Draw on my body, draw directly onto my skin without any distances or obstacles, draw, with all of your colors, all of your fingers. Draw on my body as if I am the very last of your canvases. Your drawing will erase all of the futile, stupid actions of others. I will not be the best of your canvases, Dareen, yet this canvas, me, will be one of the best in its power to move the emotions, to express meaning. Aren't you comfortable with the way my body speaks? So, then, hug me, hug me a little, no, hug me a little less than that, and then do not start searching inside my chest, do not ask me, Why is your soul not there? I have no soul, Dareen. The others have consumed it, the others who come and go, across me, these others who pass by, and those who thought I loved them and they loved me ... you consumed it, you, Dareen, or perhaps it was Nadia.

We were silent for a little, so sad that we could not rise above our sorrow. Then she punctured our silence with words.

Do you know what the song of our relationship is?

Of course, it is what you made the painting of.

And it is just ours!

Dareen, too, possessed her own particular ability to predict, and this is what she told me as she sang it.

O Time
Since these plants threw their shadow on the wall
And from before the days when these trees grew tall
O Time, light the lamps, and look at my friends
They've passed on by and I remain all alone
O friends who are leaving, and the snow that was here
You'll no longer return to my door in this drear
Howl at them, wolf, howl with the winter
Howl to my friends, and maybe they will hear ...

It was as if she were saying, I will wait for you even if you do not come, and I forgive you for being absent even if I do think it is wrong.

After we were finished I was careful not to leave anything behind me. The law says: Nothing left hanging behind you when you leave. No words lest they be said, no stories lest they be told, no needs lest they be longed for; because, most of the time, such things come back later to spoil the ambience. I was accustomed to ending my relationships in the most seemly way, what I can call *a clean kill*. I make our final day the very best day we have ever had, and I make sure that no doubt remains, not even the lightest tiniest tremor of concern, about whether the relationship deserved all that we poured into it. That way, nothing is left over that we are compelled to revisit at a later moment. And so, on that day precisely, I was fulfilling everything required of me, saying everything that needed to be heard from me, so that I could be absolutely certain of not leaving this place before seizing everything due me or paying everything I owed.

But—Dareen!

I simply was not capable of taking advantage of her heedlessness, fooling her this way, nor was she capable of playing along—of playing this game with me. I sensed that we would come together; we would find a way through this that would defuse the tension. We would make a relationship that did not leave such a heavy footfall. We would not release ourselves, such that we could be unfaithful, despite the few times, really, that we had been together, so few as to be considered nothing much at all. Times that had always come to a close with the certitude that our intimacy would not repeat itself. We had not been so caught up in our bodies; our desires had not run away with us. But this is what the impossibility of attainment, after its possibility, does. The jealousy germinating in the joints of a body which is no longer able to commit the act, to touch, to kiss; and the belated flame of desire which is fueled only by the power of that other's existence, and the fire of distance. Perhaps we would meet in paradise, where we could become light, ridding ourselves of the burden of our bodies, released finally from memory.

18

Rayyan was a story in one chapter. I do not know which one of us finished with the other one. We just ended it. Supposedly, short stories do not leave vast spaces of sadness behind. Supposedly, transients pass lightly. Supposedly, we remain friends and he leaves the lamp in his window lit for me, so that I may turn to it in my darkest nights, when I make my way along corridors that lead nowhere. But things do not match up with our *supposedlys* or our prior expectations.

The worst thing about death is dying slowly, wilting and fading away, dissolving and decomposing. The worst is to find that your every breath holds a little less air. The worst case scenario is when death does not come quickly and decisively; and that was the scenario that overtook Rayyan and me. We ended slowly, so slowly that I have no idea in what moment we actually did end it. I cannot pinpoint or even guess the time span that framed our relationship. We ended so slowly that it wasn't really an ending.

We met through pure Internet mischief in an online club. I do confess, Rayyan is one of my favorite writers. I was determined to hassle him, so I highlighted a marginal bit of information in one of his comments, and declared it wrong in a thread I added. Later on, he told me of his suspicion that I was stalking him, likely with some bad intentions. He was outraged and he decided on the spot to break my head, as he put it. Breaking a head takes time and effort, though, and we found ourselves dangling in a certain trap without having realized that we were falling into it.

When I said to Dareen, What I long for in you is a man, but it's a man who will never show up, she whispered into my ear, I wish I could be that man.

But I do not expect anyone, I answered with truly lofty hauteur.

Without knowing it, she drew my attention to the entity missing in my life. There had never been a man, never at all. In my remotest hopes, in my very feeblest and most secret thoughts about the future, there never ever had been a man. I dealt with the problem of the absent man as a foregone conclusion, a grim reality. Even when the world of the Internet opened before me in all of its tempting, enticing possibilities, that particular absence was a premise whose bases I did not contest. Umar himself was an exception—an exception far beyond the usual or the anticipated. The virtual space where our relationship played out with its natural limitations contained my awareness of him as a presence that had no physicality, no gender, no sex. I expect that if it had not been for the nature of these circumstances, which allowed him to slip easily into the tiniest crevices of me, we would not have come close to completing our second year together as buddies on the Internet.

Whenever I got close to negotiating with the idea of a certain man's existence in my life, I had to think about the possibility of there existing a man who would be right. But the sheer question of sexual nature would shove me off course every time I allowed an opportunity to perch in my mind. I am not someone to give my body to strangers. I do not invite to my bed those who will put on their clothes in the morning and go away and not come back. I cannot detach my body from my soul; I cannot fill one of them up while the other remains hungry. There is an enormous distance between releasing my body into the whirl of its desires, and being cheaply and easily available.

They say that you know love when it shows up in front of you. I do not know if this thing with Rayyan was love or if it was something else. They also say that love comes when we are really ready for it, but it comes from a direction we don't expect. I was living our relationship as if it were a tightrope on which I had to balance without any safety net below—that *below* which was deep and very dark. Our relationship took on a strange pattern of absence and presence. Boredom quickly grabbed us if we were in each other's presence too long. Desire stung us when we stayed away. So we swung between presence and absence, two dubious choices with no third way out. Without any prior accord, we seemed intent on filling an obligation to time our absences and our presences alike. That way, one of us did not have to wait and the other did not have to feel ignored. Knowing from the start that Rayyan would be absent, I did not feel any great fissure opening up behind my ribs if I did not find him there, no gap that solace could not close, no hollow that could fill up only with the muck of regret or the standing water of unbearable grief.

I always believed that I would not love. Not because love was not capable of including me, but because I was not courageous enough for it. Now, though, I seek to distort or misconstrue some of our truths, or to deflect my thoughts about them, for the sake of convincing myself that I did go through this once. The world can have its truths; I want only some peace of mind within the space of my illusions. Many times—I did not count how many—I said *I love you*, and he said *I love you*, and our voices choked on the fierceness of our desire. But these are instances I do not put much stock in. The words we say as a couple of glazed-over sots playing with their bodies across a telephone connection have no value. Many times, when we were on the edge of real grief, he would say, I want someone!

Anyone! And I would understand it as: I don't have anyone! No one is with me.

How often I have intuitively understood the notion that what begins at boiling temperature ends tepid. Whatever the qualities that create such intensity, they are consumed in that breakneck acceleration of desire, for which there can be no preparation. We are not born as adolescents ready for anything. By nature, we are creatures who develop gradually, and just as this is our nature—and the Creator's will—so it is also the nature of what we do and think and have. My relationship with Rayyan, which flared and flamed suddenly beneath our fingers on our cell phone pads in a conversation lasting no more than ten minutes, clearly was going to sink and die out just as quickly. We are not giving a relationship enough of a chance if its first moment is its best, for then there will be nothing afterward worth waiting for. And having something worth waiting for is what keeps us going. Probably our repeated truancies from each other on the Internet were half-successful attempts to prolong our hypothetical time together—the time we *should* have had!—or to grant us a little respite across which we could begin again. But it would not be easy for us to begin again, or to reset the biological clock of our relationship to zero.

I have sincerely and fervently believed at times that the grief that condemns a certain relationship is also capable of retrieving it. For that sorrow does not leave us. It alights on our pillows just before we wake up, and it seals our eyes shut before we sleep, and it brings those who have left us, or those whom we left, and who all carry that sorrow heavily. Sorrow brings them to us, coming along with them in all of its severe and inscrutable presence. We feel it is the heavy severity of things that hover because they are never forgotten and they allow us no opportunity to overlook them. From Rayyan on, every day of my life, the thought will come to me that those who do not *ever* arrive—we open a path for them by parting the waters, and still they do not come—are sources of sorrow whose impact we cannot take lightly, although I feign distance from them and claim that I can live with them perfectly well.

During one of those intervals when our relationship was flagging, Rayyan was in an accident although he was not hurt. I said to him, I do not want you to die! I do not like people who die. I remember that he laughed. That was the moment when I began to observe and count up his absences and mine. As I thought about them, I realized that I no longer found anything enjoyable and appetizing there. It was as though he filled me with stones every time he went away, and I would drown—drown! and when he went away for good, he sent me to the deep and murky bottom without leaving even a breath of air in my chest.

Our public and passing disagreement lasted a few messages and then extended to long hours of chatter on the Internet, since after all, I was such an expert at immunizing myself against strangers. I found myself opening all my horizons to him. When I heard the little bell signaling that he was entering the site and I read his screen name, *Wa-tamuut ma had diri fiik*!, "You-die-and-nobody-knows!", something told me in a whispered voice that I was being taken in by this assured longing for sympathy, and that I would definitely pay the price. I remember my first sentence: On the first of September, many things happen. And I remember his answer: But one of them is not that I will become your Black September!

It occurred to me that if I had met Rayyan only one month earlier, in August, even in mid-August, then everything between us would have been a mere summer misdemeanor. I am very good at arguing at great length about how negligible are all of the sins or errors I have committed out of pure boredom. I can argue about them and come out of it without any losses worth mentioning. The summer is good for crafting sudden provisional things that are quick to disappear. All things melt in the summer, not only ice and *gelati*. I can stand it that the ice cream I have with Rayyan melts. But I am not capable of being his tree, and he my autumn, so that I become naked and alone.

When I heard his voice on the telephone, sounding wounded for no obvious reason, I could well believe that distance creates a temptation that you never feel with anything or anyone nearby and easily available. I told myself that Rayyan was a chance at love that would not come again. He seemed such a sure thing, exactly because he was so far away. He could not really hurt me when he was 400 kilometers distant. Besides, Riyadh—which teaches its children how to be tough and severe—taught him well how to distance himself from people, among them me.

The borders around our relationship were imposed in advance, without any need on our part to interfere and make adjustments. We did not give the matter any thought. After all, we would not actually meet, and so we could not become embroiled in questions such as, Where will this relationship lead us? How far should it go? There was nothing there to merit such questions. There was no *what about later on*? to plague us. It was a beginning that had no tomorrow. This was an ideal situation as far as I was concerned, since I am someone who refuses to allow anyone to pin me down so that I cannot move. That day he had to change his name to *A safe place for love*. But he was a human being, he said to me, not a place. We are all places, I replied.

That wounded voice of his tinkered with my heart and mind and changed the whole order of things in there. It was the disordering impact of a man on a woman whose only triumphs were over ordinary matters, her only successes within tightly contained boundaries, and her only achievements governed by stern laws. This is what men are so good at, and they have no rivals. They make a woman into a woman and nothing more.

Rayyan had an attractiveness about him that I could neither resist nor outdo. He knew how to be beautiful in his sadness, desirable in his anger, compellingly extravagant in his thoughts and ideas. The Internet—that ground across which we sowed our first steps—was, as he saw it, the only space that offered women balconies for love trysts, in a country which mounted perfectly arranged conspiracies to turn its sons into deserts—dry and harsh. When I told him that his personality made him extremely good writing material, he answered me sarcastically, So will you kill me off, the way that Algerian writer Ahlam Mostaghanemi does with her heroes? Then he added, Writing does not give me glory. Only praise and women!

Rayyan is like this: he says things he does not mean, and inflates his words grandly and shoots them out, while at the same time concealing what he truly means ever deeper below the surface. His double-sidedness slays me: sometimes he is frivolous and trivial, but far more often he is incredibly stupendous.

Once the froth that floated on Rayyan's surface was swept away, what drew me to him was the fact of our difference. We were opposites who could only accommodate difference, like God's dark night and His day, woman and man, a Shi'i girl and a Sunni guy, the ancient Bedouin purity of his blood and my sedentary inheritance—for my blood runs with green heads of grain—dry and rainy, sharp and fine. Even my same-sex experiences fell opposite to his background, which was fundamentally a straight and proper line between two points, reflecting his thoroughly upright character. For him, I was something else for sure, something other, as he was for me. It was obvious from the many issues that came up and astonished us. We would talk about these things, on and on, question marks popping up to which we provided answers, each in turn; and massive differences of opinion that we argued over before giving them a figurative slap on the nape of the neck and telling them to go away. When he saw a picture of me, he said, The origins of people from the Qatif region must go back to Iran. If not, where do you get all this pale skin? *Inti haliib, ya bint*! You are milk, girl!

We advanced play by play in our game of e-absences, with its persistent rhythm of recurrences, but whenever we overdid it we returned to our policy of frugality. I recall him saying, Only with you I sense how light my absence is, how little impact it has. And I would ask myself at what point on the path of our relationship had we wrongly taken a side road that became a shortcut leading us to-ward the end—the end of us. Our absences had become something we celebrated and treated with utmost respect. Our absence became more important than our presence. This is the hardest part of it all. I don't know what was wrong. Why did we come to an end? What was the final obstacle on the road that we stumbled over? The hardest thing about it is that I search for the reasons and don't find them, and so I cannot finally or definitively escape him, nor can he truly rid himself of me. We would continually return, having conversations of an hour or two. I would go on feeling angry about our predicament. I would think, This is not where we were meant to end up. When he returned, I would still feel that I needed him, and I would shelter him for an evening or two. He did the same for me, leaving his door slightly open. I remained certain that it was not a question of one of us playing with the other, raising all of this dust in front of our steps and sending all of this inflammation into our eyes. We were still attached. We still came back. We still did not come back.

In his wallet, he kept a scrap of paper filled with notes and observations, and when he returned he would read it to me, like a sacred book, even if it only inscribed little things. "I am having a falafel sandwich for supper, I am not inviting you. Anyway, your bad blood prevents you from accepting my invitation." "I am watching *The Others*, are you still crazy about it?" "I am feeling kind of blue and I miss you." "The exams are at a bad time for me to read *Love in the Time of Cholera*, and anyway, I am longing to hear you say,

On condition that you don't make me eat eggplant. And instead of my saying, I am returning the keys to your life to you, I found myself thinking, If you cross the street you will find me dead when you come back." "I know you despise our Abbadi, as famous as he is, as great a lute player and singer as he is! But hey, listen to this … or, never mind!" "There is someone who is a lot like you and she is egging me on, she wants me to seduce her. Are you using a new nickname?" "Still love me?" "It isn't the hunting season, but I am going out into the wilds for the weekend … just so you know, my phone will be off, but don't worry."

Just little things, the things that he was going to send to my cell phone but was forced to actually write down on paper instead, to keep himself from sending them right at that moment. To cool the need in his blood, he would say. We savored our state of chastity, but at the same time each one of us was thoroughly tangled up in the other, and we also savored that to the point of addiction. One time when real stupidity got the better of me, I sent him a strong and probably hurtful message, which I started by saying, Honestly, doesn't your heart pain you over me? I did stop saving up my transient daily details to tell him, because doing so filled me with more need for him. It made me turn and turn again in the same maze, coming out one door only to find it sending me back inside the very same maze through another door. I would fill up with need that I would try to blot out, and then, when we were together again in virtual space, and close, I would start feeling sorry for myself and so I would revert back to absences.

He told me that he had been unfaithful to me for a short time at the start of our relationship. I laughed at his use of the word *unfaithful*. His girlfriend had returned to him and his longing for her had intoxicated him, and so they had had sex, he said. He tried to lighten the presumed impact of the news on me by saying it only happened two or three times, on the basis that a little unfaithfulness and a lot of unfaithfulness are not the same thing; meanwhile, I was thinking, Once is enough for it to count as unfaithfulness. But in fact I didn't consider it that. Our very ambiguous relationship did not permit me to interpret what he had done as unfaithfulness. I listened to his tale all the way to the end. Afterward, I made no attempt to cut any of the long and entangled threads of it, for that would require me to make some sort of decision, and I did not want to do that. Although he saw my reaction as a lack of interest, I considered it an attempt to remain impervious to scratches.

He was always repeating that it was up to God to put him in paradise, if not as compensation for denying him any assurance in life, then at the very least because he had repented of all his sins out of pure anxiety. We did not see eye to eye at all whenever we got onto the subject of God, nor when I would ask him, Have you visited your mother? He would respond, What you mean is, have I visited my mother's grave! Rayyan encumbered himself with other people without any of them having any right of possession over him. No one permanently inhabited him; he was a many-roomed mansion, housing others when he lived on nothing more than the screech of the wind that came in through the cracks. God moves in mysterious ways, he said to me.

Both of us hark back to the same northern region, even to the same tribe, a fact which caused Rayyan two minutes of pure astonishment and a passing cackle before he could take it in, and a coincidence which gave me a moment's doubt about the passed-down tale reciting the origins of our family. A distant male ancestor of mine, when I was only a latent prospect in God's will, left his northern home and settled somewhere near the Gulf, after switching from his Sunni-ness to the path of the Shi'is. I mull over the possibility that he was a great man. I do not care how he changed or from what or why. What is important is that he did it. It seems a great thing to me that he looked to God with his own eyes and not with theirs, a wondrous thing that he left all of his former hazy doubts and began with a new vision. It is not important that others might have seen him as a freak.

This difference between us was nothing if it was not a spur to caustic banter. We would deride even ourselves, and the stupidity that had made our difference into an instrument of so much coercion, rights put on hold, and demi-wars waged in secret. We were constantly trading jokes and jibes on the subject of our difference, even that one time when we talked in what-ifs. What if we were to get married? What if we had children? His words got lost in his laughter as he said, I am probably capable of convincing my family about my marrying a servant in the household, but a Shi'i woman? That is the most impossible of all. At his words, I felt the slap of a hot gust of wind on my temple. But I just let it go, determined to see it as simply a slightly tasteless joke. Then we disagreed on the name of our firstborn, although after a lot of banter we came to a solution: his name would be Muhammad, a name that no Shi'i or Sunni could contest. The drift of our conversation carried us further when he asked me about the religion of our children and I exclaimed, By God, what will they be! He answered me, I don't want my children to be *rawafid*.

Rejectionists! That was what some Sunnis called us Shi'is. *Rawafid*! Oh, Rayyan.

And then I said some very bad things, although I do not remember now exactly what they were. I cannot remember what I say when I am in a state of blind anger. I would have let it go as any polite person would, had anyone but Rayyan said it. But not him. The enormity of the letdown that he flung at me when he said that, the scale of the loss, the atrocious degradation, filled my eyes with tears. Later, after he had tried to excuse the whole thing by telling me that it was a bad attitude that he had been brought up with through the whole of his twenty-five years and could not slip out of easily, no matter how hard he tried, and that inside of him there would remain traces that he knew were despicable, I cut him off in mid-explanation. I will not negotiate with you over your convictions, I said, no matter what they are, but you are obliged to respect my difference from you. What if it had not been a slip of the tongue after all? I reflected.

At that moment I considered some kind of revenge that would let me get even with him. But I pulled back because I was convinced that it really was extremely difficult for him to understand what it means for your own homeland to have an exclusive vision that keeps you out. How could he really understand what it means for your neighbors to band together and conspire against you? For you to exist in an area that is something less than the land that is yours? For you to have to argue for your rights, and to feel that everything coming your way is a charitable donation, bestowed graciously, even when it is the labor of your own hands that provided it?

I am a person who forgives and does not forget, and he is one to apologize but not erase his wrong. This lapse stopped us cold. We did not refer again to what had been said, nor to the way we had exchanged jokes and drummed up bonus laughs at the expense of my sect or his. We no longer ended our messages with *A Shi'i and she's prettier* or *A Sunni and you love him*. No longer when I called him on the phone at noon on Friday and reminded him to pray, saying, Come on, get up and go pray, our Lord will be pleased with you, would he answer, I don't have any need for the Shi'i Lord! He no longer exclaimed, You sectarian-monger! when I wished him good night by saying *Masa' al-rida*, May your evening be full of peaceful contentment. That had not been his response in the beginning, only after he asked me one day what the secret was behind the label by which we were called, Twelver Shi'is. I explained to him about our twelve holy Imams, and when I was counting them off and reached the Imam al-Rida peace be upon him, my ninth Imam, he immediately picked up on it, as if he had pounced on a treasure: So that's why, *ya la'ima*, you are always saying *Masa' al-rida*! It's your Imam-of-Peaceful-Contentment! Evening of Contentment with God, how do you like that! The whole silly thing became a wall erected at the center of our relationship, behind whose curtains there was a fissure rather than a window.

After the *rawafid* incident, I stayed away for a little while. I cut myself off from him, from the Internet, our tiny virtual homeland. This was not revenge or punishment so much as it was an attempt to forget. And when I returned, someone among my net friends informed me that Rayyan had come to my defense when some anonymous user had made a comment against me. I knew what had set this off. I was aware of it because it had begun in my personal inbox with a few messages that moved gradually from greetings to open harassment. At the time, all I could do to counter them was to ignore them completely, which is all they deserved, anyway. So I knew the beginnings of it, but I remained in the dark about the ins and outs of how it ended. The topic at issue, with which that person tried to put me in a bad light, ended with suspension of his membership.

I was grateful to Rayyan for standing in solidarity with me on this. I leaned on him to give me the details, but all he said was, Their pebbles only stirred up the surface, they didn't reach the bottom. I returned to the net as if nothing had happened. Even selfless and noble behavior in the virtual world is measured by the teaspoonful. When you defend somebody and stand by him, it either signals a lot of affection and care or it tells everyone that you are part of his personal clique. Defending a woman can mean only that you are a greedy cuss who is trying his luck with her, if it does not mean that in the real world, you are a close friend and an exquisitely noble individual who carries five stars on your shoulders. It's all a bunch of electronic filth! The virtual world holds as real an opportunity for everyone to empty their trash at their neighbors' doors as it does for a person to cleanse himself, empty his trash, and start fresh. The virtual world is making its way toward resembling the real world a little more each day, losing its old gleam and ceasing to be a miniature homeland or nation or dream. But why should this not be the case, when the virtual world is run by the same minds that order the real world and mold all of its features?

Finally, it was Rayyan who said the words that formed the entire character of our relationship, after he changed his name on the chat screen to *You-are-stuck-at-the-edges-of-my-eyelashes-but-my-eyes-don't-see-you.*

There isn't anything about what is between us that is real, he said. I am only a wandering electron where you are concerned. Nothing real! I kiss you but I do not taste the wine of your lips that poets are always talking about. I make love to you but I don't know what the silk of your body feels like or the flavor of its milk and honey. I have actually smelled that perfume you wear, *Le premier jour*, but I don't know what its fragrance becomes when it is on your skin. I know now that you have blue pajamas, like the color of the sky, since you've told me so, but I do not know exactly what blue that is, or what sky exactly you have in mind, and precisely at what moment of the day. You say it looks like the sky at Qatif right at this moment, as you write, but I have not seen the sky at Qatif, ever, at any moment. I know Qatif, through you, I know it a little, and you know Riyadh, also a little. But you don't know what Riyadh really is, just as I don't know what Qatif really is. You have my pictures but you would not know my features without a square of glossy paper and a camera flash. You have my voice but you don't know what I sound like when my voice is not traveling through a medium. We have everything, almost—and we have nothing. What piece of me will stay with you when I leave? A lot of words. This is all that is between us. A lot of words. What kind of memory is this, a memory that words manufacture? And my picture, the picture of me, Rayyan, which I want to stay inside of you always, isn't even a picture. It's only a vague composite of an incomplete presence in an unreal world.

These words, which opened a black hole in my heart and did nothing to close it, these words of his seemed the ultimate and final truth with which he illuminated my nights. We are nothing but groups and series of ones and zeros, lined up, and electrified telephone lines with twenty amperes shooting through them. This is Rayyan: a memory of words, tens of words, hundreds of words ... and an image with sham features. I would read his texts over and over, endlessly, trying to extract his soul from them, but it was no use—it was hopeless to try to fill in the gaps this way.

During one of his long absences, and after I had wiped his images from my computer memory, I awoke belatedly to the realization that I did not know his face. I could describe him, sure, and with all the tiny details, but behind this description of mine there was no consistent image on which to rely in my cold and lonely nights. There was only the gelatinous image that I could not pick up with my hands. I realized that what I had been seeing was not actually him, it was only his voice, with its particular ways of speaking and its allusions. I *saw* that voice so clearly, from the *marhaba*˙ that began every one of our conversations, that I could immediately weigh how much salt or sugar his voice carried, depending on his level of emotional fatigue or comfort. It was not Rayyan's face that was fading, because the face itself was never there in the first place; the longer his absence was, the more eroded were the details. His distance made him remote at the same time that his words were many and large.

At a late point in my relationship with Rayyan, and because I was so very sure that there was no longer anything between us that was strong enough to keep us together, nor anything strong enough to

---

*   Hello.

push us apart—our choices seemed equal on both ends—I sent him a message. Xcuse me 4 showing up lk thieves of d night do! Thks 4 everythg. Rayyan, gdbye.

I hated being so stealthy, via the cold screen of a mobile, in a nighttime whose limbs trembled with the savagery of the wind's breaths. I hated it even more that he was more gentle with me than I had been with him, asking me, Do you really want to leave me? Do you want me to help you to get over me? And I hated everything that was happening even more when I found myself answering him with some swagger, I can handle my own business, don't worry. When I am one who never says goodbye because I believe that goodbye is a bullet that pierces the heart suddenly and unnecessarily, right at its center; because I believe that there are gentler ways to not be there; because I believe that there is no justification for leaving mournful elegies in our wake. With Rayyan I had reached a final conviction. I knew I would always leave the door slightly open for his sake if I did not slam it now, close and lock it firmly, and throw the key into the ocean.

The following autumn after we broke up, we were no longer friends, but I understood what it was that I suffered each time I said to him—quoting from somewhere, but I don't know from where—To love is one thing and to fall in love is something else. I am certain that it would be an excellent idea to bring in something here from the song archive of Talal Maddah with the longing in his voice, or from Abbadi with the sadness in his songwriting pen (this is how Rayyan always elaborately describes the two of them). Except, what I would choose to send to him would be the voice of Fairuz which does not know the Najd dialect with its unique accent and vocabulary; nor our vernacular Nabati poetry, which is so different from that of Lebanon; nor the hunting seasons; nor the old-fashioned "house of goat hair," the tents that our people used to live in, that you see now only in special exhibits or commercial shows. Nor the schools where children memorize the Qur'an, nor the crescent moon, nor the *istraahas*˙ that groups of friends rent to spend their free hours, nor Riyadh's famous neighborhood al-Ulya, nor the wide congested streets and narrow morals of Riyadh, which Fairuz does not know and neither do I. I sent him a song by Fairuz: *I remember you whenever the clouds come … your face is a reminder of the autumn … you return to me as the world gets darker … like the breeze that does not moisten lightly* … And I headed my message with a question that was like his wounded voice and his face wiped of features: Still, Rayyan? The song, after all, asks, *Are you still with me?* And I ended it saying, A Shi'i girl who loves you, neighbor.

˙   Lounge.

19

My ability to convey the essence of things—whether objects, events, images, places and odors—almost nil, now. Perhaps it is that my ability to communicate has all but shifted into a particular and unintended sort of lying: that is, I am hopeless at squaring the reality of any object with the transmitted images of it. There is a conspicuous lapse between the two that I do not know how to explain or interpret. It is not that I intend to say the opposite of what things say about themselves, nor to give them an aura any falser than what is already there. But that is how it always ends up; I leave that gap as well as a trail of questions about the true nature of things around me, questions about how well-equipped I am to put the truth of them to examination, or to look beyond their surfaces to their essence and spirit. And that is why often I arrive at each disclosure, each confession, with a single result: a hateful feeling that what I have drawn is an entirely new world, an ambiguous and dark world with no link whatsoever to the world that I intended originally to pass on through my mind and words.

Umar justifies this to me by saying that I am trying to preserve my image of the world for myself, so that it will go on being a complete image that nothing disfigures and that no one else can imprint with his own traces. I know in myself that his justification is not an accurate one; I know that I am the one who is not allowing the world to pass across her. Every passageway is low ground, a heavy step, and my heavy steps across low ground give me no pleasure.

I can regret, too, that as a person who will not talk about things except as a strategy to forget them, I was allowing my experiences to stay alive, if not in my memory, then in another's memory, Umar's memory, where I had extended the threads of all of those happenings that had left me so fatigued and upset. Where his mind could spin them into something more substantial.

Now, I told him the secrets—the only secrets whose doors I had closed to Umar, who was the only one, with the lightness of his being, to open them. I relived the secrets as I told them, chattering on and on wildly, unsure of whether I could really enable Umar to understand what happened, as it was not a question only of his knowledge of the events. And I was uncertain of whether I could forget them. The attempt absolves us of the failure, anyway, I said to myself.

I made a final point and came to a stop. Umar had said nothing the entire time except little mumbled exclamations that meant he was following my words, plus some questions and comments, just a few, to urge me on. He had made me halt for two seconds as soon as it was somewhat clear where my endless chatter was headed.

I'll listen to you til the end, he said, but do try to be economical with the physical details.

That's exactly what I mean to do.

He apologized for being such a lout, as he put it, and explained that it was just not a comfortable thing for his mind to play house to any fantasies about a physical relationship where I was one of the parties involved. It was like imagining your parents in bed, or like seeing the mark of a kiss on his sister's neck.

I finished saying what I had to say. As I wrapped it up, I was already worried about having to handle a moment of silence that neither of us would be adept at breaking. So I said, with an enthusiasm that

I hoped concealed my apprehensions, So, what do you think? Say something!

Do I have to?

Of course you do!

I can't stand how neutral you are when you talk about all of this.

How neutral I am?

You cannot possibly be neutral and speak with such an unemotional voice when you're one of the people directly involved. You shouldn't do that. It's not right.

It is not right either to get so tangled up in it that my eyes are blinded and I can't see the truth of what's going on.

Your eyes are wet, come on. You won't convince me otherwise.

And here I am trying to stay dry. Dry and detached.

Do you love Dai?

I am not a lesbian. So don't ask me that in such a tone of voice!

Do you hate her?

No, never!

And Dai—does she love you?

I don't think so.

Why do you insist on denying the act of love?

What's the use of it? With love or without it, we got to the same place.

Do you know what your problem is?

Tell me.

You have a kind of belief in yourself that pushes you to reject what everyone else says and does.

I believe in you.

I am your exception, and exceptions do not break the rule.

You know what? Not long ago, when I was talking to Sundus, I told her that I can't seem to hold on to anything. Friends slip through my fingers like water. Writing stops being a gift granted as compensation against my madness. And the walls of my room are closing in. Everything, Sundus says in answer to me, everything is untrue and invalid except God. She said that everything I do for any reason other than pleasing God's countenance will rebound against me. I think that is silly. God doesn't play chess with our lives according to some pre-arranged set of rules telling us to either play every move in a way that accords with what He knows is good for us, or else He will spoil our game.

Her beliefs are of the sort that give her certainty that God is a fixed and unchanging part of everything's equation, like the side of a triangle that never gets longer or shorter. Don't deny Sundus her beliefs.

Well, I could say, then, that God chose the path my fate would take, and it is not fair that I have to bear the consequences on my own.

But it is an argument that goes against your beliefs, you know that.

Do you think God will be merciful with me?

I am very sure that God is much better than what we hear of Him. A whole lot finer.

Even if I don't see what happened as sinful?

You should ask Him before you ask me.

So I would have to wait for a deferred response.

A final response.

You haven't told me yet. How do you see me?

Nothing at all has changed.

Nobody comes, nothing happens.

Samuel Beckett, *Waiting for Godot*

20

My body betrays me. It hurts—the unfaithfulness of a body that has always been neutral, even in the worst of its histories with me. It has been so balanced that I do not recall even one day when I carried it and found that it weighed me down, nor do I remember a time when I stripped it off and cast it away only to stumble over it. For so long it was silent; when my chattering was at its noisiest, my body just nodded its head to show that it understood. For so long, it was in harmony, perfectly balanced, between hunger and fullness, between a warm embrace and the frost of aversion. For so long I took it at its word, because that is the way it was. It was good to me, and it treated me fairly.

My body pains me, the kind of pain that Panadol pills do not take away, an ache that does not disappear when I try to ignore it. Pain that is like heaviness, as if I am pushing forward with difficulty across a terrain of mud and green creatures that stick to me, pain that urges me to abandon the whole idea of life altogether; a deceptive and complex pain. My head is a bullet hole around which voices buzz and the wind whips. Pain gallops through my head like wild horses. It is a pain that takes up all the space inside of me when it is here, and when it ebbs, the receding tide swallows whole my little pearl oyster shells, my sailors' boats, their fishes and their fishing nets.

When I turned to face my bedside table, I laughed. I howled as though I had lost my ability to do anything but laugh. I don't recall laughing like this, ever, except just before going into the operation room a few years ago, when I shattered my arm and it had to be set with a metal bolt so that the calcium would thicken and harden anew. I was in a huge, cold room, intensely white, with lights that were even whiter, and a lot of white coats constantly going by, their hands jerking back the curtains and then pulling them shut again repetitively, but not routinely enough to be comforting. The thought that came to me was that my shroud might not be as white as this room, and I laughed, as if someone was tickling me and would not stop. I laughed. And now, I was reading on my pillbox, in red, *400*, and I was laughing.

The bridge of confidence between me and my illness had collapsed since the scandalous seizure I had had in Hall 24 of Building No. 1. I could not get out of my head the terror on my classmates' faces, and the curiosity and sympathy that I saw there, too. My illness was kind enough to leave me some breathing room the rest of the year, during which I didn't have any convulsions worth the name. But the confidence I had had was no more than the translucent negative of a snapshot. I could not glean much substance from that, no more than a single image to keep me going. So it was very difficult to get that flimsy confidence of mine back. Confidence is a one-time thing. When we shatter it, only a miracle allows us to regain it, and for my part, I was not expecting or awaiting any miracle. I was not yet at the point of relying on that!

It was a burning hot summer, and no moisture had yet rained down to split open the roofs of the houses and break the heat on the first of June. I received my graduation certificate. The lady who gave it to me took my university ID, cut it in half, and threw it in a large faded container with other half IDs, lots of them, names and majors and university branches and classes all mixed together. She tossed it in there with no concern about what it meant, and then she gave me the document, smiled, and said, Congratulations.

I left the library where I had picked it up, my throat congealing into a lump of sorrow, and its tightness pushing that lump toward my breathing passages. I went outside and sat down on a wood bench. Salma waved at me. The time had come to act happy and pass on my good wishes. Praise God, who had restored her finally to His grace, Salma said. I said to myself, If only He had not! What is forgiveness, restoration to divine grace? It is nothing but a creepy discharge from life. What will I do now? Where will I spend my days, when there are no places where I can profitably use them, and when the days are no longer precious things to be hoarded?

I applied to volunteer at the nursery school attached to the charity association as a college graduate, though I knew that what they were looking for was high school graduates. I also presented myself as someone who had been on close terms with volunteer work for several years. My acceptance was guaranteed, though I expected to be taking on office work, not twenty-four children who would nourish my desire for motherhood. And with me came the presence of my illness, a presence that made a real difference. No heaven kept its tyranny over me at bay.

I loved my twenty-four children. I loved them each individually, even though I am a person whose memory has a lot of unpleasant collisions with people's names and who comes up with responses that are always wrong. By the end of the first week I had all of their names memorized. I was put to the test—and I passed it—when I convinced Manaaf to stop using his teeth as a fingernail clipper, and Walaya to stop using her fingernails as weapons of both defense and offense, and Ali to stop using his wicked tongue as a sharp whip, and Iilaaf to stop giving other children her most stinging lashes. The children displayed an endless succession of bad behaviors that triggered more. For the sake of stopping them, I was forced into bribery, looking the other way, and all of the familiar reserve strategies, like putting on a tape. With the children, I believed I was secure, that a part of me had been created for a role like this, an existence like this, an effort like this. Those children helped me to achieve some equilibrium. I strengthened myself through them, and I counted on them to change my mood and re-orient the path of my day in a better direction. I depended on them to create a better person out of me, outside the criteria that people—or angels—apply.

Their reactions to life astonished me. Their little details, the way they closed their eyes, the way they moved their fingers, the particular look that came over their faces when they were trying to get me to understand their need to use the bathroom—it all astonished me. The racket they made at breakfast time arrested me, as did the way their faces screwed up uncomfortably when they drank juice. Daily story time amazed me. They would pile themselves up on the floor, surrounding me from every angle, and try to guess the events of my story, try to touch the storybook. The room filled with their colors, crooked lines and the latticework on the plant arbors. When we finished telling the story they would sketch out the scenes that had pleased them the most. It amazed me when one of them would clap for himself because he knew the correct answer. When I forgot the tin of sweets, I soon saw how displeasure gathered in their eyes and disgust puckered their mouths. They were my little paradise, a heaven that every day concealed a greater surprise for the next.

They made me, the night owl, into a person who drank the morning in from its earliest dawn. Daily, I would wake up with the dawn call to prayer, bathe, dress, listen to my mother's morning bits of news as we waited for the bus to the nursery, which came at 6:30. It would honk for me and I would come out of the house, ascending two steps with my hand—soon enough to be grasped by little Hawraa—on the metal railing. The minute I took a seat in the next to last row, Yusuf would cling to my jean skirt—always a jean skirt—and yank it—he would always yank it.

But this time that seemed like it would never end was doomed to come to a close. My illness, which had been playing games with me from a distance, was no longer content to peek at me from behind the door or through the window shutters. It had to declare itself, to show up with definite and final demands. It was not a question of the size of the damaged pit in my brain, which was not growing. For me, the important issue about the absence or presence of my illness was how often I got seizures and how bad they were. That was a message I could not ignore. My disease was announcing that it was here to stay. I had to begin taking appropriate measures.

Was my leaving the nursery a precautionary measure? God alone knows. The only thing I know and am certain of is that I could not gamble on the consequences of something as frightening as this for my twenty-four children. Life would terrorize them enough as it was, and I had no right to load their tender hearts with anything more. I submitted a rather misleading excuse to Najat, our director, known as Umm Hashim. My excuse was that I was going to apply for an MA program at King Saud University, and that meant I would have to study English intensively for the TOEFL exam. I was not lying, but I was seeking an excuse. Results were never confirmed until months after the exam, and my English was not so poor that I would have to devote all of my time to it if I took the test. At the end of the academic year, acceptances to the program would be posted without our having to have already passed the TOEFL. My name was not on the list.

Umm Hashim responded to me with her usual kindness, restricting herself to asking whether I would stay until the end of the school year so that my children would not face the disruption of a new teacher. She was holding back the stream of my excuses, meaning to spare me having to justify myself. Just beneath the surface of her sweet, light face, compassion hovered, mingling with affection. It was the same look of concern that I saw in the faces of the other teachers and the women on the cleaning staff.

I knew that talk would fly around fast. My seizures would soon become the stuff of whispered gossip. My spells had been coming insistently, surprising me at any time of day, in the bathroom, in the teachers' room, and even in the one meeting of the association's women's committee that I attended. Sometimes, the seizure was so light that I barely felt it. It appeared in the guise of a lump in the throat, a light choking sensation, or a cold little slap of breeze. It would inject my eyes with tears and my throat with saliva. Sometimes it would repeat itself, with a clear border marking off the waning of one seizure from the beginning of another. And sometimes, it was so violent and intense that it would put me into a faint and wipe my memory. I had not had memory lapse problems before. This new element frightened me. It scared me not to know what had just happened. It frightened me that I had no idea of how I came to be where I was, to have blankness in my mind around the details.

I finished the school term with a little farewell party, the crying of Yasmine, which left a spot on my jean skirt, and little gifts: a Pooh-shaped eraser, an old issue of the children's magazine *Maajid*, a hair tie, sugarless gum.

I called Muhammad from my room.

I'm really tired.

Do you want to go to the hospital?

I took an extra pill. Or two.

Don't close your phone. Get up right now and open the door.

I got up, but it was difficult. I was able to estimate distances. More than once, I sensed that I was about to bump into the wall. I felt as though the floor was opening under my feet and swallowing my steps. I constantly had to repeat to myself what I was about to do so that I would not lose myself halfway and forget. I had to fiddle with the key several times to be able to open the door. I came back into the room with my vision blurry and the fogginess of the encroaching illness stealing my senses. I picked up the receiver and before I said anything, Muhammad said, Just wait a little and mother will be there.

He told me to keep talking to him. I think I raved plenty, my words broken, unlinked sentences without meaning.

Finally, a prime opportunity for my mother to care for me had come. My seizures could keep coming in quick succession for however long my damaged brain wished as long as my mother would be there to help in the end. She would keep feeding those ropes of conversation to me, the cords that had broken between us. As long as she would stop looking at me as if I were not even there, and busying herself with any old trivial thing whenever we happened to be together, and talking, waking, and feeding me by means of the maid, Edna!

Then, I could tell that the level of whispers and furtive talk with which I always lived had become unusually high. The repeated visits from Fatima stirred my suspicions. Every time I went in to where mother and Fatima were, they stopped their whispering abruptly and immediately made up some new topic of conversation that they stuck to until I went out of the room. I knew that there was something going on. My mother said, Your aunt is going to visit us on Thursday. Her sister. I said to myself, My aunt visits us every day, so what is new?

And the girls, your cousins, my mother added. Uff! I completed the thought for my own benefit. Another family gathering to kill off boredom.

And don't come up with excuses to be away, as you usually do, she said. For shame!

Of course. For shame! Shame! Shame!

That night I did not sleep. Hamza getting engaged to me! They must be joking. Why would he ask to engage himself to me? All I am is a sick and defective girl. I am a girl who cannot get along with the world nor even come to terms with the expectations she is supposed to have as a reasonable and well trained daughter, but who is every bit as incapable of throwing herself under the wheels of a train, because she is so afraid that it might miss her. All I am is the girl whom writing and hours on the net and the company of young men there have corrupted and ruined. That is the way my aunt sees it, and she has managed to get my mother to see it that way, as well. My aunt would always set strict limits on how much her daughters could mix with me, so that the rotten apple wouldn't spoil the crop.

Moreover, in combination with *him*, I am nothing more than a collection of bad genes, I thought to myself. What was in his mind? Was he thinking that we would hatch damaged children who would spend their lives moving between hospital rooms? Or maybe he was thinking that God would spare them the curse of our blood? And then what if we did marry, and in an intimate moment he saw me clinging to his nakedness, my longings overpowering me, and suddenly, I would be nothing more than *a woman*, a body erupting with passion, a being of deficient understanding!

What if we got married and I had a child, or more than one? How would I bathe it without being afraid, how would I hold it and carry it down the stairs and not be afraid, how would I give it my breast when my seizures will not stop coming? How would I put it to my chest and comfort it so that it would sleep? How, when this body was not ruled by my will in any condition? If this is a joke, I do not understand what is funny about it, and if they are serious, then I am almost certain that I am the only sane and rational one among them all.

My aunt, who would present her son to me with obvious benevolence, as if she were sacrificing him, and my mother, who believed that she would achieve her goal in life by guaranteeing me eternal happiness with Hamza, agreed on one matter. They agreed that I would agree to this. Indeed, I had no reason to refuse. The two of them had spent days planning out our life, where we would live, the hall in which we would get married, and the timing of everything, all the way to the names of our children, how many there would be and the spacing of each. That is why it would be truly hard on my mother to believe that I would say—and in such a loud voice—No!

Perhaps I really do give my illness an opening to stop my life cold. But that is because I figure this is the only way that I can get the better of it. I will not allow it to continue through my children or because of them. I do not want to be a transit lounge for this disease, nor to live my mother's life all over again. After every spell that electrifies my body, she is powerless to make anything happen that would absolve her of her sin, just as she was powerless faced with the death of Hassan. I am grateful to God for this lovely chance, but I am not kicking His grace in the face if I say no. In other circumstances, perhaps I would have considered Hamza one of the best opportunities to come my way; he would be a good companion for a life, a whole life. But I live here, suspended in this body of mine, with its limited possibilities, and I cannot gamble with future lives for the sake of my life here and now.

As soon as I heard my mother's steps on the staircase I turned toward the wall. I did not have it in me to bear up under her sorrow. She came and pressed herself against my back and began to stroke my hair, weeping over her powerlessness and her weakness. With every seizure—these seizures that seemed to reoccur at fixed and regular intervals—I would feel the convulsions of my body stripping me naked. It was a nakedness that left me powerless to cover myself, a nakedness that meant there was no point in pulling the cover up and over me or clutching my clothes tightly. It was the nakedness of exposure, need, and weakness. I heard her sobbing but it was hard to make myself feel it, for my seizure enveloped me in a stifling sheath and took me to a place of total isolation. It took me far away.

I was empty, and among the things that had left me was my desire to stop the seizure. I was reaching the moment where everything was absolutely like everything else, since my head was vacant and my spirit was quenched completely. I was so weary that I let the thread of saliva stream across the pillow. My mother's sobbing, growing louder, and the rattlings in my throat, sang their parts in turn, like a chorus, and I was seeing myself from the inside, and hearing myself from the inside, and my temples were throbbing inside the walls of my chest and echoing back, and the echoes were spreading to the deepest recesses of me. Every seizure settled deeper inside of me, leaving more residue.

Muhammad, who could transform any event into gripping entertainment, inventing jokes from it and making me laugh, was hiding his worry under an artificial calm. He asked me rapid-fire questions the whole way there. When had I eaten? When did I wake up? What time did I go to sleep? What did I do today? All in an effort to keep me with him, but my drowsy state kept me from responding beyond a few unconnected words. The letters I did try to enunciate would drown in the saliva of my seizure, and that was enough to distort my few words beyond intelligibility. My head was very heavy and my sleepy state pushed me to hallucinations. Sometimes I was trying to answer questions that had already been superseded by other questions, and sometimes I was answering the same question twice in a row. When I could not speak because the words only gurgled in my mouth, or when I stayed still, quiet without a sound or a rustle because I was so fatigued, he would put his hand out to me and say, Squeeze my hand. Out of weakness or pride, I did not much give him my hand.

For so long I had been sure that I—rather, I and my illness—were standing on the rim of a dangerous precipice, and if we fell we would fall together. I believed that the impact our crash made would resound in my ears for a very long time. I would know then, and for certain, that we had indeed fallen. What happened, though, was that when we fell, my senses and the cracking sound of my bones lied to me. What happened is that I exchanged that gigantic blackness swallowing me at the opening of the precipice for mere everyday darkness, which I handled by saying nothing and claiming that nothing had happened, while in fact this descent was burying me alive little by little. We had really fallen, and my new belief was that every fall concealed behind it another drop that was even worse, that would take me down a steeper incline and further into the abyss. I knew I was threatened with more.

When I was in the sixth grade, aged eleven, the first signs of my illness came in the form of light, uncomplicated spasms attacking me as I slept, giving me a bout of fright or a nightmare, some tremblings and a choking sensation, and then I would wake up bewildered. My mother carries the disease in her genes, so she had always been immediately suspicious of anything at all that afflicted us, no matter how short-lived. We would not let her watch any medical program, because that would mean a new name, a new disease, to add to her already rich vocabulary, as well as another round of anxious suspicion about every passing cold that would inhabit our bodies. When my mother saw those nighttime seizures, she willed herself to believe that I did not suffer from any diseases. It was not possible for her cute, sweet little girl to really be sick. But after three years of it, seeing the way I would shake uncontrollably in the middle of a seizure, she could no longer deny it. The results of the EEG were enough to prove it.

I remember her face, when she was sitting in front of me as I was undergoing X-rays. I could see her face in a little mirror opposite me, as I was encased in that huge disk, an enormous white coffin. She was moving her lips with verses from the Qur'an and was all but crying. I remember how she questioned the doctor fiercely as he wrote out a prescription and said that if I stuck to the medication it was very possible that we could control the seizures and stop the disease from progressing any further. She was arguing with him about entrapping my blood with tranquilizers and turning me into a girl from whom all life had drained. Meanwhile I was laughing. Epilepsy. The doctors are really something, coming up with names for sicknesses that sound so hilarious when you repeat them.

My mother believed that the sum of all the changes she was making would lessen the possibility that any of this would hurt me. She bought me a new bed with really low sides and corners, and no bedposts, and she populated it with a whole tribe of pillows. She covered the floor of my room with a fine blanket, since during my seizures I often fell out of bed. Whenever I fell, she would question me about my head. Whenever I was about to go in for another examination, she would be terrified at the thought that they might find a tumor in my brain, even though those falls of mine did not even bruise any bones. I had to stick to a few rules: I was not allowed to have a bath in the bathtub, or cross the main street by myself, or lock the door to my room. Some of her rules were illogical, and some of them I didn't bother to carry out.

We did not have any fights over my disease until I graduated from high school and decided to apply to King Saud University. If my mother did not feel confident about what my disease might do and what it might mean for us when I was with her, how could she feel comfortable if I were so far away! I found myself explaining and talking and coming up with lots to say with the aim of confronting her fear and apprehension. I asked her not to put obstacles in my way, to let me run my life as I wanted to. But she deserted me. And so, for four years I studied a stupid trivial subject in a stupid college, with no opportunities to achieve anything with my diploma. I studied because that was what I had to do. And I succeeded and passed because that was what everyone did.

I knew that the moment my feet stepped through the hospital

doors, my seizures would stop—seizures that had gone on relentlessly for some ten hours or more with no more than five minutes separating each one from the next. I knew exactly what would be said to me. It is one seizure, they would say, one continuing seizure! Sure, I know! And I don't want anyone to remind me. I only want them to take my body and try it out for just one day. For three or four seizures. Then I will leave them the freedom to choose their terms and descriptions and names and cold drivel.

The seizures really did stop. The on-duty doctor came. Before she began talking, I was all set to address her aggressively, hostilely—the one tool I possessed by which I might defend my own body, in light of the feeling of violation and the sense that any space of my privacy had disappeared. She asked me what was wrong, and I said, I took one pill more than the max dose. As soon as I said it, Muhammad was on the point of jumping in with *maybe two pills* but he sidestepped when I gave him a couple of really angry looks. Answering her, I prepared a logically connected equivalence: my usual dose of Tegretol, the orange pill, as my mother calls it, is 200 mg. I used to take two pills every day, but my doctor combined the dosage into one pill, and I forgot. My seizure didn't stop, so I thought that taking extra pills would improve things a little. The maximum dose was eight of the old 200 mg pills, or 1,600 mg, and since I took five pills each of 400 mg, that meant I had taken 2,000 mg.

I used up every last bit of my energy presenting her with this detailed explanation. Her response stunned me with cold suspicion: But since getting here, you haven't had any seizures at all! The questions that followed confirmed my misgivings. She asked, Had I had a fight with anyone? Did I have any family problems or pressures at home? Was this the first time I had taken more than the usual dose? Had I played around with any other medications? Was I seeing a psychiatrist? From time to time she would check my answers with Muhammad, talking to him in English as if I were a stupid girl who would not understand, and as if her expressions did not reveal clearly, even to a blind person, what she meant. I locked down my mouth, biting on my lips to keep my anger inside, until I found myself exploding at her doggedness. Write in your report that it is a failed suicide attempt! I don't care!

She resumed examining me in silence, an atmosphere of tension closing in on us. I hated specifically the hammer that they used on my legs, the soles of my feet, and my elbows to check my nerve responses. And I hated it when the doctor asked me in the first examination whether my seizure made me urinate uncontrollably. As much as I hated it, I had to let my leg react, and I had to answer no. A firm no, but a very faint one. The nurse ordered a blood sample. She called Muhammad over and told him it was necessary to wait for the results of the blood test to be sure. The whole thing was more than a matter of one night's observation in the hospital, she hinted, even if the overdose was small and the passage of a few hours since taking it had allowed my body to get rid of it, most likely without any permanent damage.

The whiteness here is unbearable! I clung to Muhammad's hands, saying, Don't leave me! Please. I will die if you leave me alone, don't leave me! The first thing he would do tomorrow would be to come to me, he said, and he promised me things as if I were a little child—a box of Mackintosh chocolates, Baskin-Robbins ice cream. All that was lacking was a doll with blonde hair who would sing *The fox is gone away ... he circled round seven times today*. Muhammad thinks that being born first gave him precedence—which should have meant he would be the one to receive the defective cells that sit in my brain, and the unfaithful blood of Hassan that would not clot. Like my mother, he carries guilty feelings about not getting sick instead of us, which would have allowed him to settle all the family debts at once, by means of one person.

The whiteness here is unbearable! But I give in to Muhammad's will, and I put on a white shirt that is barely there, and I lie down in the bed with white sheets, in a room whose walls are white, whose curtains are white, whose doors are white. Everything here is white with a sharpness that makes you dizzy, and brings fear and dark nightmares. How can a whiteness like this be anything other than death, that whiteness in which we shroud our dear departed? In one of these white rooms, Hassan grew two wings and flew away, no longer weighed down by his blood, no longer under the control of his body. He was released, a luminous spirit. On that day, a shooting star fell and wounded my eyes—the shooting star of a short life. I missed distancing it from my vision with the shade of my hand, just as I missed the chance to charge it with a wish, as if it were Hassan, as if he would return, a star to hold suspended in the skies, from a long thread whose end would be in God's hand.

My mother says, The good folks—they are the ones the world does not want! My mother is always smart about inventing philosophies that convince her of God's perennial justice in anything involving her. She does not run down His judgment, does not speak disparagingly of the trials He visits upon us, never blasphemed him, not even once in her whole life. It is He (as I convince myself) who will bring Paradise to her, as the Qur'an says. For those who earn Paradise on that day, says God's Holy Word, will find a better abode, and a fine place of repose.

I am not a good enough person for the world not to want me, but I am weary enough to want my death. I would embrace death, if Death were anything like Joe Black. Maybe Death is really like the guy in *Meet Joe Black*, handsome and tall, and fond of the creamy inside of peanuts. I will not bargain with Death to obtain a few days more, and if he wishes to divide with me whatever part of my life is left, I will give him all of it. I am ready to believe any legend that will lead me into an easy death. Like the ancient Babylonians, I will have coins placed on my closed eyes, coins to consume my sins and return me to the whiteness of my purity. I will believe in the boatman of the underworld, who guarantees me a safe passage to the Bank of Death. I long for death, but I fear the look of the world over there. I am afraid to knock on the door and find no one there to open it. I am afraid to go on, after the door locks behind me, and find that there is nothing but darkness and loneliness and many people entering whose faces I do not know, and a time without end. I want Death to be a little bit nice to me, to take me without hurting me, to take me gently and lightly, to take me without stuffing me into a space smaller than my body, to take me with my filth and black spots and the mire in my soul, to take me and raise me on his wings, to lift me outside and above my body, above the world, above, where God is. I want to say goodbye to my body, but without death I will never be able to leave it.

I add the twenty-seventh star to the calendar of my nights in white rooms, but I am still not used to this. The odor of cleanliness here is loathsome. All alike in their dull stupid looks, the faces inspire sarcasm. It is exactly the way things always are, and always have been, on most of these white nights of mine, ever since I was old enough to know where I was. I have spent most of them singing, as swans do before they go away, the singing that I saw in Hassan's eyes during his final illness, and then I knew he would be fine. He would get well as he had promised me, and he would no longer be exhausted by his body, and the failures of his blood. His promise was made good. He was cured in the only way he could manage. Death. I have spent this night humming and murmuring an old song by Fairuz. I can only remember a whole line from it with difficulty. If only its sound, if only her voice, which lives in my memory, would not sting me so, as it goes round goes round goes round ... something about a big girl in a big world and absence no longer frightens her but she will be afflicted there's no doubt about it with sad longing.

The whiteness here is unbearable! My own room tonight must feel the loneliness like I do. My phone cries and no one hugs it; my little things scream, trying to get someone to pay attention, but nobody gives them even a passing glance. I am alone except for the songs, in the isolation of my light weeping. The lights from the window pound in my eyes, and the silly movements of the nurse around me or in me, every hour, keep me from going to sleep, and anyway I cannot go to sleep in a strange room.

At five o'clock the next evening I left the sinister whiteness. Every added hour I spent there meant someone else getting the news in all of its details, and extracting whatever seemed useful, putting the proper expression on his face, and putting on some old stinking clothes and coming to the white room bearing a prayer. But they were prayers that these people did not really intend to send upward, and so they sat heavily and painfully on my soul. Walking away, my visitors sliced off parts of my soul carelessly. If the white room had a door, I slammed it shut, time after time, declaring, I did not want to see anyone! And a virtual window whose luster was extinguished by the red writing bore the word *overdose*.

21

Taking Stock: My Year[*]

... a single reason[†] gives me justification for plunging into a balance sheet of this year, which is almost over; only one reason but, it appears to me, a very important one: I have the feeling, without any proof to confirm my intuition, that each of my coming years will be an exact copy of the one before, with a few small made-up details on the margins that will not require or attract much attention. Thus, the reason for taking stock of this year is so that I will know for sure that I lived it. It is true that I will not forget the grand turns it took, but I am not positive that there are rooms in my memory to house this year with proper hospitality. I want to convince myself that I lived it in the best possible way without feeling any regret that I let pass by some different possibilities according to which I might have lived it.

A few hours separate me from the end of the last day in my twenty-second year. I have no intention of transforming this stock-taking into a long-winded elegy. I know how much we tend to recall things in an idealized way, simply because the fact of their endings makes us more gracious toward them, to classify them under the

---

[*] You are supposed to read this in the Internet club a few hours from now. Leave the icons however they happen to be, and read it in light of them. I know that you know that I do not like the Hotmail icons.

[†] The truth is that I became aware of that when you asked me: What happened in this year of yours? And what changed in you?

forceful admonition, "Remember the merits of your dead." Or the opposite, since we do examine the scratched-out side of the tablet. I will try not to fall into that trap.

The first impression I can cull from this year is that things were not great. Things were not warm to me, in response to my having ignored them. I will not start by complaining, for I do respect the complexity of those things' position. Many things happened to me, and many things struck me—poems, songs, beginnings of musical phrases, beginnings germinating inside of me, and my two fish, Yaza and Nala, with their gold and orange hues. But they all faded quickly, and no traces remained. Everything leaves me before I can close my fingers around its shadow. Swiftly, the songs would depart, exhausted by being sung and heard so constantly, and the poems became banal, the poems themselves no longer felt any joyful surprise at life, and one certain day both of my two little fishes were floating on the water's surface, even though I had not skimped on changing their water and feeding them once a day.

The prevailing characteristic of this year is that I was busy. Very little time and many postponed projects. I got my tasks done at the last possible moment: my final paper for graduating, studying for my final exams, picking up my diploma, applying for the job, and then leaving it. My pace this year was accelerated and I moved to a loud beat, so that when I finally stopped I no longer knew how people spend their days when they do stop!

I added only two kilograms to my balance sheet this year—and the credit for them goes to bags of m&ms and long hours on the Internet—and I lost them in the second half of the year with my disturbed sleep patterns and sharp mood, in addition to not having partners to share the dining table with me at two o'clock in the morning, eating two fried eggs with cheese and a round of bread. Most of my losses yielded to the same reasons: a bad mood and a messed up sleep schedule, plus missed conversations left on the screen of my cell phone and angry friends.

But overall, my relationship with sleep this year was pretty good. Waking, also, was fine, accompanied by a less sharp mood and the heightened possibility of hearing three particular words and seeing half a smile before brushing my teeth. I finally did away with the ticking of the alarm clock, since I did not have any important appointments that required my waking up at specific times. The new thing was that my dreams seemed attached to my eyelids with steel forceps whenever I slept, and they remained fixed there until after I had awoken. For a person who has never remembered dreams, it is not comfortable to acquire this new habit of remembering them.

I still have my old doggedness about every no I have said and my hesitation before every yes. I all but leave those *yeses* silent. Sometimes. This year I believed that I was living according to a plan I did not understand, and so I would end up with more spontaneity, and absurdity, more isolation, and fear, more likelihood of dedicating myself to desires that my personal shortcomings would not allow me to transform into reality. I was more compliant this year, sometimes going beyond what I was expected to do, and I turned into a wall for others' graffiti. There were many unintelligible writings, and others that were good, and some sculptures. And likewise there was some foul graffiti and offensive words.

I do not want to make excuses for what I was, nor for what I was not. I grew up a lot this year. I grew up more than three hundred sixty-five days' worth. I accommodated my fragilities and achieved some balance with my failures. I came to terms completely with my receptivity to defeat and my propensity for setbacks. I came out of it in a way different than I went into it. I am no longer concerned with counting up my nose dives or lying in wait for my losses or beheading the scarecrows in the fields of my fear. I no longer have any desire for immediate gains or enjoying the limelight or making new friends.

There is no almanac whose days I would study, no miracles to fortify my certainty, no anticipated victories to include among my winnings. I grew up, like other people grow up. And—even if this comes in the category of belated confessions—this was the year of my weakness, the year of a devastated harvest, the year of ruin and a wrecked soul, and the tetanus that eats at the edges of the heart.

It was the year of the one and only one error, and the open curtains, and the few quarrels with Mama. The year of navy blue, of irrefutable books, of the printer's screech. The year of Herbal Essences shampoo, ads for CloseUp toothpaste, Galaxy chocolate. The year of the Internet, deservedly—MSN chat windows and all of the imaginary users with their imaginary names. The year of French fried potatoes, cans of green beans, sandwich crumbs wedged down between the keys on the keyboard. The year of evil desires and lack of resolve, of a total inability to make my mind up about anything, and wrong hypotheses. Right now, the hypothesis that I am putting to the test is the following: If I was able to reserve myself a preferential seat in a doubtful year like 1400, it will not be impossible for me to reserve an even better seat, with a comfortable cushion and footrest, in every year to follow.

This year I loved Grenouille a lot, so much that I did not find his crimes scandalous at all. The only crime that left me raging was his death, arranged with the lowest imaginable level of savagery. I mean the kind of savagery that the death of a *lord* deserves, and not a simple savagery of dogfights and cleavers, even though I understood why Patrick Süskind wanted to grant Grenouille less glory and a death that would not make him into a legend. I loved Kundera. I would not forgive him at all if he had chosen to not limit the forlornness of this world with his lightness that is unbearable. I loved especially his surpassing ability to introduce the world to me, and to push me to put my questions—every one of them—on the table. I loved

Nietzsche because of the one and only line of his that I've ever come across, that to bear double pain is easier than bearing a lone pain.

I loved the crying of a little boy, a long and silent crying because he was so overwhelmed by the wide gap between his imagining of the world and the truth of it in *Almost Famous*, and I loved when they all sang "Tiny Dancer." I loved Michael Nyman's brilliance and his earthy soul in the music to *Gattaca*. I loved Tom Cruise in *Vanilla Sky*, even though everyone I talked to about it badmouthed the film and insulted him. I loved him in *Magnolia*, and I loved the intersecting lines of the film, and his genius in convincing me that he was not coming out of a screen but rather out of houses and streets and bars, coming from the backdrops of real places and their vestibules, and from the eyes of those who lived in the film and their tired hearts. I loved the man who said, *I have a lot of love, and I don't have anyone to give this love to.* I loved him and I hated the rain of frogs at the end of the film. I loved Westlife for their song "Soledad," about the singer's absence and the streets that were empty without her, and the feeling that those whom we miss are a loss hard to replace. I loved them too when they sang "My Love," which goes, "where the skies are blue ... where the fields are green, to see you again."

I had a friend,* what a friend, an unconditional friend, a friend for the difficult times and the dreariness at the end of the night, and urgent calls. A friend for playing XO, and erasing from my mind the poems that upset me because they were so sad, and going broke before half the month was over. A friend for deterring ambiguous questions, subjugating time, and flinging insults back and forth. A friend for sharing insomnia and complaining and exchanging the last page of the newspaper with the sports section. A friend who does not stop being lovely no matter how hurtful I am, how vulgar, how bad-natured. A friend who points to vague places in the distance and

---

* There is no need for me to tell *you* who it is, right?

says, One day we will be there, my friend. A friend who generally nods his head these days, and thinks about how it is that I am impelled by gratitude and the way writers exaggerate to make a hero of him. That is what he is, *wAllahi*, that is what he is, by God.

What do I hope for this year?

To answer this question I have to digress and talk about the song I was addicted to this year. Maybe most people don't listen to country music; there is no harm in passing on a bit of information about "I Hope You Dance." It is sung by a good-looking woman named Lee Ann Womack. If the links were not down, I would have sent it to you. The song talks about keeping a sense of wonder, and not taking things for granted, and it expresses the hope that there are always doors opening for every door that shuts. We should not let love go out in our souls, nor keep faith from having a fighting chance to prove again how important it is for us to hold fast to it. Here is the song's refrain (I remember it well):

And when you get the choice to sit it out or dance
I hope you dance
I hope you dance.

What do I hope for this year?

I can toss out some easy hopes: that I will learn French, travel to Italy, find some Andumi brand pasta so that I do not die of hunger. But my true hopes are four: I hope that my fear does not remain a rock of Sisyphus that I bear, with one feebleness of mine atop another, so that it destroys me. I hope that my passion for life does not melt away, nor my love of experience with all of the enormous costs it brings. I hope that I am not included on the list of poor miserable wretches, defeated people who are more numerous than the earth's expanse is broad. I hope I do not commit the sin of death. With the exception of that, I can deal with death, cleverly or stupidly, according to whatever circumstances require, although I cannot manipulate the great fates which I do not comprehend, whose free flow I have no power to redirect, and whose passage I cannot deter.

My overwhelming desire right now is to dance. I hope I go on dancing.

22

I often cling tightly to the idea that tomorrow will be better than today, no matter what this day held. And even though I have met with many failures and disappointments, when the features of my tomorrow are not different, I still hold fast to the one certainty that I possess. Despite my being the only one who can govern the details of my day, I do not know how days are crafted. How are they kneaded? How are they baked? How do you prepare that spoonful of yeast?

All of my days pass by this way station: my daily venture from home just before the late-afternoon prayer. Whenever the emptiness and boredom of my life overwhelm me, the streets are my only escape. Every day the streets carry different smells, different children playing different games, women's voices I have not heard before, and birds lighting up the horizons with singing the more the day darkens. Although I am not in need of regaining my old longings or my tenderness, I have found myself walking in the very streets that Dai took me to in the winter before last, and I head for the same promenade, passing opposite the window of her room without giving it a look.

Today I left home earlier than usual, and without any advance planning I was standing there in front of the door to her home, my finger pressing the bell. One of the *little devils*, as she called her brothers, came to lead me to her room. There, I waited five minutes, heavy and disconcerting minutes, hearing her voice in the bathroom and tracing the sound of her steps: she cleans her teeth, she washes her face, she moistens her fingers and pokes them into the locks of her hair, she dries her hands, she lifts her arm and smells herself, she examines her pajamas, she turns the key in the lock and comes out. After taking two steps more, she is standing doubtfully inside the door to her room, staring at her visitor who has come without letting her know in advance.

I was thinking of all sorts of things to say, bits of news, little thoughts. I probably shouldn't have come and bothered you! Are you annoyed that I came? I guess I should have called first. I'm here because ... I need you, I mean I miss you! Don't refuse to see me. I hope my timing isn't bad, maybe you have other obligations. As soon as she was standing in front of me, I couldn't say a word; my language was entirely gone, and my ability to take any sort of stance was gone, too. I had not prepared for this, I hadn't practiced for it, it just came as pure need, and I cannot always control my needs.

I had very low expectations. Maybe she would gracefully get out of receiving me. Maybe she would treat me cautiously and with reserve. Maybe she would talk to me, but coldly. Maybe she would start blaming me out loud. Maybe she would hurl all her anger onto me. But my expectations were not borne out. She smiled as if one of her miracles had come to pass. She took me by the hand and we sat down on her bed. She was staring at me as if I were about to slip from her grasp, as if I would disappear, the parts of me scattering into thin air—indeed, as if I were unreal and she was imagining this. I was following her actions as if she were not really there. A part of me was withdrawing from this scene, shrinking into a ball somewhere inside of me, and I was trying hard to hold on to that part of me.

She didn't say anything and I didn't either. She just went on staring at me and smiling. When I was tired of feeling how very enormous was the distance between us, I whispered into her ear, Will you do something?

It's your turn to say the secret password, she said. Secret password? What secret password? If she was testing my memory, though, apparently I passed the first test. I whispered, Hold me. She said, I can't hear you. So she was testing the depth of my need for her. Don't be stubborn with me, Dai. Hold me.

I was on the point of saying, Hold me really tightly or Hold me as hard as you can! But I left it to her to hold me so firmly that she could feel my ribs, my shoulder bones, and then more to caress my neck, my jaw, and my forehead. Her eyes held a huge question. Are you really here with me? The moment she was ready to hug me she would get her answer, I thought, and she did. She hugged me as she'd always hugged me, in the same hard way, as if she were saying, I want you to melt in my arms.

You haven't changed, I said.

But you have.

I have changed!

You're older.

What happened while I was away?

Pretty much nothing.

Don't you want to hug me?

Yes, I do.

She put her hand under my shirt.

Why do you torture me?

Here I am, close to you.

I didn't come here to have sex with you.

She waved her hands around in front of me as if to say, See, I don't have any weapons in my hands!

I know. I just want to see you and touch you.

It feels like forever, this long time that has passed since I was naked with her. Under all this bright light, I have lost that familiar habit—that is, if I ever really did get used to being naked before. She got up and took off her clothes, with her usual calmness that I knew so well. Dai who has no problem with the nakedness of her body. It is impossible for her to hesitate more than once when I say to her, You first!

As she was about to come back to me, I moved away from her, rubbing my thumb against the raised paint on her wall. Turn out the light and bring me a cig, I said.

She turned it out and came back quickly. She wanted to light me the cigarette. The lighter's flame as it flew up in front of her face cast a sharpness over her features that I had seen only in her moments of anger. I took her by the hand and moved her until I got the best shadow I could, where her eyelashes appeared longer and her eyes turned into tiny pearls.

Are you trying to scare me?

But you don't get scared.

Didn't I tell you that you've changed?

I smiled. The feeling came over me, unbidden, that I was making light of her. She said, Give me a kiss before the cigarettes ruin the taste of your mouth.

She kissed me, but our kiss died out quickly. All of my attention was focused on my need for a cigarette, on the bubbly feeling in my head and the pulsing in my veins. She moved away, disappointment showing on her face. Her irritation was clear in the light sarcasm of her voice, as she muttered, It's like boiling an egg!

I left her and went toward the bathroom where I spat her kiss into the basin. I asked myself angrily what had brought me here. What had been my motive? I returned to her room, my mind pounding and echoing, as if with the ferment of just beginning to form some decision. I turned on the light and opened the curtains of her west-facing window. Nothing had changed at all. It was as if I had been here yesterday and the day before. I sat on the floor almost against the bed and I stretched out my hand to her. Come. With the obedience of someone who does not understand her role in a presumed scenario, she came, searching in my face for some reasonable answer. I patted my stretched-out legs. Sit down. She sat. I took a long drag on my cigarette and followed it with a gulp of Pepsi. All of my motions were deliberate; I was seeking an escape from her kisses. I stuffed the cigarette into the Pepsi bottle and pushed the bottle away, under Dai's bed.

I hate seeing my cigarette ends. They remind me that I have sucked out their souls completely, burned their embers, and when I have finished, I abandon them, cigarette butts massed together and yellowed like someone hugging himself as he wilts, for there is no one else there to share him, to huddle in the empty space between his arms.

I stared at her body out of sheer curiosity. She really hadn't changed. Then I looked at her and shrugged. She was opening the buttons on my blouse, moving from bottom to top.

I dropped my head onto her shoulder. I could not bear the way her burning gaze fell over my body. I couldn't bear the air conditioning's stuttering. I couldn't bear it as she turned into a little finger, feeling me millimeter by millimeter.

Lie down.

I lay down.

How much I had always hated the moment when she reached my lower body, making it necessary to go further, to bare more expanses; and where my cooperation appeared to be something agreed on in advance, waiting only for her to ask, or even for just a little hint. How much I had despised discovering, once we had reached this point, that I had become naked, as if being completely naked was not inevitable, given what was taking place.

I do not know how people deal with their bodies. I don't know how they see those bodies in the mirror. I don't know how they preserve their own private boundaries when they ride in buses. I don't know how they avoid the embarrassment of two bodies touching. I don't know what feelings they have about their own nakedness, how they overcome that oppressive sense of being naked. I know only that the nakedness of my body cannot be appealing and beautiful as long as it is shameless, as long as I am well aware that my body was not created for this exposed and indecent role. I have gone through the same moment time after time after time, and I still feel that my body is mine, it is for me, and I cannot put it out there in the open for others to share, even if it is only one other. I still feel that there is nothing quite as exhilarating as keeping my body a sacred secret. Maybe the fact that I bathed in my underclothes until five years ago lost me the ability to let anyone share in this secret and for me to enjoy sharing it.

Open the doors to your wardrobe, I said.

For every wall and in every corner of her room I had a story—except for those mirrors on her inner wardrobe door panels. For them I had memorized a single story, the story of the beginning. She got up and opened them, and so suddenly I found my body all over her room, the whole length of that wardrobe and four of its six doors and three fourths of the wall supporting it. I glanced at the mirrors. There I was, many times over. If I were to pick up a rock and throw it at the mirror and my body shattered, would the pieces even have any substance? I mocked myself: slivers of glass? What kind of pain am I still intent on gaining? Then a thought occurred to me. Perhaps that old soul of mine which had been imprisoned in the mirror ever since Dai had first touched me would come out!

Did I cry? I asked her. The memory of our first time was sealed off in red in my mind. It was a secret memory with a door there was no reason to knock on, with a keyhole there was no need to spy through. When the mirrors were out, I went blind for a moment because of the light, and then all of a sudden I could see everything, and the images came down on my head until they drowned me, I remember. She was licking my face and eyes, and I was crying and saying to her, I am dying! I am dying! And she was saying, Everything will be fine, don't be afraid. And now I think, maybe my memory is distorted, maybe I have gotten things all mixed up. I must not have cried, my memory must be leading me astray. Dai was looking at me, looking for an explanation. With my eyes I signaled her to look in the mirror. That day, was I crying?

Yes, you were.

I was counting on her proving my memory false. I don't cry with anyone, I was thinking, I don't cry at all, ever. And if I were to cry in front of someone, if it were up to me, it would certainly not be Dai! But, if I could not even remember crying before, then perhaps nothing about anything was really up to me.

Really?

Really.

So what happened?

I was taking off your clothes.

Then what?

Then I touched you.

And then what?

Then I touched you again!

Then what?

What are you getting at with all of these questions?

Did I come?

Only at this moment was I discovering that none of this seemed to resemble the image I had been carrying in my head. New pictures I had never seen before were taking over. She answered me.

No ...

No what?

You didn't come.

The circles of astonishment were widening and widening in my mind until they precipitated a collision with a thousand exclamation points attached. No, I hadn't ... ? Where had I been as she penetrated me? And why, that evening, had I spent the entire night washing myself, over and over? All the while I washed, I tried to bring myself to prayer, but couldn't because I felt so guilty. I remember very clearly that I could not perform the prayers for several days thereafter. She added, You were in shock, you didn't really know what you were doing. That usually happens when it is the first experience. At that last phrase, I laughed, but in disgust. She looked bewildered, even stunned. Was it such a trivial moment that it deserves to be forgotten? she seemed to be asking me. My laughter made a larger question inevitable behind her perplexed face. Wasn't I the first one who touched you? Answer me, don't leave me in such doubt about something like this. Don't rob me of the truth of you!

But as she did not dare to actually ask her questions, I did not care about giving her any answer.

I put my hands out toward her, crossing one wrist over the other. Handcuff me!

That isn't necessary.

Do what I ask.

But ...

Don't argue with me.

She tried to deflect me, claiming that she didn't have anything that would work as a rope. Nervously, she opened her drawers, scattering what was in them, grumbling. It was clear that she felt caught in a dilemma. She was giving me pleading looks, asking for my sympathy, asking me to save her from this.

What's your waist size? I asked her.

What!?

Bring the measuring tape.

I know Dai's infatuation with her body measurements, exactly how many kilos she weighs, the portions of food she eats. Anything having to do with numbers and her body puts her in a fever. She treats her body according to mathematical formulae that are extremely difficult if not impossible to maintain. She is so parsimonious with her body that it is all but a heap of bones. I would not be surprised if the measuring tape were folded up carefully and concealed under her pillow.

She walked toward her wardrobe and took out the measuring tape, which was hung over the wooden rod next to her shirts and trousers and dresses.

Tie me up! She hesitated again. I crossed my wrists even more insistently, and directly in her face, but with a gesture more like a plea than a clear threat or an order that could not be disobeyed. Tie me up!

It was not in my power to say to her, Give me back my confidence, my faith, my certainty, my purity, although she would certainly have been the first to understand what I meant if I had been able to ask. But I had come to the conclusion that it is not in our power to have something better than what was before.

She was on the verge of crying as she did it. Whenever I closed my eyes I could hear her breathing, as if she were sobbing. I threw my gaze to the darkness under her bed, protecting myself with it in compensation for the insolent light of her room. She treated me gently, not as she would if she were rediscovering my body, but rather with the sad softness which we sometimes feel when things stolen from us return, but which we had no power in us to bring back ourselves. The more she got entangled in my weak points and the hidden places of my pleasure, the more I pulled back, although there was nothing but the hard floor and the shattering of my bones to receive me.

I was crying, too, or rather, I was leaving it to my body to cry, to clear a space for its grieving: my body and I, we sit together on the steps and we cry. So many words my body had said to me as she touched it, before it went insane with desire, before it had been warned away from sin. My body was far away, and only its filthy memory existed, below an imperfect sky aborting its clouds so that not enough rain could fall for it to become clean. My body was crying, as its griefs reproduced themselves, each one calling out for nourishment, for water. My body's loneliness, its fear, its doubt. My body screams whole words, though letters are lost amidst the tears, and I cannot understand what it says. I am afraid to pat my body on the shoulder to make it stop crying. I do not want it to stop before its sadnesses are consumed. I do not want to console it with cheap words, cheap excuses. I want it to heal.

Why aren't you breathing?

There's no reason.

You frighten me!

Don't be frightened.

My mind wandered, and I did not come to until she was undoing the yellow plastic tape numbered on both sides in inches and millimeters. She began to kiss my wrists, moistening me with her saliva and the trembling of her lips.

You didn't have to push me to that.

It's what I asked.

You don't see what I see.

So, what do you see?

She lifted my hand in front of me. This!

It's just a mark, it will go away.

She stared at me as if to say, You don't understand! You won't understand!

Don't scold yourself. Nothing happened to make you scold yourself.

I decided to face her contempt for me head-on. I took out a tissue and wiped her sticky saliva from my body. She had never before allowed me to do anything like this. When she came close to kiss me, I stepped back and said, Wash your mouth, first! I was inclined to really push her around a little, to make light of her, even as her gazes showed just as strong an inclination to show herself humble. I lay down on her bed, covered myself with the sheet, and tucked its edges beneath me, so that she would not come and join me there, sharing the sheet and pressing herself against my body. I left my shoulders showing and my arms outside the sheet. I did it deliberately instead of putting on my clothes and leaving. I wanted her to see my body in her bed naked and close by, but beyond her reach and beyond what she deserved. And I ignored her. I turned on the little radio that always shares her bed with her and began rummaging through the stations. Defeated, she left me there and went into the bathroom.

As soon as she came back, she lay down, next to me at first, staring attentively at the sheet that covered me. Then she rested herself on my chest and began to cry. If she had left me a choice then I would have chosen to put off her crying until after I had left. I couldn't stand this role any longer, this usual and often repeated role, but I did not know how to explain that embracing the crying of others simply weighs me down more each time it happens. It is not easy to be alone with the weeping of others, to make yourself into a tissue upon which they dry their grief, leaving in your heart the echoes of their sobbing. They fill your darkness with voices that are difficult to listen to, and they coat your fingers with bitter salt.

Faced with the pain of her crying, I could not remain unconcerned but I could not feign anything or appear as if I truly sympathized with her. It was simply that side of me that cannot maintain silence for very long if it is drawn in, and I was implicated in her crying to the very core of things. I pulled up the blanket and covered her trembling. I wiped her sweaty forehead and her cheeks. Dai was clinging to me as if I were all she possessed, and the last thing she would possess, and I could not disentangle myself from her arms. I was forced to wipe her tears with my bare hand since the box of tissues was out of my reach. The sight of Dai weak was pounding at me. She has no right to be weak! She has no right to be a mere ordinary person, soiled by what dirties ordinary people. Ordinary people who grow weak, are defeated, know pain, and cry. This was Dai! And Dai was the mistress of my angels and my devils all at once. She had no right to be anything other than that!

What's wrong? Why are you crying?

Because I love you so much, because you don't love me at all. I always knew that you were going to leave me! Why did you have to draw it out, why did you stay so long?

I am still not sure what it was that brought me to her, but what I was sure of was that I had not come to open any more doors. And if I were to allow my reaction now to cleave a hole and escape through it, without a doubt I would leave a lot of filth on the walls of her heart and chaos in her mind. I suppressed my irritation and my strong desire to scream at her, I loved you to the point that my bones hurt! To death, to the point of worship I loved you! What did you do to me, then, Dai? You shattered my heart.

Instead, I smiled lightly and answered her. A few months is not a long time, I said.

But you are a lot, even for a few months.

She lifted her head off my chest. She was dizzy from so much crying. She raised her head and laughed. I hate it a little bit when she overdoes the crying, and I hate it a whole lot when she follows crying with laughter. What justifies her digging into herself? If I have enough reasons to make light of her, why does she do it too? She said something in the way she always does, to make fun of her crying, a joke I didn't hear, and then she giggled nervously.

I felt in need of doing something to regain my good mood. Let's do something. Something we've never done before.

Marry me.

What?

Marry me.

You're joking!

Not at all! Marry me. I won't hurt you. I won't be unfaithful to you. I will do everything exactly the way you want it. Just, marry me!

I did not know how to escape from the hysteria that surrounded this request of hers.

Say something sensible!

Like ... like that I will strip off the extra hair on your legs.

The hair on my legs hasn't even sprouted yet!

Marry me.

In Paradise.

When I woke up this morning I had no determination to make the day any different than the pattern of other days, days so similar as to be copies of one another. I woke up early in a troubled mood, the only reason being the way my mood has of not coming as I expect. I didn't care. I just left it to treat itself until it got well.

And now, as I place my kiss on Dai's cheek, and withdraw her arms from around me, and press my finger into her dimple to make her smile, and tell her that I still owe her the clothes in which I left the house the last time, fifteen months ago—in this good mood of mine, I am incapable of explaining to her that coming here this time is not coming back, and that I was using her to cure myself of her, to absolve myself of all of the pain that she left in my mind and existence. Trying her for one last time to make sure for myself that I do not want to come back to her.

I stare at her as if we are strangers, while she is engrossed in tugging on my wrists. I ask myself, did I know this girl once? Where does she get all of this simultaneous delicacy and harshness? She wraps round my wrists two black bracelets that look more like cloth ties.

Don't wear them when you are with strangers.

Why not?

So that no one thinks you broke your wrist.

At the door, my grip was loosening as hers tightened, and my fingers were slipping outside of her palm as her fingers stayed clinging to mine. She said a lot of things that I do not remember, something like goodbye and sorry. I remember how very pretty she looked, pretty and sweet, despite her sadness. A razaqi flower, very white, hung down alongside her face. She grasped it with her fingertips and stroked it before picking it and presenting it to me as a final gift.

23

Umar, kiss me right now!

Why right now?

I won't ask you that again.

Are you sure?

About the kiss or about asking?

Both.

I'm sure.

What if the kiss were to ruin our friendship?

It's supposed to ruin it, somehow. Anyway, we are adults enough to repair what is ruined.

What if you are just saying it on a whim and later on you regret it?

I won't regret anything that you're a part of if I'm the other part! And anyway it's not a whim.

And what if I were out of control and I wanted more than a kiss?

Nothing guarantees that I won't want the same.

What if I don't please you?

You will.

I might not be *a good kisser*. He finished his sentence in English.

I'll teach you how. Now, kiss me.

If I don't?

Let's just say that if you don't kiss me within seconds I will take that kiss myself.

Yesterday we were together, too. He called me to tell me that he was about to board the airplane, and then he called again to tell me he had arrived safely, and then again to tell me he could get a room in the hotel right next to the one I was staying in. We were practically facing each other, and the breeze that was leaving my window behind was passing on to his window. I was just as certain that the day would not pass without my seeing him as I had been doubtful two weeks ago about the possibility of our meeting at all. On that night, and after I said to him, Come, I put down the phone to find myself suddenly struck with guilt about burdening him with such a heavy mission, and I called him a second time. I'm withdrawing my offer, I don't want you, don't come! But after a few days, he was so out of control that he canceled his summer classes and traveled to Lebanon to attend one of the concerts in the Beiteddine festival series.

I will not do irreparable harm to the world's teeth if my schedule is packed for one term and I study those subjects poorly and not very conscientiously, he said. And then, nothing rivals *West Side Story* and the violinists of Bond, not even the two hundred dollars that I will pay!

And so we met here in Medina. I gave my mother the excuse that I had to buy a toothbrush. Don't be late, she said. In the trade center, which is always full of crowds and commotion, we met. All I saw of him was his back, and all I could hear in the sea of chaos and crowds was the sound of my confused steps on the tiles, which were out of sync with the rhythm of my pulse. I thought my heart would stop completely at the rate it was pounding. A shop window crammed with colors and goods and perfume bottles, all glass. Lots of glass. I do not know how I walked those twenty steps to Donut House without the slightest turn toward the dark green hue of The

Body Shop façade. I found myself behind him exactly, pressing my fingers into his palm, his warm palm, like two old friends, or a pair of lovers, and as if I had done the same thing a million times before. He was startled for a moment, I think he was startled, and then he said, I don't know which one you prefer, choose yourself, and I pointed randomly. I felt the whole world staring at us. They all must know that we had an assignation. He took his wallet from the pocket of his olive-green trousers and paid, and pushed the glass door leading to the street so I could go through, and the breeze went straight to my heart, and without any reason for it I loved him more, and I don't know why I remembered something he had said to me many times. *I will always be concerned with you, and I will work to make sure no harm comes to you.* We went outside and sat at the fountain and I laughed, because I don't eat doughnuts, nor does Umar, and we had not cleaned off the spot where we sat down, and there must have been a terrible gray stain now on his pants and my *abaya*. A few meters from us stood a policeman next to a No Smoking sign. Next to us was an Iranian family taking pictures of the fountain and the tiles and the walls of the sacred enclosure where the Prophet is buried. For a moment I thought I was in one of Ally McBeal's craziest, most hysterical made-up scenes.

Umar was exactly like himself, exactly as I had seen in his pictures and via the webcam in the few times he happened to be at an Internet café. Here were the same facial expressions and gestures, the same sharp aspect with the fine protruding nose ending in a tip that needed only an index finger poking playfully at it, the same dark complexion and deep brown eyes, the hair whose blackness the breeze made fly, his long fingers always ready to sketch shapes in the air, his reserved smile that waited until his face was turning in the other direction to complete itself, his laugh like the breaking water in the fountain nearby, and his broad forehead, which offers an abundant destiny for someone wanting a full life to immerse them. There was his smell mixed with Calvin Klein cologne, his smell that God did not duplicate in anyone, and the warmth of his body, too, which no technique could dispel.

My entire world had withdrawn into the confines of virtuality, where my features are embodied icons, my voice a "respond" box, and my room a chat window where time falls away and place goes missing. My friends, my little homelands, the man whom I thought I loved, my mailboxes, the cafés where we would meet—it was all virtual, even our names. My cousin's names were no longer what they had been twenty years before, but had changed to Hiba and Sundus and Aqil, even before the Internet when we had pseudonyms for the magazine. Dareen first introduced herself to me using her Internet name, and then apologized, smiling, and replaced it with the name on her birth certificate. She loved the Qatif region so much, she said, that she had chosen the name of a coastal part of Qatif's body. She said to me, I wanted a name that would unite the memory of my homeland, Qatif, with Nadia. "Nadia" and "Dareen" share letters. Rayyan chose the name that no one called him by except his mother—and it appears that my luck at its best was with people whose names contain the letter R. Dai said, By pure coincidence my eye fell on the word Dai at the very moment I was registering, and there wasn't any other name in my head at the time. Only Umar was a fact that virtual reality did not demolish, nor did distances, nor my fear.

On the horizon of my expectations, the possibility of our meeting as quickly as this had not occurred, nor had the possibility of it happening again this fast. I returned with my head spinning, searching for a way out. Umar would not stay for more than five days, and I would have to make up some convincing reasons to cover two or three meetings during that time without stirring up my mother's suspicions. My mother—who doubts even her own doubts, and who does not impose enough logic on her rules—did not even allow Salaam to drive me to the college that was outside Qatif, for everything outside of Qatif in her view amounted to nothing more than unknown, foreign towns. Even here, in the city that I had visited some dozen summers in a row, and whose map might as well be drawn on my palm, I knew it so well, and which became every summer another Qatif, so that wherever I turned I would see someone I knew—even this remained for my mother an unknown, foreign city—and no one can trust foreign cities.

My only way out was Salma. I figured that God loves me and so He sent Salma to me. I called her and I told her a double lie. I asked her to help me claim in front of my mother that she was inviting me to lunch, because, I told her, I was going to meet up with Nuuf, a net girlfriend, and my mother would give us a hard time, and so would Nuuf's mother, and we wouldn't be able to find any middle ground to meet on. I was only half lying, because I really was going to meet Nuuf, and we were searching out a secret way to meet without having to get into an argument with my mother and hers which would end with the mothers opposing the idea or expressing their displeasure at our relationship altogether. A little while later, Salma called me back, so that the idea of the invitation would not appear to have been arranged in advance. We talked for a few minutes and then I gave my cell phone to my mother. I know Salma's way when she is going after something she wants. So I knew that my mother would be embarrassed enough that she would agree without any back-and-forth or bargaining. I got what I had been strategizing for, even though my mother gave me no more than three hours. That was not a problem; I had learned how to bargain with her for more.

I couldn't sleep. I stayed sitting up in my bed, staring out the window to the glass façade where Umar was asleep behind one of its windows. Tomorrow seemed very far away and it was taking its time about arriving. It is only 2 a.m., I thought, so hopefully he is not asleep yet, and if I were to wake him up he would go back to sleep. No doubt he is tired enough to fall asleep again. So I called him, and thank God he was not asleep. I told him my naïve need to know which window he was sleeping behind, so he turned the light on and off several times until I was able to find his window. I reminded him not to put on any cologne tomorrow so that my mother would not smell its scent on my clothes. I wished him a sound sleep and clean sheets and a pillow that didn't hurt his neck, and I hung up.

In my dreams, Hassan came to me. He had never before visited me in my sleep. His face was covered with a small piece of white cloth that I pulled away, but it returned to cover his face again, growing larger, reaching for his limbs and his whole body. I pulled it off but it came back and grew still larger, and so it mutated from a handkerchief into a *ghutra* like men wear over their heads, and then into a sheet and then a shroud. I was asking him, Have you forgotten me, Hassan? Why don't you come? Come with me, okay? Get up from death, and come. All he did was smile, a long and sweet smile, not the kind of smile that indicates the helplessness of the dead when their shrouds bind and incapacitate them. And before the dream was blotted out, he said to me, This is not the right of the dead over the living. What do you mean by that, Hassan? What do you mean? What? and I found myself tumbling into a foggy wakefulness and the room.

At midday, as soon as I stepped into the elevator alone, I called Umar to open the door for me. As I walked through the door to Room 1407 he put out his right hand to me. Men shake hands, and we girls kiss each other, and sometimes we hug. I gave him my left hand, since my right one was not free. He took the two plastic bags I was carrying. I went to the window, pointed out my window, the open window on the ninth floor, and said, I am five floors beneath you, and he laughed. He always laughs when a possibly suggestive expression slips out of me. Just as yesterday we sat next to each other at the fountain, where his trousers and my *abaya* got soiled, today we sat beside each other on a sofa the color of soil under yellow lamplight. He hoisted one of the bags.

A bottle of beer and strawberry gum ... what made you late?

Two minutes aren't *late* unless you are going by Greenwich Mean Time, I said. Often I say any old random thing when he has me cornered and I can't find words to finish my sentence. In the second bag was a sealed bottle of ∏ cologne.

Why ∏? he asked me.

I can always love a man who wears ∏. Another random sentence, I guess.

In bed, he asked me, Do you love me?

Since when do you use love as a way to something else?

Don't be pedantic—answer me.

I sang something about waiting for opportunities that always come late, and things that keep you from being well, and your need for a compass that isn't broken down, for an angel to come and take you from your cold dark room, to empty your veins of memory and make you light, snatching you from your lowliness and making you forget the fear of endings, an angel who flies you somewhere high, to where you are in a safe place.

Am I your angel?

More than that, Umar. There is a sentence in the film *City of Angels*, if you remember it, the angel said something like, *he'd rather one breath, one touch, one kiss, than eternity ...*

And you are the one to whom I voluntarily cede my eternal angel-ness, if I were an angel, for the sake of human-ness.

He smiled. We had not put out the light, and I saw how he smiled.

I love you, Umar. I love you a lot. By the Lord of the Heavens, I love you.

And although I had said it before, *I love you Umar*, in tens of circumstances I had said it, these circumstances had never come my way before. I had never said it as a young woman ready to love, a young woman at ease with a guy she trusted and amazed by all the little signs of his guy-ness: his beard, the whiskers on each side of his face, the hair on his chest, the different proportions of his body, his heavy smell—as a young woman who had always been searching for solutions and discovers now that all her possible solutions were there beneath her hand, but she never noticed.

He asked me if I was afraid. No, I responded. He laughed, for the glint in my eyes gave me away rather scandalously. So I pulled back a little and said, Fine, yes, I am a little anxious. The question was flowing along the edge of my tongue as Umar took it between his lips. Will you be disgusted if I get a seizure when I'm in your arms? I could ask it, knowing that he would close my mouth with a firm hand, and say in a firmer tone, Don't say that, don't think about it, okay? Or that he would lightly bite the tip of my forefinger like he does with Jawd, his littlest sister, every time she memorizes a bad word and repeats it without understanding what it means.

With the kiss, he spread his hands across me and lifted my clothes off. Slowly he lifted them after I had undone the buttons on his shirt, my reaction growing along with every new part of my body he revealed, and as I saw my reflection in his eyes desire burned over me. I had never seen myself reflected in another person's eyes. His fingers moved down over me and then up—Umar, whom I thought would rip across my body like a sandstorm but who in reality moved more like the ebb and flow of a tide.

He tried to take off the necklace around my neck and I refused. I had not taken it off for five years—as of last Muharram it was five years—and I could not take it off. It would be as if I were taking Hassan's hands off me, Hassan who told me as he clasped it around my neck that the angels would protect me as long as I wore it, Hassan, who never for a day believed in the protection of amulets or in summoning angels. I refused, and he murmured, unconvinced, Never mind.

When he slipped his hand beneath the flesh of my legs, I said, Don't do that, don't touch my leg like that. He took a long breath and drew nearer.

Do you trust me?

You know the answer without asking.

I need you to trust me now more, a lot more than ever before.

I was chewing on my nail and he took it out of my mouth.

I need a cigarette.

No, no you don't need a cigarette.

I need the bathroom, then.

I got up quickly, slipping out from under his hands. I went into the bathroom and locked the door behind me. I opened the tap. I stood in front of the mirror. I feel as if I am spoiling these moments, and I don't understand why I am doing it, and why now I feel that I am weighed down by my memory, possessed by all that has gone by and everyone who has gone by. The old murmurings are hurting me, and the whispers of the darkness, and the vapor of breaths on my face, and my underwear twisted at my feet or thrown carelessly against the bedpost, and panties damp in their stickiness and odors that choke me, and the hand circling the flesh of my leg as I suppress my fear and my crying that must not be heard, I repeat, I do not see, and so there is nothing happening. I do not see anything, and so nothing is happening. Nothing.

I heard Umar's footsteps, he must have been spying from the bathroom door.

Umar, go away.

What are you doing in there?

I have to pee, I said in English.

Why the embarrassment?

It's all about dirty words.

Haven't we said words this dirty and shrugged them off?

We'll say them *in English*. Now, go away.

I am tired of my old features. I want to wipe them away, I want a clean memory, and a body without traces of anyone's passing across it, a body free of sobbing and oblivious. I washed my face. I washed it several times. And I came out of the bathroom.

I went to Umar, sitting on the edge of the bed, and stood between his legs. He wrapped his hands around my waist. I withdrew his right hand, put the necklace in his palm, and folded his fingers over it.

Take me, Umar. Take all of me!

And he did. Not as Dai did in all of our scrabbles in bed, nor in the state of lightness I had gone through with Dareen, nor in the fear and shame I had felt having a strong and forceful heel pressing down on my body for years. Now and then, out of an extreme of desire or love, I would be on the point of saying, Don't stay outside of me! Don't steal your children from me! But I held back, afraid that such big words would frighten him.

And my virginity, which had never meant anything to me, not since some woman came to our home one day when I had not yet changed out of my blue school uniform, and I did not let my mother see the white ribbon knotted into a flower shape that the teacher had attached to my collar in recognition of my excellent work. I sensed a strange aroma in my mother's behavior. She was enticing me toward something I knew was frightening and terrible, except that I didn't know what it was. Enticement gave way to the chase, and when they seized hold of me, the strange woman cooperated with my mother to strip me naked, pull my legs apart and disfigure me with her fingernail scratches before stuffing a piece of my flesh in a handkerchief and throwing it into the waste can in the bathroom. I had not yet begun my periods but now I saw the first sign of blood. I understood then that everything my mother said about modesty and covering the body and the privacy of its parts was meaningless.

She would warn me, Don't let anyone put his hand on you! to the point where I would no longer put my own hands on my body, but it was all meaningless. In my feverish, reckless play, I didn't care about my virginity, except in the narrow limits within which I had to remain sealed. And now, at the beginning of things with Umar, I wanted to say to him, Take it! I don't want it, take it! Then he kissed me and asked me, Do you love me? and I answered, More than you can possibly imagine, Umar. I wanted to say to him, I want you to put your children in their home, come! but I knew it was not in his power to do so.

We spent ourselves and he dozed off immediately on my belly. I could not believe that Umar would sleep the minute his desire was met. I don't know why, but I could not believe it, even though I had heard so many bizarre stories that by comparison this was ordinary. After all, he did not eat an apple after making love, nor was he addicted to yogurt.

As I restrained my breathing to not disturb his sleep, his features were calm. If I had the power to spy on his dreams, if I could intervene and change their colors and smells and venues, if I could simply live in his eyes, and open them slowly, drinking in his face, and his eyes drink in the light ... he opened them, and smiled. His smile kills me, and he knows it.

You miss a lot here, when you're sleeping.

Since you aren't being unfaithful to me I am not missing anything.

How do you know?

You can't be unfaithful when I'm asleep on your body.

He reminded me of a saying: Go to sleep on my body, and implore God that daylight not come! I don't know where I picked that one up, among the many Internet sites I've visited. Although I am certain that my supplication to God will not be answered, I will not stop trying. There is one difference, though. It is not daytime that I want to keep from arriving, but rather the night.

Tell me, what did I miss?

Seeing yourself asleep.

My eyebrows are like this and my mouth is like that.

He was crooking his fingers over his eyes, and stretching out his lips in a laughable way.

You are so good to be true! I said in English. Maybe my English wasn't perfect but the sentiment was real.

Did I please you?

I could praise you all the way until tomorrow, but you will not judge yourself or base your self-esteem on my opinion.

Don't go back to being pedantic.

You know you pleased me.

And do you still love me?

Even more.

What didn't please you? Don't make a fool of me and say, Nothing! I won't believe you.

You have to let me try you out again so I can judge.

Let me try you again!

I thought, we might not be here again, Umar, we might not meet, Umar, I might not see your eyes again, Umar, and you might not smile in my face, Umar, and I might not be able to cling to you and say, Save me! And ...

Umar?

Yes?

I love you.

I feel like I'm hearing, "I love you, but ..."

Like a night of firecrackers, things I had read with Umar flared and exploded in my mind, leaving behind a smoky film and the terror of loss. They were sayings like,

My hands open the curtains of your existence.

I love you to exhaustion.

Someone who looks like me greeted me and passed on, leaving me here on earth alone, isolated, and broken-hearted.

Soon the full moon will come out and every one of us will lose our chance to remain alone, and our need for regret.

If only love were a matter of words. My nearness to your body creates a language.

The windows will fall one after another and what will remain is a building of wind with its thousand floors.

My scattered thoughts ended with the memory of a poem I had read to Umar. He had imagined that behind the emptiness of my voice lay a story called "All of Those I Love Change!" I pressed up against him.

Umar, don't leave me! And don't—

I won't. Trust me.

And you won't die! I don't love those who die. Say that you won't die.